Eric
Wilder

Half
Past
Midnight

Other books by Eric Wilder

Gondwana Press
1802 Canyon Park Cir. Ste C
Edmond, OK 73013

Front Cover by Gondwana Graphics

ISBN: 978-1-946576-16-3

Acknowledgments

I wish to thank Linda Hartle Bergeron and Don Yaw for beta reading, editing, and providing valuable input involving timeline and character development.

for Marilyn

"You only live twice. Once when you are born and once when you look death in the face."

–Ian Fleming

Half Past Midnight

A novel by
Eric Wilder

Chapter 1

There's no odor like the stench of death. Doctor Wayne Pompeo knew as much, the pungent smell of disinfectants accosting his senses when he unlocked the door to the autopsy room. After fifteen years as the hospital's chief pathologist, he'd participated in hundreds of autopsies. It didn't matter because he'd never gotten used to the putrid odor.

Jack Dugas, his autopsy technician, suffered no such problem as he switched on the overhead lights. He and Doctor Pompeo had different backgrounds, though they had lots in common.

Pompeo lived in a million-dollar house in the Garden District. Jack Dugas had a small house in the Seventh Ward. Pompeo owned a Mercedes, Dugas an old Ford. They could have passed as brothers, both short and bald. Dugas liked raucous zydeco music, while Pompeo preferred Mozart concertos. Music by Rosie Ledet or Clifton Chenier usually flooded the autopsy room during dissection.

Dugas glanced at the chart on his clipboard when Pompeo asked, "Who we got today?"

"Robert Blanchard, Jr., Male Caucasian, age twenty-three."

Dugas laughed when Doctor Pompeo said, "Twenty-three? What the hell killed him?"

"Hell, Doc, that's for you and me to find out," Dugas said.

"The name sounds familiar," Pompeo said.

"It should. His daddy's a state senator. Ran for governor last year."

"Too damn conservative for me," Pompeo said. "I didn't vote for him."

"Didn't know you was a socialist, Doc."

Pompeo didn't react to Dugas's political comment. Instead, he crossed himself and said, "What a horrible tragedy for parents to lose a son so young."

"You been doing this longer than me, Doc. You know you can't look at it that way. He's just another stiff," Dugas said.

"Suppose so," Pompeo said.

Dugas glanced at his watch. "We got nothing scheduled after this. It's Friday, and I plan to go home early."

"I got lunch at Antoine's. Can we finish by then?"

They laughed when Dugas said, "Hell, Doc, you got the fastest scalpel in the whole damn hospital. Drink a brandy milk punch for me."

"Will do," Pompeo said. "Let's get to it. I got Antoine's on the brain."

A body bag on a gurney waited in the hallway. Dugas wheeled it into the pathology lab and unzipped the bag to reveal the body. Using practiced leverage and balance he'd developed through years of practice he lifted the shoulders of the deceased young man and slid the body onto the dissection table he called the chopping block. Though Dr. Pompeo hated the crude synonym, he'd never mentioned his dislike for the term to Dugas.

As Dugas returned the gurney and empty body bag to the hallway, Doctor Pompeo glanced up at the overhead LED modules. Vision is critical when performing an autopsy, and modern lights are more efficient than fluorescent illumination. He wondered how they'd managed before the hospital had outfitted the dissection lab with advanced lighting. Dugas returned with pen and clipboard as Pompeo began his examination.

The pathologist adored the functional stainless steel table. Its design allowed blood and other fluids to flow away from the body, containers under the cutting surface collecting them. Soft light from the LED modules provided all the vision Doctor Pompeo needed to complete his task.

Dressed in faded blue jeans and a purple LSU tee shirt, the deceased wore a braided leather bracelet on his right wrist. He wore no shoes or socks. Pompeo cradled the man's head and began rubbing his fingers through his short brown hair.

"Cuts and contusions on his scalp. From the looks of the bruising, he might have taken a fall and hit his head." Pompeo used an Archimedes

Screw to open the man's jaws. "Full set of adult teeth. Looks like he had a high-dollar dentist. Recent shaving cut on his right cheek. Let's get him undressed."

Dugas set his clipboard and pen on a cabinet and unbuttoned the shirt. When he had the body undressed, Doctor Pompeo examined the man's neck, quickly working his way down the body.

"It appears from the bruises he was in a fight and got the worst of it," Dugas said.

Doctor Pompeo ignored him. "Let's not get ahead of ourselves," he said.

Dugas wasn't convinced. "Just saying."

"Old appendicitis scar. Normal male genitalia."

"What about the bruises?" Dugas asked.

"Football player, most likely," Pompeo said.

Dugas was skeptical. "What makes you think so?"

Pompeo pointed to the cadaver's left knee. "Hasn't been long since he had his knee scoped. He's too muscular to be a runner and too short for a basketball player."

"It's April," Dugas said. "Football season's long gone."

"Spring training. Don't you keep up with sports?"

"Saints and Pelicans," Dugas said.

Dugas grinned when Pompeo said, "They're pros. They don't have to practice."

"Is that a tattoo under his left nipple?" Dugas asked.

"So strange," Pompeo said. "Looks like an Auschwitz tattoo."

Jack Dugas focused on the dark tattoo. "M1231," he said. "What does it mean?"

"Don't know," Pompeo said.

The music track had ended, morphing into swamp rock that Pompeo detested even more

4

than zydeco. He poured a cup of coffee from the pot on the cabinet while Dugas flipped the body and then centered it on the dissection table. When he turned away from the table, Pompeo handed Dugas a cup of steaming coffee.

"Break time," he said. "How's the wife and daughter?"

"The old lady's good. My little girl ain't little no more. Got my fingers crossed she don't have me a grandchild before she graduates from high school."

Pompeo grinned. "My daughter did. Sissy's a freshman at Tulane, me and Melissa raising her baby while she's screwing God only knows who at the sorority party of the week."

"What's she majoring in?" Dugas asked.

They both laughed when Pompeo said, "Partying one oh one."

"Hell, Doc, we was young once."

"I barely remember that far back," Pompeo said.

After setting the half-finished cup of coffee on the cabinet, Pompeo pulled on another pair of gloves and returned his attention to the job at hand. He lifted a leg to examine the soles of the feet. The bruising on the young man's back appeared to confirm the injuries occurred from something other than a beating.

"Forceps," he said.

Dugas handed the instrument to Pompeo, watching as the pathologist dropped something into a metal collection pan.

"What is it?" Dugas asked.

"Tiny shards of glass in the soles of both feet," he said.

"Damn, that must have smarted," Dugas said. "Maybe that's what caused him to fall."

Pompeo was rubbing something between the thumb and index finger.

5

"Lacerations on both feet, and there's more than glass in the cuts," he said.

"What?"

"Sticky brown powder," Pompeo said.

"The glass is in the powder? What would have caused that?" Dugas asked.

"Not what; who? Hand me a tube."

Dugas handed the pathologist a collection tube and watched as he began scraping the powder out of the raw wound.

"You think somebody put the ground glass in the powder?" Dugas asked.

"It didn't get there by itself," Pompeo said. "Another tube."

"Same powder?" Dugas asked.

"No use speculating until the results come back from the lab," Pompeo said.

Pompeo spent the next ten minutes cleaning out the cuts on the feet. After capping the two collection tubes, he handed them to Dugas, who labeled them with a marker and dropped them into a tray. After removing his second pair of gloves for the day, Pompeo poured another cup of coffee.

"Java's good today," he said. Dugas smiled when he added, "Damn obvious you didn't make it. Want a cup?"

Dugas stripped off his gloves and said, "You don't like my coffee, Doc?"

"You kidding? I've had tastier castor oil."

"Hell, Doc, nobody drinks castor oil anymore."

"Just saying," Pompeo said.

Dugas took a sip of the coffee. "It is good. Don't know who made it, but we need to hire them permanently."

"Got that right," Pompeo said.

"I think our deceased stepped on glass, tripped, and fell, hitting his head. The fall killed him," Degas said.

"The bruising on his head and face isn't that severe," Pompeo said. "Something else killed him."

"Maybe he had a heart attack when he hit his head," Dugas said.

"The brown powder wasn't something someone dropped and then forgot to clean off the floor."

"Then what is it?" Dugas asked.

"Voodoo powder," Pompeo said.

"Did you learn that in med school?" Pompeo wasn't smiling. "Hell, Doc, you don't believe in voodoo?"

"I've seen a few things I can't explain," Pompeo said.

"Everyone in New Orleans has. But voodoo powder?"

"I had a black nanny growing up. Her name was Mirlande Casseus, from Haiti," Pompeo said. "She always threatened to turn me into a toad when I misbehaved. She carried a vial of brown powder in her purse. Voodoo powder. Same thing I swabbed out of the cuts on the cadaver's feet."

Dugas rolled his eyes and turned away so Doctor Pompeo couldn't see the smirk on his face. The swamp rock tape had ended, and the autopsy tech loaded a Mozart rendition.

Pompeo smiled when Dugas said, "Hell, Doc, I should have brought a Congo Square drumming session."

"Mozart will do," Pompeo said.

"Say, Doc, you're joking about this voodoo thing, aren't you?"

"I'm dead serious. Anything Mirlande didn't like had a way of disappearing," Pompeo said. "My ferret, for one."

"You had a ferret?"

"Mirlande made it disappear."

7

"You mean like a magician?"

"The woman never liked me, and the feeling was mutual. She was pissed off at me one day for something or other. When she pointed her finger at Jacques, he went "poof" and disappeared."

"Just like that?"

"Right before my eyes."

"Maybe she hid him under her shirt."

"She was on the other side of the room," Pompeo said. "I searched everywhere. My ferret was permanently gone. Jacque wasn't the first nor the last thing of mine she made disappear."

"Hell, Doc, I believe I'd have said something to my parents and had her fired," Dugas said.

"I did. My daddy whipped me for my trouble."

"He didn't believe you?"

"Though I never caught them in the act, I've always suspected Dad and Mirlande were having an affair."

"Your mom didn't know it?"

"Maybe, though it wouldn't have mattered. Mirlande had a spell on everyone in the family. My younger sister adored her."

"I never knew you had a sister," Dugas said. "What's she do?"

"Her name is Pearl," Pompeo said. "Pearl Pompeo. Recognize the name?"

"Surely you don't mean Pearl Pompeo, the president of Southern United Hospital and the boss of both of us," Dugas said.

"Exactly who I mean," Pompeo said. "Little sister Pearl is my boss."

"Damn, Doc, are you trying to scare me or just pulling my leg," Dugas said.

"Mirlande watched me once while my parents were away. She put something in my orange juice that immobilized me for almost eight hours. It was the most frightening experience I've ever had. Pearl adored Mirlande."

"Damn!" Dugas said.

"I could hear and see just fine, though I couldn't utter a sound or move a muscle. Mirlande left me that way, not giving me an antidote until just before my parents returned home."

"Double damn!" Dugas said. "What did you do about it?"

"Nothing," Pompeo said. "Mirlande told me if I ever breathed a word to anyone about what she had done, she'd do it again and leave me that way."

"Hope she never finds out you told me," Dugas said.

Doctor Pompeo cracked a smile. "She's probably dead. At least, I hope so. Let's get a move on, or I'm going to miss my lunch at Antoine's, and you won't be going home early. Turn over the body, and let's get to cutting."

"My favorite part," Dugas said.

Dugas flipped the body and then placed a dissection block under the back of the cadaver to facilitate the flow of blood and fluids. After arranging the body the way he wanted, he handed Doctor Pompeo a scalpel. Pompeo began the incision at the right shoulder. He didn't get very far.

When the scalpel bit into flesh, the cadaver's eyes opened. Rising into a sitting position, the body that was suddenly very much alive grasped Pompeo by the neck, lifting the diminutive man into the air. A muffled scream died in Pompeo's throat as he clutched his heart and crumpled to the floor.

Chapter 2

Early morning sun had begun filtering through the front window of Bertram Picou's French Quarter bar on Chartres Street as I exited my upstairs apartment. The first person I saw was Tony Nicosia, a former N.O.P.D. homicide detective talking on his cell phone. He didn't notice my arrival until I touched his shoulder.

"Was wondering if you were going to sleep all day," he said.

I returned his smile, "It's not even seven yet."

"I been up since five," he said.

"Lil, kick you out of bed?"

My bantering words didn't offend him. "Hell, Cowboy, at least I got a wife to kick me out."

"Lil's a sweetheart," I said. "If I could find a woman like her, I'd have remarried years ago."

Even though the hour was early, Tony was nursing a tall scotch. He hadn't bothered removing the ubiquitous straw fedora he favored to cover his thinning hair. Fat Tony had been his nickname when a lieutenant in the N.O.P.D. Though still stout, he'd lost fifty pounds and had managed to keep it off. Like a pair of Tony's old pants, the moniker no longer fit. Bertram Picou, the bartender, and my landlord joined us.

"It ain't Cowboy's fault he's not married. He so needy, no woman wants to take on the task," he said.

"You're one to talk," I said. "At least I once was married."

"Bartending's a hard life," he said.

"You're so set in your ways. The only female that will ever put up with you is Lady."

Hearing her name, Lady, Bertram's beautiful collie and constant companion, began thumping the oiled hardwood floor behind the bar with her long tail.

"Don't know why I even put up with you," Bertram said.

"You make out like a bandit," I said. "I'm the only person in New Orleans who gets charged four bucks for a glass of lemonade."

"Knock it off," Tony said. "You two sound like an old married couple."

Tony's comment rendered Bertram and me speechless.

"Hitting below the belt, aren't you?" Bertram finally said.

"But true," Tony said. "Charge Cowboy double for his lemonade and put it on my tab. I got business to discuss with him."

Bertram's eyes lit up. "Now you're talking," he said.

"Bring our drinks to Wyatt's table," Tony said. "You haven't changed these barstools since I've been drinking here. They're so uncomfortable my butt's rebelling."

"New furniture costs money," Tony said.

Tony didn't stop walking to comment. Instead, he gave Bertram a backward wave.

"Tell it to my sore butt."

Bertram smiled as he said under his breath, "Can't please everybody."

I had a booth in the back for meeting new

clients and hearing their problems. It wasn't free. Never missing a way to earn a buck, Bertram added an extra hundred dollars a month to the rent on my upstairs apartment. Just one of the reasons Bertram was rich and I wasn't. Tony slid into the booth beside me.

"You were a bit harsh on the Cajun bartender," I said.

"With the money he charges for drinks, he could at least afford comfortable furniture."

"Those stools are antiques," I said.

"Got that right," Tony said.

"This bar is on the National Register. Bertram has to get permission to change anything about it."

"Even the padding on the stools?"

"Anything," I said.

Bertram brought our drinks, Tony remaining silent until he'd walked away.

"You working?" he asked.

"Between jobs," I said.

I hadn't worked in forty-five days, and my meager bank account was rapidly shrinking.

"I have something for us. You interested?"

I was more than interested. "You bet. What's cooking?"

Instead of answering my question, he said, "Can you leave the city for a while?"

"Depends," I said.

"On what?"

"Where to, and how long is a while?"

"Not far," he said. "The North Shore. I can't tell you for how long because I don't know?"

The North Shore is the area across Lake Pontchartrain from New Orleans and includes the towns of Slidell, Covington, and Mandeville. The towns featured good restaurants, great neighborhoods, and a slower pace of life. Many people who work in New Orleans commute to and from the bedroom communities across the lake.

"My cat doesn't like it when I don't feed her."

"Hell, Cowboy, none of us do. Take the cat with you."

"Whose going to care for her while I'm working?"

"Trust me. You and your kitty have nothing to worry about," Tony said.

"What will I be doing?"

"Can't tell you?"

"Is it illegal?"

"It's legal," he said.

"Dangerous?"

Tony took a drink of his scotch before answering.

"Maybe," he said.

"How dangerous?"

"You asking questions I can't answer."

"Why the secrecy?"

"Orders. Interested?"

"How much does this gig pay?"

Tony counted out ten hundred dollar bills on the table.

"Just a taste of what you'll earn," he said.

Tony knew he had me when I smiled and reached for the cash.

"When do we start?" I asked.

"Right now. Get the cat."

"I'll have to pack some things," I said.

"No, you don't. Someone will provide everything you need."

Sliding out of the booth, I headed upstairs to get my cat Kisses while Tony tabbed us out with Bertram.

We were soon on the Causeway, the longest water-crossing bridge in the world. The weather was beautiful, with no clouds and several distant sailboats. The top of Tony's red convertible was down, and Kisses was asleep in her picnic basket converted to a cat carrier. Tony hadn't spoken since we'd left Bertram's.

"No one's here but you and me," I said. "Can you at least tell me where we're going?"

"Frankie Castellano's horse farm north of Covington. He woke me this morning at five and said he needed to see me. For a retainer, he wired money into my bank account. He asked me to bring you along."

"What if I were busy?"

"Frankie don't take no for an answer. I'd have had to kidnap you."

Tony didn't sound as if he was kidding.

"If he needs a private dick for something, you're as good as they come."

Tony glanced up at a flock of seagulls flying overhead.

"I got no clue what that man is thinking. If I did, I'd be as rich as he is instead of working P.I. cases until I drop dead."

"You know you love it," I said. "You'd be working cases even if you had all the money in the world."

"Maybe," he said. "I wouldn't be driving the Causeway. I can tell you that."

"Longest bridge in the world," I said. "At least over water."

"Yeah, well, no one ever climbs Mount Everest twice. Once you've done it, driving the Causeway's nothing more than a pain in the ass."

"Been a while since I've been to the North Shore," I said.

"Growing fast though it still looks pretty much the same," Tony said.

The Causeway, as Tony had said, dragged on forever. He'd grown silent as the miles passed. Easing against the comfortable bucket seat, I closed my eyes, enjoying the sunshine and salty breeze. I awoke when Tony slowed to exit the

Causeway.

Frankie Castellano's horse farm was north of Covington, the area highlighted by pine trees and rolling hills. We passed a sign on the highway that said Murky Bayou Farms, home of thoroughbred champions.

The front gate was majestic, a brick-lined road leading toward a house in the distance, acres of manicured grass, beautiful horses, regal barns, and stalls as far as the eye could see.

The scenic road led us to a sprawling, single-storied structure that seemed like a cross between a Texas ranch house and a Louisiana plantation home. A man with a shotgun in his lap sitting on the porch informed us this wasn't the home of the local Baptist preacher. Frankie Castellano came outside as we approached the porch.

"No need to check I.D.s, Gus. I know these two."

Unlike the pin-striped suit and polished brogans Frankie wore the last time I'd seen him, he seemed relaxed in a colorful Hawaiian shirt and Bermuda shorts exposing his bony knees. One thing hadn't changed: the tumbler of scotch in his hand.

"Quite a spread," I said as Frankie pumped my hand.

"The best Louisiana thoroughbreds in the world," Frankie said. "How you doing, Wyatt?"

"Couldn't be better," I said.

"Thanks for coming."

"No problem. Hope you don't mind that I brought my cat."

Frankie took the picnic basket from me and handed it to the man with the shotgun.

"Take this pretty kitty to Toni, will you, Gus?"

"Her name is Kisses," I said.

Gus nodded as he disappeared around the

corner.

Frankie gave Tony's shoulder a friendly slap. Except for his casual clothes, he'd changed little, tall and regal-looking even in his shorts, bare legs, and expensive sandals. His thinning hair was still dark, though it had grown longer, framing his bulldog face that made him look fierce even when he was smiling.

"Come in," he said. "I'll get us something to drink."

The place was stately, with expensive rugs covering the floors finished in marble and polished hardwood. Paintings of champion horses decorated the walls, and slow-moving fans ceiling barely rustling the room's open curtains.

"You've outdone yourself, Frankie," I said. "This place is gorgeous."

"Josie found it for me. Adele loves it."

Josie was Frankie's daughter and the mother of his grandson Jojo. Adele was his wife and mother of Toni, who was now looking after my cat.

"How they doing?" Tony asked.

"Well. Jojo and Josie are in town shopping with Adele. They'll be back before we finish our business. You'll see them."

From speakers hidden somewhere in the walls, light jazz began to emanate. Frankie poured another scotch for himself and one for Tony. He and Tony tapped tumblers and sat on an oversized leather couch as Gus appeared with a pitcher of lemonade for me.

"Cheers," Frankie said.

I'd known Adele, Frankie's wife, for years. She was arguably the best Italian cook in Louisiana. It didn't matter because Frankie thought she was. She and her father, Pancho, and daughter, Toni had run the Via Vittorio Veneto in Metairie for years. Adele and I'd met Frankie the same night when he stopped by to sample the fare. Romance had ensued.

That night, someone had been with me: Eddie Toledo, my best friend, and valedictorian of his law class at the University of Virginia. He was the assistant Federal D.A. in New Orleans when I'd first met him. He was also the best lawyer I'd ever known. As intelligent and talented as Eddie was, he had a fatal flaw: he'd never known a woman he didn't lust after and couldn't keep his pecker in his pants.

Eddie and I had met Frankie's daughter Josie at a horse race at Fair Grounds in New Orleans. Josie looked so much like the former love of my life that her appearance caught me by surprise. Though I'd never had any romantic relationship with Josie, Eddie had.

Eddie and Josie's relationship had progressed to the point where they'd gotten engaged. Frankie was on cloud nine, anticipating Eddie becoming his consigliere. It never happened, nor did the marriage between Josie and Eddie.

Unable to consummate a permanent relationship, Eddie spoiled his engagement when he had an affair with another woman. Frankie and Adele loved Eddie as much as Josie had. Frankie gave Eddie a second chance by making him a part-owner of a restaurant and casino. I'd only seen Eddie once since he'd moved.

I forgot about Eddie when Frankie said, "I got a job. Nothing big. You interested?"

Chapter 3

After Frankie had put me on the spot, he and Tony waited for my answer.

"Why are you grinning?" Frankie asked.

"Good thing you aren't a salesman," I said. "You'd starve to death."

"I didn't want you going into anything without knowing the ramifications."

"I need the work. Tell me what the job entails, and let me decide if it's too dangerous to risk."

Frankie's smile returned. "You're right about my sales ability. Adele says I'm too blunt."

"I like blunt," I said. "Tell me what you want me to do."

Frankie stirred his drink with his finger. "You know what omerta is?"

"Code of secrecy," I said.

"This is a secret. Even if you don't take the job, you can never tell anyone about this meeting. Understood?"

"Though disbarred, the attorney-client privilege is still the rule I live by."

"That's what Tony told me," Frankie said. "There's someone I want you to meet. You'll work through me if you take the job, though he will call the shots. What's your political persuasion?"

"I have none," I said.

"Sure about that?"

"In my line of work, it's best to be apolitical."

Frankie grinned. "Same goes for me. I can't afford to piss off someone in a position of power to put me in jail."

I tried not to smile. Frankie didn't mind as he took Tony's empty tumbler and returned to the wet bar to refresh their drinks. Instead of two scotches, he mixed three. I understood why when someone appeared from down the hallway. I recognized him even before Frankie made introductions.

"Gentlemen," Frankie said. "This is Robert Blanchard."

"Don't get up," the man said.

Blanchard was a state senator with higher political aspirations. He'd run for governor in the last election, narrowly losing to the popular incumbent. As the grandson of a former governor, I was well aware of the games public servants must play to survive life in office.

Blanchard was forty-something with brown hair touched up to hide any gray around the edges. His short-sleeved sports shirt and khakis made him look younger than in a suit and tie. Though it looked forced, he was smiling as he sipped his scotch.

Tony and I nodded when he said, "You may have heard my wife and I recently lost our son. The papers said the cause of death was a drug overdose. That's a lie propagated by my political opponents."

"You want us to find out who's spreading the lies?" Tony asked.

"Anyone into social media knows the answer to that," Blanchard said. "I have reason to believe my son is still alive, and I want you to find him for me."

"Maybe you better explain," Tony said.

Blanchard's smile had disappeared. He drew a deep breath and then sipped his scotch.

"Bobby was the starting quarterback at L.S.U."

"Now I remember," Tony said. "I didn't make the connection."

"Though Bobby had a hell of an arm, he was probably too short to succeed in the pros. The rumor was I'd paid to get him on the team."

"No one who has seen him play would believe that," Tony said.

"You'd think," Blanchard said. "Football wasn't Bobby's main passion. He majored in journalism as a straight-A student. He told me he was working on a story involving certain things I'd find hard to believe."

Tony glanced up from his note-taking. "Such as?"

"He never had the chance to explain. He only said whatever or whoever he was dealing with was dangerous, and he didn't want me or his mother hurt."

"Not much to go on," Tony said.

"I had nowhere else to turn, so I talked to Frankie about it," Blanchard said.

Senator Blanchard's admission made me wonder what connection a state politician needed to have with the Don of the Bayou. I kept my mouth shut and continued listening.

"Tell us why you think your son is alive," Tony said.

"Bobby was only twenty-three and in perfect health. I requested an autopsy to determine the cause of death."

"Understandable," Tony said.

"The medical examiner had a heart attack and died during the procedure."

"Damn!" Tony said.

"It's what caused the unnerving heart attack,"

Blanchard said. "When the medical examiner made the first cut, Bobby sat straight up and grabbed him. The autopsy tech jumped back, tripped, and banged his head on the floor. When he recovered, he found the medical examiner dead and Bobby missing."

"Why wasn't any of this in the news?" Tony asked.

Blanchard sat his drink on the coffee table. "I've used all my political connections to suppress the story."

"Because?" Tony said.

"I believe Bobby is in grave danger. I don't want to jeopardize him if he's still alive."

"We're here to help you," I said. "Please share your plan with us."

Robert Blanchard fished in his pocket, removed a keychain with a single key attached, and handed it to me.

"We saw him shortly before authorities found his body. This keychain fell out of his pocket while sitting on the couch. Alice, my wife and Bobby's mother found it the next day."

The tag on the keychain said Bell House Bed and Breakfast, Coffee Street, C. 1884, Mandeville, Louisiana, Room 1.

"What am I supposed to make of this?" I asked.

"Bobby stayed there for some reason," Blanchard said. "It's the only clue I have."

"It's not where he lived?" Tony asked.

"He had an apartment on Conti in the French Quarter. I don't know what he was doing in Mandeville. I suspect it had something to do with his story."

When Senator Blanchard stopped talking, Tony said, "That's it?"

I could tell from Blanchard's expression he didn't like the tone of Tony's question. After twenty-five years as an N.O.P.D. homicide detective, Tony had developed an in-your-face demeanor that scared people half to death and often prompted them to blurt the truth. His line of questioning didn't work well with prospective clients, and I'd counseled him on more than one occasion to moderate his technique.

"I already told you it's all I have," Blanchard said in a huff.

Seeing our potentially lucrative assignment fading away into the sunset, I interceded.

"You'll have to forgive my partner's bedside manner. He sometimes forgets he's no longer an N.O.P.D. homicide detective. He means no harm and gets results like no other detective in the city."

"I can attest to that," Frankie said.

"Sorry if I offended you," Tony said.

Blanchard lowered his head and put his hand over his eyes. When he moved his hand away, his smile had returned.

"My fault," he said. "I'm distraught and having a hard time functioning. Still, a politician can't afford to be thin-skinned."

When Blanchard glanced at his watch, Frankie put his arm around his shoulder and pointed him toward the door.

"These boys will handle your problem. Go home, forget about it, and enjoy the rest of your day. We'll find Bobby and return him to you."

We had almost nothing to go on, and I wondered how successful Tony and I would be as we watched Robert Blanchard walk away down the hall.

"What now?" I asked.

"You in or out?" Frankie said.

"In," I said. "I'm too broke to be out."

"Good," Frankie said. "You got the money Tony give you. Here's another thousand to tide you over. I got business in town. Adele will be home shortly. She knows the story and will take it from here. Until then, help yourselves to the bar."

Tony was mixing another scotch in a go-cup when I said, "Too bad I don't drink anymore."

"Quit bitching, Cowboy. Sobriety is your choice, not mine."

"We don't have much to go on," I said.

"If it was easy, someone else would earn the big bucks. I'm heading back to town to question the autopsy tech. I'll check in when I'm on to something."

"How will I know?" I asked.

Tony handed me a key. "Frankie rented a post office box in Covington for me. If I have something or need to see you, I'll leave a letter in the box for you. Check it every couple of days. I left a pay-as-you-go cell phone for you to call me."

Tony was naturally suspicious and gave me a backward wave as he walked out the door. I reclined on the comfortable couch, resting my head on a soft cushion and listening to the piped-in music until someone I barely recognized interrupted.

"Toni, is that you?" I said.

The young woman smiled and hugged me. "It's me. Have I changed that much?"

She had. The last time I'd seen Adele's daughter, Toni Bergamo, she'd had long black hair and ample curves. Her hair was now short and ash blond. Cutoff jeans highlighted her tan and toned legs. The jean shorts and sleeveless tee shirt she wore revealed she was no longer the curvy woman I remembered. She'd probably lost thirty pounds though her muscled body was anything but emaciated. She could see me staring and did a pirouette for me.

"You like?" she asked.

"You were always gorgeous," I said. "Now, you look as if you could run a marathon."

"I'm exercising horses for Frankie and training to be a jockey," she said. "I tended to sample the cannoli when I worked at Via Vittorio Veneto for Mom and Gramps."

"You look great. You must love it here," I said.

"It's a dream come true. I've always loved animals, and now I have a place to keep them. There's an old ranch house on the property. My two dogs and three kitties love the house and yard. Your baby likes it so much you may have difficulty convincing her to leave."

"I was worried about her," I said. "How's your mom doing?"

"In heaven since she met Frankie. She loves it here as much as I do."

"And Pancho?"

"Gramps moved in when they sold the restaurant in Metairie. He never got used to it here and was moping around, everyone worrying about him until Frankie bought him a little hole-in-the-wall café in Covington. Mom and Josie redecorated it. Pancho lives in a small apartment above the café, and now he's over the moon."

"Wonderful," I said.

"Frankie wants me to alter your appearance," Toni said. "You ready?"

"No one knows who I am on this side of the lake," I said.

"Frankie doesn't take chances."

Toni grabbed my hand, nudged me off the couch, and led me to a chair in the kitchen. After putting a barber's apron on me, she buzz-cut my hair. I raked my hand through what hair she'd left as she held up a mirror for me to see.

"What now?" I asked.

"Ever been a blond?" she asked.

"Nope," I said.

Toni led me to the sink and bent my neck over it.

"I'm not bleaching you, just adding enough dye to turn your hair from dark brown to ash blond, like mine."

When she held up the mirror this time, I didn't recognize myself.

"I've never had hair this short, even as a kid."

"You like it?" she asked.

"No. It feels like I'm looking at a stranger in the mirror."

"We're not done yet. There's a change of clothes in the bathroom down the hall. Put them on."

Dressed in khaki shorts, a red-flowered Hawaiian shirt, and sandals with no socks, I looked like a tourist when I returned to the kitchen. Toni fitted me with a pair of granny glasses and a Panama hat. When I looked in the mirror, I was looking at someone I didn't know.

"Well?" I asked,

"Perfect," Toni said. "Even your mother wouldn't recognize you."

"You think?"

"We'll soon find out," she said. "Mom and Josie just drove up. Keep the hat on and stand by the bar. Mix a tonic in a glass, so you don't look like a teetotaler."

Toni cleared away her clippers, dye, and barber's apron as I added ice and tonic water to a tumbler. I stood at the wet bar, sipping the tonic when Josie and Adele came through the front door.

Adele had put on a few extra pounds since the last time I'd seen her. She looked enough like Toni to pass for her older sister, except her hair was still dark, and she hadn't lost any of her curves.

Josie's beauty always made me feel

25

uncomfortable. She looked enough like my former girlfriend Desire that I felt uneasy every time I saw her and didn't know how to act since Eddie had jilted her.

Josie and Adele's black dresses draped to their calves. They were in an animated discussion about a designer purse Josie had just bought and didn't look up until they'd dumped their shopping bags on the kitchen table adjoining the living area. Their smiles disappeared when they saw me standing at the wet bar.

"So sorry, Toni. We didn't realize you had company," Adele said.

Neither Toni nor I spoke. Adele almost fainted when she walked over to introduce herself, and I hugged her.

Chapter 4

Adele's reaction to my hug was swift and unexpected. After pushing me away, she slapped me hard enough to send my granny glasses flying across the room.

Her expression was priceless when I said, "Did I do something to piss you off?"

Adele's hand went to her mouth. "Wyatt, is that you?" she said.

"You don't recognize me?"

After giving Toni a look, she rushed to me with open arms.

"Wyatt," she said. "I'm so sorry. Are you okay?"

"Except for my burning cheek and bruised ego," I said.

"You look so different. I didn't recognize you."

"Toni performed her magic. Guess it worked."

Josie had watched the entire scene. She was smiling and shaking her head when she joined Adele and put her arm around my waist.

"I wondered what Toni was doing, letting a stranger mix a drink from Papa's bar."

"It's tonic water," I said. "I haven't tasted any in so long it almost made me tipsy."

"Sit," Adele said, pointing to the couch. "I'll get you some lemonade."

"I already have a pitcher," I said. "You two look great. Living on the farm must agree with you."

"I have never been so happy in my life," Adele said.

"Toni told me about Pancho's new restaurant," I said.

"It's little more than a hole in the wall," Adele said. "Frankie bought the place for him, and Pancho is finally happy."

"Does he have help?"

"Pancho's doing everything himself. I'm worried about him."

"He's fine, Mom," Toni said. "Pizza is the only thing on the menu. I go by almost every day to help him."

"You didn't tell me that. Now I feel guilty," Adele said.

"He's happy, Mom," Toni said. "The word is out. People are coming from all over the parish to sample his pizza. Pancho's in heaven."

"Almost no one makes better pizza than Pancho," I said.

"It was Josie who found the place and negotiated the deal," Adele said.

"Brains and beauty," I said.

"Don't start," Josie said. "After my experience with your buddy, I'll never trust another man for as long as I live."

Josie grinned when I asked, "Seen Eddie lately?"

"I'm so done with that man," she said. "He taught Jojo how to fly a kite the last time I saw him. I still love him, but leopards don't change their spots."

"Where have I heard that before?" I said.

"What about you?" Adele asked. "Is there a new woman in your life?"

"I feel the same about women as Josie does

about Eddie." They laughed when I added, "I don't trust any of you."

"Let's quit talking about relationships," Adele said. "We brought pizza home from Pancho's."

I was soon eating the best pepperoni pizza I'd had in years. Toni, Josie, and Adele drank Chianti and giggled like schoolgirls.

They stopped chattering when I said, "There's only one other person I know who makes pizza this good."

"No one makes pizza better than Pancho," Adele said.

"Mama Manetti does," I said.

"Who's she?" Toni asked.

"The mom of one of my exes."

"Can she cook Italian better than Adele?" Josie asked.

"Carla and I were a number for four years. Her mom was such a wonderful Italian cook I did my best to keep the relationship from failing."

"Is Mama Manetti married?" Josie asked.

"Widowed," I said.

"How old is she?" Toni asked.

"About Pancho's age," I said.

"Maybe we should do a little matchmaking," Adele said.

"Wouldn't hurt," I said. "Meantime, please tell me what I've gotten myself into?"

Adele grew somber; her smile had disappeared.

"Alice and Robert are friends," she said.

"Alice?"

"My best friend. Alice and I grew up in Metairie."

She nodded when I said, "The Blanchards?"

"Bobby was a change-of-life baby. Their only child. To say they doted on him is an understatement. They were devastated when they thought they had lost him."

29

"Is that a fact?" I said.

"Maybe," Adele said. "Alice and Robert are clinging to the hope a miracle has occurred. Frankie and I are doubtful; Frankie called Tony when I reminded him about you."

"I'm not a miracle worker," I said.

"Josie," Adele said. "Tell Wyatt about the area he may not know."

"The towns on the North Shore are laidback, a place for families with kids," Josie said. "The shops and restaurants are eclectic and cater to a population wealthier than most parts of Louisiana."

"What's the deal with the Bell House?" I asked.

"A bed and breakfast closing in on two-hundred-years old," Josie said. "A lovely place. I've never heard anything bad about it."

"Does this area have a dark side?" I asked.

Josie glanced at Adele. "Such as?" she said.

"Drugs, gangs, or weird political groups, maybe?"

Josie and Adele both glanced at Toni when she said, "Drug use is rampant in high school. The kid's rich parents either don't care, look the other way, or are unaware of the problem."

"I've never heard that," Adele said.

"It's true, Mom," Toni said.

"Blanchard mentioned his son Bobby was investigating a story while he was staying at the Bell House. Is there something I'm missing?" I asked.

"There's a nightclub in Abita Springs that's like no place on earth," Toni said. "Word on the street is it's owned by organized crime."

Adele and Josie glanced at the floor at the mention of organized crime. Toni didn't seem to get the connection between a random crime family and her stepfather Frankie.

"Where did you hear this?" I asked.

"So the story goes, the mob owns the new nightclub on the outskirts of Covington," Toni said.

"Tell me about the nightclub," I said.

"A large building designed for big crowds and specialty acts," Toni said. "Voodoo dolls and amulets are part of the decor. They serve drinks like voodoo landmines and zombie bombshells. It's an advertising ploy that draws the crowds."

"Who owns it?"

"Not my dad, if that's what you're getting at," Josie said.

"There's nothing illegal about owning a nightclub," I said. "If Frankie doesn't own it, I'm sure he knows who does."

The conversation had suddenly grown contentious, both Adele and Josie showing signs of irritation.

"Frankie has nothing to do with Bobby's disappearance," Adele said. "I promise you that."

I raised my palm in a sign of truce. "Frankie hired me to get to the bottom of Bobby's disappearance. No one knows better than I that he has nothing to do with it."

Adele's arms were folded tightly across her chest, her smile gone.

"Exactly," she said.

"It does seem logical he may know something which he hasn't conveyed to me," I said.

"Adele and I will broach the subject with him," Josie said.

When Adele let one of her hands drop to her side, I grabbed it and squeezed.

"Adele, I wouldn't do anything to harm Frankie in a million years," I said. "There's no doubt in my mind he's not responsible in any way for Bobby's disappearance. Will you help me with this?"

"We're all family," Adele said. "I know you wouldn't harm Frankie."

Toni grinned when I asked, "Have you been to the new nightclub?"

"Me and everyone else within a couple of hundred miles. People come from New Orleans, Baton Rouge, Biloxi, and as far away as Lafayette to hear the touring groups. The drinks are expensive, and there's a cover charge at the door. They must be making a fortune."

"You've never told me about this place," Adele said.

"I'm going on thirty, Mom. There are lots of things I haven't told you."

Adele let the matter drop. I had a few things to which I needed answers.

"So, what's your plan?" Adele asked.

"Check in to Bell House for as long as it takes," I said. "What's my cover story?"

"You're a travel writer working on an article about the North Shore," Josie said. "Bobby made a connection concerning his article while staying there. Maybe you will too."

"I have no car. How will I get around?" I asked,

"The Tammany Trace connects most of the towns around here," Toni said. "Heard of it?"

"Not really," I said.

"A railroad once connected the towns on the North Shore. Contributions purchased the easement, removed the tracks, and replaced them with asphalt. It's now one of the finest biking trails in the country," Josie said. I smiled when she asked, "Can you ride a bike?"

"That's something you don't forget," I said.

Toni had disappeared down the hall. She returned toting a large backpack which she sat on the couch in front of me.

"Clothes, toiletries, maps of the area,

notepads and pens, and business cards establish you as a freelance writer. Your name is Thomas Wyatt."

"Easy enough to remember," I said.

"And you'll react appropriately no matter how someone addresses you," Josie said.

"Smart," I said. "What if someone checks the information on the card?"

"Frankie owns several publications," Josie said. "Thomas Wyatt is now a reporter for the magazine Travel America. If someone calls and asks for you, you are on assignment and out of the office. If they leave a message, we'll have their contact information."

"Sweet," I said.

"You can contact us by cell phone," Josie said.

"Bad idea," I said. "Too easily stolen and checked. I'll leave it here."

"Then how will we stay in touch?" Josie asked.

"We don't." I showed them the notch missing from my left ear. "I lost this doing undercover work. The cover story was perfect, at least we thought."

Adele poured a shot of cognac and drained it in one gulp.

"I'm having second thoughts," she said. "Frankie will have to hire someone else to do this job."

"No, he won't," I said. "We have no idea if there's danger involved. More than likely, it'll be a walk in the park."

Adele embraced me, resting her head on my shoulder. "What if it isn't? I'd never forgive myself if you got hurt."

After kissing her on the forehead, I pushed her away.

"This isn't my first rodeo," I said.

"Bell Place has bikes for their guests. We'll drive you over and drop you off," Josie said.

"Not a good idea. Is there a bike here I can use?"

Toni grinned. "About two dozen," she said.

"Then I'll use one of yours," I said.

"It's a long way to cycle," Adele said.

"Not that far on a bike," I said.

"I'll ride with you to the outskirts of Mandeville," Toni said. "Show you the way."

"That'll work," I said.

"Before you go, I'll fix an Italian lunch you'll never forget," Adele said.

I shook my head. "I'm ready to start now. Plenty of time for your wonderful food when I finish the job."

"Sorry, Mom," Toni said.

"One thing before I go," I said. "If you see me, go on with your business. Don't act as if you know me. We'll have plenty of time to visit when this is over."

Josie and Adele hugged me before I followed Toni.

"Wyatt," Adele said. "Be careful."

"I intend to," I said as the front door shut.

Toni led me to a prefab metal building large enough to house fifty full-sized cars.

"After unlocking the door, she said, "Frankie's toys."

Inside the building were jet skis, all-terrain vehicles, mopeds, go karts, motorcycles, and bicycles. I zeroed in on one I liked: an immaculate red bike with a front and rear basket, foot brakes, a headlamp, and taillight.

"That's for old people," Toni said.

"I love it," I said. "Reminds me of the one I had when I was a boy."

Toni grinned when she said, "Must have been a while back."

"I can still beat you in a race."

"Not on that old thing," she said. "Check out my bike."

Toni beamed when she showed me her specially built racing bike, complete with an expensive frame, wheels, and gears.

"How much did that baby set you back?" I asked.

"I don't even want to know," she said. "Frankie gave it to me for my birthday."

"Probably more than I make in a year," I said.

"Close to it," Toni said. "I'm almost afraid to ride it."

"Frankie would buy you ten more just like it if you asked him."

Toni didn't reply, straddling the bike and riding it out the open door.

"Try to keep up," she said.

"Wait," I said. "What about the backpack?"

Toni returned to Frankie's toy shed.

"We can put it in the basket in front and attach it with bungee cords," she said.

"It's not that heavy," I said. "I'll wear it. That's where it's supposed to be, anyway."

We hadn't gone far when Toni turned off the paved farm road onto a much narrower dirt road. Toni's fancy racer didn't like it though it was no problem for the big wheels on my old clunker.

Toni shook her fist at me when I said, "I'll race you to the end of the dirt road."

"That's the only way you're going to win," she said. "This is a shortcut to the Tammany Trace."

Though the terrain was flat, the pine trees growing everywhere prevented seeing far into the distance. We'd gone less than a mile when Toni got off her bike and began walking it into the trees. I followed her, bees and other insects buzzing around our heads.

"Hope we don't cross paths with a

rattlesnake," I said.

"I'm deathly afraid of snakes," she said. "You could have gone all day without saying that."

"Sorry," I said. "You sure about this shortcut?"

"Quit carping. We're almost there."

Toni was right. As we pushed through the pines, we reached the Tammany Trace, thirty-one miles of manicured asphalt surrounded by a scenic pine forest.

"I love it," I said. "How far is it to Mandeville?"

Toni pointed in the direction I needed to go. "About twelve miles," she said. "I can easily make it in a half hour. It'll take you twice that long on that old bike."

"I better go alone from here," I said. "How will I find the Bell House?"

"Keep going until you reach the Mandeville Trailhead. It's a renovated train station with restrooms, pavilions, and picnic facilities. Take a right when you leave the Trailhead and keep going until you get to Coffee Street. Hang a left. The Bell House overlooks the north shore of Lake Pontchartrain."

When Toni started to peddle away, I stopped her. "You heard me tell Adele how possibly dangerous this gig is. It goes for you, too. This is the last time I see you until I finish the job."

"No, it isn't," Toni said. "You're taking orders from Frankie. So am I."

"And?"

"Frankie is not only my stepfather. He's my employer. He wants me to keep tabs on you and report your progress to him."

"He said nothing to me about it."

"I'm telling you now," Toni said.

"How am I supposed to report my progress?"

"I'll be around."

Chapter 5

Tony shook his head as he exited the Causeway toll booth and headed toward the New Orleans hospital district. He needed to interview someone who worked there and wished he still had his police badge.

After leaving the N.O.P.D. and becoming a private investigator, Tony quickly realized how easy he'd had it while working for the police. All he usually had to do to gain access to a witness was to flash his badge. As a P.I., things had become more complicated.

Now, Tony had to deal with privacy rules. If someone didn't want to answer his questions, they could tell him to kiss their ass. He'd had that happen on more than one occasion. The chance he'd locate his witness and get no answers crossed his mind as he entered the hospital and approached the front desk. The woman's nametag said, Millie.

"Hi, Millie, I'm Tony, Jack Dugas's brother-in-law. We're going fishing. Can you tell me how to find him?"

Millie's smile never disappeared as she pointed to the bank of elevators beyond the front desk.

"Pathology is in the basement, at the end of

the hall. Catch a big one for me," she said.

"You got it," Tony said.

Tony punched the down button at the bank of elevators, happy he wasn't claustrophobic when he entered the windowless hallway leading to the pathology department. The nurse at the front desk wasn't smiling.

"Hi, Gloria. I'm looking for my brother-in-law Jack Dugas. Is he around?" The large woman in blue scrubs pointed to the break room down the hall. "Thanks," he said.

Only one person occupied the break room, and he fit the description of Jack Dugas. The little man with thinning hair glanced up from his coffee when Tony approached his table.

He nodded when Tony said, "You, Jack Dugas? I'm Tony, a private investigator. Do you mind answering a few questions?"

"About what?" Dugas asked.

"The death of Dr. Wayne Pompeo."

"You with an insurance company?" Dugas asked.

"Maybe," Tony said. "This is part of my job I don't like."

"Which is?" Dugas said.

"Obtaining witness testimony so my company don't have to pay out a big claim."

"How is interviewing me going to affect that?" Dugas asked.

"Today it ain't," Tony said with a smile. "The company decided against giving me my yearly bonus. Because of their generosity, I'm going to shove it up their ass." Tony put money in a vending machine and waited as coffee filled a paper cup. "Mind if I join you."

"Sit," Dugas said. "I was getting lonely."

Tony made a face as he sipped his coffee. "This shit never tastes any better, does it?"

"That's a fact," Dugas said.

"I told the lady at the front desk I was your brother-in-law, and I was here to take you fishing. I have to lie every day in my shitty job. I hate it."

"I wish you were here to take me fishing," Dugas said. "It's my favorite thing to do."

"You got a boat?" Tony asked.

"A 23-foot runabout with a 50 horsepower Evinrude. It's old as the hills, but it runs, and I don't owe a penny on it," Dugas said.

"The kind of boat to have," Tony said. "Wish I had one."

"What's your name?" Dugas asked.

"Tony," he said.

Dugas extended his hand. "I'm Jack. Pleased to meet you, Tony."

"Same here, Jack. Mind if I ask a few questions about Pompeo to hold on to my shitty job?"

"Why not?" Jack said. "Pompeo's family is so wealthy it don't make no difference if he gets a penny of insurance money."

"Thanks," Tony said. "You were performing an autopsy when Pompeo had a heart attack. Did something that happened during the procedure result in a heart attack?"

Jack grinned. "I'll say."

"Tell me," Tony said.

"The man we were about to autopsy was young. His chart said twenty-three."

"Too young to kick the bucket," Tony said.

"Got that right. He had cuts on his scalp and bruises all over his body. Looked to me like he'd taken a fall and hit his head."

"What did Pompeo think?" Tony asked.

"He believed they were football bruises. The man looked too small to me to be a football player."

"What else?" Tony asked.

39

"He had a tattoo on his right wrist. Some symbol."

"What did it look like?"

Jack had a manila folder under his elbow. He opened it and handed Tony a sketch of the symbol.

"This is the autopsy file. I found it today."

"Found it? Where was it?" Tony asked.

"Doc's death traumatized me more than I realized. The head nurse sent me home. I took the file with me and threw it in the backseat. After Dr. Pompeo's death, I decided to take some time off from the job. Today is my first day back. I found the autopsy file a minute ago when I went out to the car to smoke a cigarette."

"The hospital never missed it?" Tony asked.

"Nope," Jack said.

"Why is that?" Tony asked.

"Maybe because we never completed the autopsy," Jack said. "When I tried to return the report, I was told the case is no longer in the system."

"That's strange," Tony said. "Have you seen the police report?"

"I don't believe anyone called the police," Jack said.

"Sure about that?" Tony asked.

"As I said, I wasn't around."

When Jack handed him a drawing from the folder, Tony was making a note. "Here's the sketch I drew of the tattoo," he said. "The doc said it was a voodoo symbol."

"How would he know?" Tony asked.

"He told me he had a black nanny from Haiti when he was growing up in the Garden District. He said she practiced voodoo."

"Mind if I keep this?" Tony asked.

Tony folded the drawing, preparing to put it in his pocket, when Jack said, "I was getting ready to toss the file into the trash. You can have the whole damn thing if you want it."

"If the hospital doesn't need it, you can bet I do," Tony said.

Jack slid it across the table to him. "Knock yourself out."

Tony returned the drawing to the file and thumbed through the other documents. "What else is in here?"

"The name of the doc's nanny, for one thing," Jack said.

"Mirlande Casseus?" Tony said.

"Yes."

"Did the doc tell you about her when he saw the symbol?"

"Later, he began scraping ground glass and brown powder from the cuts on the soles of the man's feet."

"Brown powder?"

"Voodoo powder. There's a sample in the file. Doc told me his nanny Mirlande gave him some once, and it paralyzed him for hours," Jack said.

"Pompeo told you his nanny paralyzed him with voodoo powder?" Tony said.

"That's what he said. He couldn't move or speak though he was fully aware of everything around him."

"Makes you wonder why he didn't tell his parents about the incident," Tony said.

"He did," Jack said.

"And?"

"His dad punished him. The doc told me his nanny had everyone under her spell. Even his sister, Pearl."

"What's the significance of his sister?" Tony asked.

"Pearl Pompeo is the chief administrator here at the hospital."

"Why did Pompeo have the heart attack?"

Tony asked.

"When he used his scalpel to start the first cut, the cadaver rose into a sitting position and grabbed him by the neck. Must have scared the holy hell out of him because he clutched his heart, collapsed, and died."

"What happened to the cadaver?" Tony asked.

"Don't know," Jack said. "I fell back and hit my head. The cadaver was gone when I got off the floor, and the doc had no pulse."

"Guess the cadaver wasn't a corpse," Tony said.

"That's a fact. The young man was alive," Jack said.

"But comatose until Pompeo cut him with the scalpel."

"That's the way I see it," Jack said.

"Could be Pompeo was right about the powder," Tony said. "Maybe it was voodoo powder in the cuts on his feet that anesthetized him."

"You don't believe in that bullshit, too, do you?" Jack asked.

"I'm just connecting the dots," Tony said. "One thing puzzles me."

Jack grinned when he said, "Just one?"

"The man was naked. When he arose from the dead, so to speak, he disappeared. Don't you think someone would have seen a naked man with a bleeding shoulder running down the hall and reported it to security?"

"You'd think," Jack said. "Didn't happen that way. He went missing, and no one has seen him since."

"Strange story," Tony said.

"Hell, Tony, you should have been there." Jack got up from the table. "Have to get back to work. Hope the file helps you. You got a card?"

Tony dug in his wallet and gave him one of the cheap business cards he'd had printed when he became a private investigator.

"Sorry about the dog ears," Tony said.

"No problem," Jack said. "Want to go fishing sometime?"

"Love it," Tony said.

Jack stuffed Tony's business card into the pocket of his scrubs.

"I'll give you a call."

"I look forward to it," Tony said. "Nice meeting you, Jack, and thanks for the information."

"One more thing," Jack said. "The body had another tattoo under the left nipple."

"Tell me about it," Tony said.

"It said M1231," Jack said.

"What does that signify?" Tony asked.

"Doc Pompeo said it looked like an Auschwitz tattoo."

"You mean like in the Nazi concentration camp?"

Jack nodded, and then Tony watched the little man disappear out the door before opening the folder. Born in New Orleans, Tony had lived there his entire life. Like everyone else who lived there, he knew at least a little about voodoo.

His good friend, Mama Mulate, was an authentic voodoo mambo and knew more than most. Thinking he might catch her at Bertram's, he punched her number on his cell phone. She answered on the first ring.

"Tony, I was thinking about you."

"In a good way, I hope."

"Always," she said. "What's up, honey?"

"Wyatt and I are working on a missing person's case. There's voodoo involved. I have questions, and I was wondering if I could get your perspective."

"Of course, you can. Where are you?"

"In the basement of a hospital over here in the hospital district. You?"

"At home," she said. "Between semesters, bored to tears and drinking vodka."

"At ten in the morning?" he asked.

"I began pouring vodka in my coffee when I awoke this morning."

"Hardcore," he said. "Can I come by?"

"I'll leave the front door cracked. I'm sitting on the back porch with my kitties. Join us," she said.

"Be there directly," he said.

Tony put the folder under his arm, hurried to the bank of elevators, and pushed the up button.

Mama's house wasn't far from the hospital district or the French Quarter. She lived in a Creole cottage in a rundown old neighborhood. The car on blocks across the street was still there, just as the last time he'd visited.

Mama liked living under the radar and didn't mind it a bit. Unlike the neighbor's, Mama's tiny front yard was freshly mowed, the path leading to her porch lined with yellow flowers he didn't recognize growing in terracotta pots. Vines covered with purple clematis climbed the stockade fence on both sides of her house, ferns and other hanging plants accompanying the lone rocking chair on the rustic porch.

Mama had cracked the door, and he entered without knocking.

"Is that you, Tony?" Mama called to him from the back porch.

"It's me," Tony said. "Need anything from the kitchen before I come out?"

"Get a tumbler from the cabinet," she said. "There's ice in the fridge, and I already have a bottle of scotch waiting for you."

"You're a princess," Tony said, looking in Mama's cabinets for a tumbler.

When Tony opened the door to the back porch, he found Mama sitting in a rocking chair, her three cats playing with a rubber ball. Instead of her old blue bathrobe, she was nude.

Tony grabbed his heart. "Whoa!" he said. "I wasn't expecting to see you naked."

Chapter 6

Tony quickly turned away. Mama's laughter stopped him.

"Where are you going? You've seen me naked more than once. Stop acting like a prude."

"Sorry," he said. "I feel as if I'm intruding."

Mama got out of the chair and hugged him. "Am I making you uncomfortable?"

"You kidding? I almost had a heart attack."

"I'm the one who should be sorry. When I'm home alone, I rarely bother wearing clothes."

"I see that," Tony said.

"I've been an exhibitionist since I was a little girl, embarrassing Mom more than once. Sit. I'll put on a robe."

"Please do," Tony said. "Unless you want my jaw dropped and eyes popping out of my head while we're trying to talk."

An ice bucket, a pitcher of water, bottles of vodka and scotch, and their tumblers sat on a little table between two rocking chairs. Mama was still laughing when she returned wrapped in her old blue robe.

"Sorry, Tony," she said. "Sometimes I forget not everyone is as liberated from common norms as I am."

"Most people don't have bodies like yours. I

need that scotch now," he said.

"You should have helped yourself," she said. Ice?"

"Straight up," he said.

He laughed when she said, "And you call me hardcore?"

"Being a homicide detective for twenty years will make an alcoholic out of a choir boy."

"I hear that," Mama said. "Relax and tell me how I can help you."

Tony issued a sigh of relief when he sat in one of Mama's comfortable rocking chairs.

"Love your covered deck," he said. "I could fall asleep in this chair in about a minute."

"Not until you tell me how I can help you," Mama said.

The ball Mama's cats were playing with rolled beneath his feet. Retrieving it, he tossed it across the floor.

Mama nodded when he said, "You're a news junkie, so I'm sure you heard about the death of Senator Blanchard's son."

"Yes," Mama said. "So tragic losing a son at such an early age."

"Wyatt and me are working for the senator through Frankie Castellano. Maybe Blanchard's son isn't dead, only missing."

"I haven't heard that," Mama said.

"Because it isn't public information."

"Why not?" Mama asked.

"Senator Blanchard requested an autopsy to discover why his healthy, twenty-three-year-old son had suddenly died. When the pathologist made the first cut, the cadaver arose from the dead, sat up, and grabbed the doctor by the neck."

"No way!" Mama said.

"The autopsy tech fell backward and banged his head. The pathologist had died from a heart attack, and Bobby Blanchard was missing."

"What does all this have to do with voodoo?" Mama asked.

Tony opened the manila folder and handed Mama the drawing of the symbol.

"Bobby had this symbol tattooed on his wrist. The autopsy tech seemed to think it was a voodoo symbol."

"Exactly what it is," Mama said. "A Baron Samedi veve. Samedi is the guardian of the dead."

"Why would Bobby Blanchard have a voodoo tattoo?" Tony asked.

"No idea," Mama said. "What else do you have?"

"Bobby had cuts on the soles of both feet. The pathologist scraped brown powder out of the cuts. Here's a sample."

Mama opened the small envelope and tapped some on her saucer.

"Zombie powder," she said.

"What the hell is that?" Tony asked.

"Mambos and houngans use it to create a zombie from a normal human."

"You're kidding me," Tony said. "I thought that was all mumbo jumbo."

"Hardly," Mama said. "Zombies are real."

"I'll take your word for it," Tony said. "What's the significance of the ground glass?"

"The mambo or houngan sets a trap by placing the powder where their victim might walk without shoes. The powder is useless unless it gets into the blood. The glass lacerates the bottom of the victim's feet."

"What is in zombie powder?"

"If I told you, I'd have to kill you," Mama said.

"This isn't a joke," Tony said.

"Sorry," Mama said. "Why do you need to know what's in the powder?"

"I probably don't. The pathologist called the

brown stuff voodoo powder. He told the tech his Haitian nanny had paralyzed him when he was a boy making him unable to move or speak."

"That's what zombie powder does," Mama said.

"Really?" Tony said. "The nanny's name was Mirlande Casseus. Ever heard of her?"

Mama shook her head. "One thing about your story has me puzzled."

"Which part?" Tony asked. "Everything about it puzzles me."

"You're saying the young man was naked and bleeding, and no one saw him after he left the autopsy room?"

"Correct," Tony said.

"Seems impossible unless someone helped him escape," Mama said.

"Probably so," Tony said. "But who?"

"Whoever zombied the young man would have known where he went," Mama said. "Maybe they were waiting to assist in his escape."

"If that's true, they almost waited too long."

"Even if aware of someone cutting on him, he wouldn't have been able to do anything about it," Mama said.

Mama nodded when Tony asked, "Zombie powder's that powerful?"

"Someone must have given him the antidote and had expected it to work sooner than it did," Mama said. "When he came out from under the drug and bolted, they were there to corral him."

"Makes sense," Tony said. "I interviewed the autopsy tech. I don't believe he had anything to do with it."

"Wouldn't not reporting the incident go against hospital protocol?" Mama asked.

"Since they didn't complete the autopsy, Dugas seemed to think the hospital forgot about it," Tony said. "He also told me no one called the police."

"Highly unlikely," Mama said. "The hospital could have their socks sued off for not complying with the law."

"Maybe Jack Dugas wasn't aware of the police report. I'll call Tommy and get a copy."

"Call him now," Mama said.

Tommy Blackburn. Tony's former N.O.P.D. partner still worked there. Tony punched in the number on his cell phone.

"Tommy, it's Tony. Got a minute?"

Tommy Blackburn had taken Tony's old job when Tony departed. They'd grown up in the Irish Channel District and remained close friends. It didn't affect their friendly bantering whenever they conversed.

"Don't you ever call to see how I'm doing and not for free information?"

Tony knew what was coming. "Lil's cooking meatloaf tonight. Come over about seven. We'll catch up on things."

"You'd better call and ask Lil first," Tommy said.

"You always have Lil's green light," Tony said. "Other than me, she's your biggest fan."

"Okay," Tommy said. "You know I can't resist Lil's meatloaf. What do you need me to look up for you?"

"You at your computer?"

"Here in front of me," Tommy said.

"Check if you have a police report on the Robert Blanchard, Jr. autopsy."

Tony waited while Tommy keyed the information into the computer.

"He died at his apartment near Conti and Burgundy in the French Quarter," Tommy said. "The N.O.P.D. filed an accidental death report. I can get it for you."

"What else?" Tony asked.

"That's all we got."

"That's it?"

"I'll bring the report with me tonight."

"Was he alone when he died?" Tony asked.

"His live-in girlfriend found him unconscious and called 9-1-1. The hospital pronounced him dead."

"Have a name for the girlfriend?" Tony asked.

"Stevie Jones," Tommy said.

"Thanks, Tommy, you're a sweetheart. See you tonight."

Mama had only heard Tony's end of the conversation. "Well?" she asked.

"His girlfriend found him and called 9-1-1," Tony said. "The E.M.T.s told the police he was dead."

"Zombie powder renders the heart rate so low, it's impossible to determine death by normal means," Mama said.

"Somebody knew he wasn't dead," Tony said.

"It makes sense why the hospital didn't call the police," Mama said. "Let me see your folder."

While Mama studied the report, Tony made another scotch and occupied his time watching Mama's three cats playing with the rubber ball on the back porch. After pushing the report aside, Mama poured more vodka.

"Find anything?" Tony asked.

Still digesting what she'd just read, Mama didn't immediately answer, a slight sway of her head Tony's only clue she'd even heard his question.

"There are notes in the margins," she finally said. "One note mentions Dr. Pompeo's sister Pearl's relation to Mirlande Casseus."

"What does it say?" Tony asked.

"Nothing much," Mama said. "In parentheses beside Pearl's name, it says Pearl Pompeo, chief administrator at this hospital."

"Dugas told me everyone in Pompeo's family except him loved Mirlande Casseus and seemed to be under her spell," Tony said. "That included his sister Pearl."

"Could be our connection," Mama said. "Better check it out."

"You're good," Tony said.

"Your job to find out. Not mine," Mama said.

"You know more than you're telling me?" Tony said.

"Voodoo practitioners create zombies for use as enslaved people. Maybe what we are dealing with is human trafficking."

"Slave trafficking is common," Tony said. "Why bother using voodoo?"

"Total control," Mama said. "Zombies don't require much attention. You don't have to worry about them escaping or reporting their condition to the authorities."

"When I think of zombies, I envision a dead person with body parts falling off."

Mama laughed. "You've seen too many movies and T.V. shows. Zombies aren't dead and can do anything someone living can do. The main difference is the person who zombied them also controls them with the zombie powder."

"Like Mirlande Casseus paralyzed Dr. Pompeo when he was a boy?" Tony said.

"Exactly," Mama said. "We need to speak with Pearl Pompeo."

"I'll run her bio," Tony said.

"And Mirlande Casseus's bio," Mama said. "I'll check with my counterparts and see if I can find anything about her."

"Something I didn't tell you. Bobby had two tattoos. The second was M1231 below his nipple," Tony said. "Dugas told me Pompeo described it as an Auschwitz tattoo."

Mama topped up Tony's scotch tumbler.

"What's Wyatt's part in all of this?" Mama asked.

"He's in Mandeville, working undercover and staying at the Bell House."

"Why there?" Mama asked.

"Bobby's parents found a key to a room there after his last visit to their house. Bobby was studying to be a journalist and was working on an article in Mandeville. He told his parents he couldn't talk about it because it could put them in danger."

"Hope Wyatt avoids the danger," Mama said.

"Wyatt's a pro. He's worked undercover and understands the risk. He'll be fine."

"Tony, I told you I'm bored to tears. Let me help you on this case."

"I don't know," he said.

"My services are free."

"P.I. work can be boring," Tony said. "And sometimes dangerous."

"If it's dangerous, then it's not boring," she said. "Please?"

"What's your idea?" he asked.

"Then I'm in?"

"Why not? You've already helped me. Tell me your plan."

"Visit Bobby's apartment on Conti and question his girlfriend," she said

"We'll have to do it tomorrow," Tony said.

"Why is that?"

"Tommy. He likes Lil's meatloaf and my liquor. He'll head to my house soon as he gets off work," Tony said.

"We're not far from the French Quarter, and it isn't even noon. We'll be back in plenty of time for dinner with Tommy."

"Sure about that?" Tony asked.

Mama was already hurrying to change clothes.

"Have I ever led you astray?"

Chapter 7

Tony had ridden in Mama's car on several occasions. He didn't like it. She had frequent bouts of road rage, and her erratic driving drove him bonkers. She tended to race from one stop sign to the next and slam on the brakes at the last moment. Tony kept his mouth shut after deciding he didn't want to get into it with her.

Mama ignored Tony's silence. She thought of herself as an excellent driver and dreamed of racing professionally. Her car was a fully restored vintage Bugeye Sprite. The little car had two leather bucket seats, and Mama lowered the convertible top when they got into the car.

Seeing the scowl on Tony's face, Mama said, "You don't like my little car, do you?"

"I love it," he said.

"Then why are you frowning?" she asked.

"Forgot my sunglasses. It only looks like I'm frowning."

Mama let the matter drop as she headed toward the French Quarter, slowing on Canal Street when she reached Chartres.

"I'm going to find a place to park near Bertram's," Mama said. "We can walk to the apartment on Conti. When we finish, we'll have drinks at Bertram's."

"I'm too old to hike all over the French Quarter. Can't we drive?"

"Nonsense," Mama said. "Though I wasn't going to say anything, you're starting to get your belly back."

"I've gained a few pounds," Tony conceded. "I'm not as heavy as I once was."

"When was the last time you exercised?"

"Don't remember," he said.

Mama parked the car, raised the top, and locked the door.

"We're walking. It would help if you had the exercise, and I'm not taking no for an answer," she said.

"My knee still gives me problems," Tony said.

"Give me a break! Competent doctors surgically repaired your ACL. You've had months to heal. We're walking."

"Okay, drill sergeant," Tony said.

"Don't be condescending," Mama said. "I'm here to help and not to take verbal abuse."

Tony rolled his eyes and followed the attractive voodoo mambo/Tulane English professor with a killer body.

Mama turned and gave him a dirty look when he said, "Yes, ma'am."

Mama moved at a race walker's pace and said, "Try to keep up."

"You're going to give me a heart attack."

"A fat lip is what I'm going to give you," she said.

Mama stopped when they came upon a pretty blond girl in a flower-print dress selling single roses from a bucket of water.

"How much?" Mama asked.

She smiled when the girl said, "Ten dollars."

"Give you five," Mama said. When the girl handed her the rose, Mama looked at Tony. "Give

55

her five dollars."

"Me?" Tony said. "You're the one who bought it."

"We may need it for our investigation," Mama said. "You're on the clock. Pay the young lady."

Tony reached for his wallet. The girl kissed him when he handed her a ten.

"Thank you," she said. "That's the first sale I've had all day."

Tony handed her another ten. "Then give me another," he said.

The smiling girl kissed him again before he managed to pull away and chase after Mama. When he caught up to her, he handed her the rose.

"What's this for?"

"For you," Tony said.

"You didn't have to do that."

"I'm on the clock. Frankie Castellano paid for it."

"If I didn't know better, I'd think you were trying to get into my pants," she said.

Tony didn't bother replying as he hurried after her up the sidewalk.

After several weeks of daily rainfall, the sky above the Quarter was blue, not a cloud anywhere. A brass band belted out a rousing jazz favorite on the sidewalk as a flock of seagulls flew overhead on their way to Lake Pontchartrain.

There wasn't a single frowning face in the people they passed on the street. With the spicy aroma of gumbo and jambalaya wafting from the open doors they strolled past, how could there be?

When the Americans bought Louisiana from the French and began moving to New Orleans, outbreaks of malaria, cholera, and yellow fever were rampant. No one knew what caused these deadly plagues. The common belief at the time was bad air called 'miasma' caused the epidemics.

Americans saw the Creoles living close together in the French Quarter, usually residing above the shops on the second floor to avoid the bad air. The Americans decided to do better.

In a new neighborhood known as the Garden District, they built multi-storied houses surrounded by big yards and tall fences separating them from their neighbors. The gardens they created as 'miasma moats' helped coin the name 'Garden District' as it is known today.

One thing every resident of New Orleans soon learned was there was no guarantee you'd survive much past the beginning of adulthood. Residents lived for the moment, learning to party and celebrate as if there were no tomorrow. In New Orleans, there often was no tomorrow.

Tony was grumbling when he and Mama reached the old apartments where Robert Blanchard Jr. had lived with his girlfriend, Stevie Jones.

The apartment complex was almost as old as the French Quarter. This complex had three apartments on the second floor, surrounding a tiny courtyard. To enter the courtyard, a resident had to buzz you in. Mama punched Apartment 3 and waited for someone to answer.

"Who is it?" a female voice said.

"Professor Mulate," Mama said.

When the heavy door into the courtyard buzzed, Mama pushed it open and started upstairs, where a smiling young woman waited. When Mama reached the top of the stairs, the young woman hugged her as if they were long-lost friends.

"Professor Mulate. What are you doing here?"

"Wondering what happened to the most

promising poet I ever taught," Mama said. "Stevie, this is Tony Nicosia."

Stevie was chocolate brown, her eyes sparkling and hair braided in tight cornrows. Her cutoff jeans almost made Tony blush and showed off her athletic legs. Her bright red, low-cut blouse identified her as an outgoing person. Stevie had yet to let go of Mama, and Tony wondered why she hadn't invited them into her apartment.

"Hi, Tony," she said. "Tulane's expensive, and I ran out of money. Got a job I hate and met an unlikely man who rocked my world."

Stevie nodded when Mama said, "Robert Blanchard?"

"I've never loved anyone like I loved Bobby," Stevie said.

"Can we talk to you about Bobby?" Tony asked.

"You a cop?" Stevie asked.

"Used to be," Tony said. "I'm a private dick now."

Stevie glanced at Mama. "Bobby was the only white man I ever trusted," she said. "You can see what it got me."

Mama handed Stevie one of the roses. "Tony's a little rough around the edges sometimes, but he's good as gold and a black man in white skin," Mama said. "He bought us these roses."

Stevie gave Tony an assessing glance as she put the rose under her nose and inhaled its fragrance.

"Is he your boyfriend?" she asked.

Mama laughed out loud. "Just a friend. No sex is involved. Well, maybe once during a voodoo ceremony."

"Then you're a lucky man," Stevie said.

"I have no recollection of having ever laid a hand on Mama," Tony said.

"Every wife in America has heard that excuse," Stevie said. "Are you really into voodoo, Mama, or pulling my leg?" Stevie asked.

"She's a mambo," Tony said. "If you need to put a spell on somebody, Mama's the one to call."

Mama laughed and said, "Tony's being dramatic. I'm still the caring English professor you knew."

"You're kidding me," Stevie said. "I've never thought of you as anything but a straight-laced classical English teacher," Stevie said. "What do you know about Baron Samedi?"

"He's the keeper of cemeteries and the dead," Mama said. "What about him?"

"Bobbie," Stevie said. "He came home one night with a Baron Samedi tattoo on his wrist. He called it a veve."

Stevie shook her head when Mama asked, "Did he say where he'd gotten it?"

Realizing they were still standing outside her open door, Stevie said, "I'm so sorry. My little apartment is a mess."

"We can talk here if you want," Tony said. "No big deal."

"I'm working in thirty minutes and need to change clothes. Please come in."

Stevie's apartment had no windows and was dark as well as tiny. She pulled a screen in front of her while she changed clothes. She pulled back the screen, dressed in black shorts and a yellow tee shirt emblazoned with the name of a Bourbon Street nightclub. Tony pulled out his wallet and showed Stevie two one-hundred-dollar bills.

"Call in sick," he said. "My employer is more than happy to pay for your time."

"You sure?" Stevie said. "I don't make this much in two shifts."

"We're desperate for information about the disappearance of Bobby Blanchard, and our employer has ample money to fund the investigation," Mama said.

"I'd be cheating you because I told the police all I know," Stevie said. "I'd offer you something to drink though all I have is tap water."

Seeing a tear forming in Stevie's eye, Mama hugged her and didn't let go.

"Baby, you need to return to school. Have you written anything lately?"

"I haven't been worth a damn since Bobby died. My very soul is destroyed."

"We have reason to believe Bobby isn't dead. Come with us to Bertram's Bar on Chartres," Mama said. "We can talk more comfortably there, and a few drinks will make us all feel better."

"My client is buying," Tony said. "Only problem is we'll have to walk."

"I have wheels," Stevie said. "The fenders don't match on the old bomb, but she always gets me where I want to go. I'll drive."

Stevie's dented Toyota got them to Bertram's in short order. She parked beside Mama's Bugeye Sprite.

"Tony will also pay for parking, won't you, Tony?" Mama said.

"Happy to," Tony said.

They were soon sitting on barstools at Bertram's bar. Still early, Mama, Tony, and Stevie were the only customers.

"Who's this pretty girl?" Bertram asked.

"Stevie Jones," Mama said. "The Big Easy's best poet."

"What are you drinking, pretty Miss Stevie?" Bertram asked.

"Something sweet," Stevie said.

"How about a lime mojito?" Bertram said. "I already know what these other two yahoos want."

Bertram began fixing Tony's scotch, Mama's martini, and Stevie's mojito as Stevie squeezed

Mama's hand.

"I've given up on poetry, Professor Mulate," she said. "Survival is my only interest now."

"Nonsense," Mama said. "I'll help you get a scholarship. You need to be creating and teaching and not waitressing for fifteen bucks an hour."

Stevie laughed. "Try living on twelve dollars an hour. It ain't pretty."

Tony handed Stevie another hundred. "You and Mama work on your poetry career. My client is paying for info on Bobby Blanchard."

Stevie's smile disappeared. "He was the love of my life. When he died, I didn't think I'd survive."

Bertram had pushed their drinks toward them. Stevie smiled when she tasted the mojito.

"Tell us about your relationship with Bobby Blanchard," Mama said.

"He didn't have a racist bone in his body," Stevie said. "We were a number long before I realized he was the son of a prominent state senator. Bobby's parents weren't so forthcoming."

Stevie laughed when Mama said, "His parents didn't like you?"

"About like the plague," Stevie said. "My parents were as bad."

"It's a tribal thing," Mama said. "As primitive as first life on earth."

"If you say so," Stevie said.

"What happened to Bobby?" Tony asked.

Stevie waited a long moment before she began speaking. When she did, emotion wracked her voice.

"We were asleep in the apartment when someone buzzed in. I was half asleep when Bobby got out of bed and went to the door."

"Did he recognize who was ringing in?" Mama asked.

Stevie slugged her mojito. "I was only

subliminally aware of Bobby getting out of bed to answer the intercom. He must have recognized the voice of the person buzzing to get into the compound because he let them in."

Tony glanced at Mama. "Them?" he said

"I couldn't hear what was going on, though I had a feeling of dread," Stevie said. "I don't know what came over me, because I was afraid to go outside."

"Did you hear anything?" Tony asked.

Stevie was crying again. "I felt as if I were dreaming though I sensed Bobby was confused. The men had done something to him."

"Like what?" Tony asked.

"I don't know," Stevie said. "As I said, I couldn't hear what they were saying."

"Can you tell us anything about what happened?" Tony asked.

"My neighbors arrived home from work," Stevie said. "They spooked the three people."

Tony gave Mama another glance. "Your neighbors?"

"Bruno and Harvey," Stevie said. "They live next door. They scared off the men."

"What do you mean?" Tony asked.

"The three men left when Harvey and Bruno arrived. They helped me call 9-1-1 and stayed with me until the EMTs arrived."

As Tony and Mama squeezed her hands, Stevie could no longer contain her tears.

"I know this is tough. Can you tell us the rest of the story," Tony said.

"The EMTs said Robert was dead. I was beside myself when they took his body away."

"We need to talk to Harvey and Bruno," Tony said.

"They're not straight like you are. They are cross-dressers and work in a drag show in the French Quarter," Stevie said.

"Will they talk to us?" Tony asked.

"If I ask them to," Stevie said.

Hours had passed, and Bertram's regular customers were beginning to appear when Tony's cell phone rang. It was Lil."

"Tony, where are you? Tommy's been here for more than an hour."

Tony opened his wallet and cleared the tab with Bertram.

"Keep the tab open for these two," he said. "I'll square up with you next time I'm in the bar."

Mama was smiling as Tony disappeared out the door.

"Bring Stevie another mojito and me a double, Bertram," she said. "Sounds like the party is just beginning."

Chapter 8

I followed Toni's directions to the Bell House. The old bed and breakfast sat on the north edge of Lake Pontchartrain and afforded a grand view across the vast lake. I parked the bike in front and didn't bother locking it as a flock of seagulls flew amid the puffy clouds overhead.

The old wooden structure was square-shaped and two and a half stories tall. Large windows displayed the beautiful lake—at least the first two stories. A tower above the top floor housed the brass bell which gave the building its name. Green storm shutters covered all the windows on the top story. I wondered what might be lurking on the mysterious floor as I strolled up the path to the front door.

A bell tinkled when I entered the antique entrance of the bed and breakfast, an attractive older woman standing behind the counter greeting me with a friendly smile.

"Help you?" she asked.

"Thomas Wyatt. I have a reservation."

The woman was tall, voluptuous, and too old to wear her hair in braided pigtails. Her low-cut peasant's dress revealed more than a glimpse of her ample breasts, the twinkle in her big brown eyes telling me she'd caught me looking.

"I'm Tiana Brown. Glad you could make it, Mr. Wyatt," she said. "I have you booked for our main suite on the second floor."

"Wonderful," I said. "How many rooms do you have?"

"Four, all with a view of Lake Pontchartrain," she said.

"There are no windows on the third floor. Have something you're keeping secret up there?"

"Only ghosts. Mystery and fantasy are part of the adventure when you stay at the Bell House," Tiana said.

"The lakefront is gorgeous," I said. "I brought my camera. When's the best time for great pics?"

"Dusk or dawn, and anytime in between. It's quite spectacular when a storm brews out over the lake."

"I can imagine," I said.

"Have a family waiting at home?"

Tiana's question didn't catch me by surprise. "Single," I said. "No wife or immediate family. My parents live in Alaska."

"You're a long way from home, Mr. Wyatt," she said.

"My job keeps me on the road. I like it like that," I said, handing Tiana Brown the credit card Toni had given me.

"We have unadvertised amenities not found on the Internet," Tiana said.

"Such as?"

"If you aren't out and about, we bring dinner to your room at ten," she said.

"How nice," I said.

"It's always home-cooked. My daughter will bring it to you if you're awake and in your room."

Tiana handed me the key. "Great," I said. "Can you give me directions?"

"There's a stairway outside the door. Your room is at the top of the stairs."

"Thanks," I said.

"Wait," Tiana said as I started for the door. She handed me a small box. "Complimentary chocolates. Hope you'll love them."

I took the little box from her, opening it as I climbed the stairs. The small portion of the chocolate truffle had a definite metallic under taste, and I spit it out. I had a plastic baggie in my backpack and put the truffles into one for Tony to check for drugs. When I reached the top of the stairs, I rested my elbows on the rails and stared across the lake.

A rocking chair and a potted palm tree occupied much of the deck. I started to sit but decided first to check my room. Someone had turned up the air conditioning, and the temperature was almost tolerable when I entered.

I headed back down the stairs, opening the door to the office.

"I'm going to do some exploring," I said. "I'll be back."

"Enjoy," she said.

I spent the next few hours biking along the Tammany Trace. The day was delightfully sunny and warm. Months of little to no exercise had left my muscles stiff, the burn reminding me of my inactivity as I pedaled past joggers and other bikers. When I reached the rustic North Shore town of Covington, the position of the sun and my growling stomach reminded me I hadn't eaten in a while.

Nothing moves fast in the south, and Covington was no exception. I hadn't visited the little gem of a town in years. Little had changed, and I found the unique layout of the streets and houses as confusing as ever. The palm trees lining the historic district streets reminded me the little Louisiana town was semi-tropical. A smiling stroller pointed me toward Pancho's

Place. I found Pancho waiting at the door.

"Come in," he said. "You're my first customer of the day. You hungry?"

"Starved," I said.

My disguise was working, Pancho unaware he knew me. He was short, probably no taller than five-two or three. I didn't know how old he was though he still had all his teeth. They were on full display beneath his bushy mustache as he led me to a corner table.

"You want pizza?" he asked.

"I love all Italian food, and I want to try the pizza. I hear it's the best on the North Shore."

"What you drinking?" he asked.

"Lemonade if you have it. Tea, no sugar if you don't."

"Do I know you?" Pancho asked.

"We've never met," I said.

"You look familiar. I can't quite place you," he said. "You know my daughter, Adele?"

"Never had the pleasure," I said.

Pancho didn't catch my lie as he headed toward the little kitchen in the back. He returned with lemonade and two slices of pepperoni pizza. Not leaving the table, he waited until I'd proclaimed the pizza the best I'd ever put in my mouth, nodding as if he already knew what I was going to say.

My appetite was satiated when I walked out of Pancho's. The little café began filling with diners, making me happy I'd gotten there early. Unlocking my bike, I took an exploratory ride through the old neighborhoods.

I found Vodou Nitz, the popular nightclub on the edge of town. I wondered what I would find there when I visited. The parking lot was already half-filled. A stretch limo entered the parking lot as I watched. I thought I recognized the man exiting from the back of the vehicle, though I couldn't be sure.

I spent the rest of the day exploring the Farmer's Market and many local attractions. It was late when I started toward the Bell House. The sky was growing dark as I parked my bike, locking it for the night.

The skies above Pontchartrain had turned crimson, an eagle swirling in and out of the hypnotic clouds. Glancing up at the shuttered third floor of the Bell House, I decided I needed to see what was up there.

Crouching in the shadows beneath the drooping branches of a live oak, I felt invisible. I remained cloaked in darkness, studying the old bed and breakfast structure while deciding what to do. It didn't take me long; the question was how I planned to do it.

A cool breeze was blowing off the lake. The Bell House, like most of the buildings constructed before the age of air conditioning, had used its design to take advantage of everything nature offered to combat the region's often demanding heat and humidity. This included circular porches to escape the heat when temperatures inside the houses became too damn hot.

Roofs did more than cover the houses; they extended far over the porches, ensuring no direct sunlight entered the house. They also had storm shutters, closing to protect the building from storms and opening to direct a breeze into the place.

The third floor of the Bell House had shutters but no porch and no obvious way to access it. The third floor was only accessible inside the Bell House, with bolts securing the shutters. I guessed there were no open shutters. I would never know unless I crawled up on the roof above the second story and checked them.

By now, it was dark, and no one had seen me

arrive. Moving out of the shadows, I climbed an adjacent tree until I was high enough to access the steep roof. My tennis shoes allowed me to ascend the roof without falling until I'd reached one of the dark green storm shutters. Storm bolts secured the first shutter I tried to open, and I inched slowly to the next one.

I found the next two shutters also bolted and was almost back to my original starting point when I struck pay dirt. The last shutter moved when I gave it a yank, old wood creaking as I opened it enough to slip inside.

The room was dark, the temperature warm and heavy with humidity. I let a minute pass before I moved away from the wall. The darkness disappeared when I flicked on my miniature flashlight and shined it around the room. The large room was empty. Almost.

Lying on the wooden floor near the opposite wall was a naked woman. The floor creaked when I went to her. Two things caught my attention: the woman was someone I knew, and she seemed dead.

The woman was Latitia Boiset, the lead singer for a Vegas show band named Brass & Sass. Curly hair draped to her bare shoulders, her pouty lips and obsidian eyes needing no makeup. Her dark eyes stared at me when I placed my fingers on her jugular, trying to find a pulse. I kissed her on the lips.

"Damn it, baby! How the hell did you wind up here."

Though she had no vital signs, I felt she wasn't dead and could hear every word I said. She had a tattoo I didn't remember her having under her left breast. It was F1232.

"Latitia, it's me, Wyatt," I said. "I'm going to get you out of here though I can't do it now. I promise I won't let this stand. Stay strong, baby.

There was little I could do as I climbed down the roof and back to the ground. I ascended the stairs to my room on the second floor, my eyelids drooping as I put my backpack on the floor and lay on the comfortable bed. It was the last thing I remembered until I heard a knock on the door.

A young woman in a low-cut dress similar to Tiana's entered without knocking. After placing a food tray on a wooden stand, she sat on the edge of the bed and began spooning tasty soup into my mouth. When I gazed up into the young woman's eyes, she showed no reaction.

"Are you Tiana's daughter?"

"Yes," she said.

"What's your name?"

"Eshe."

"I've never heard that name," I said

"It means 'life' in Swahili," she said.

While Tiana's café au lait skin seemed to indicate mixed heritage, Eshe's was ebony, her hair done in intricate cornrows and not pigtails. I didn't protest when she spooned more soup into my mouth.

Eshe was young, certainly no older than twenty, and sat so close to me that I could feel the heat emanating from her body. Whatever somnolent drug was in the soup prevented me from moving away.

"How old are you, Eshe?" I asked.

"Old enough," she said, putting her willowy arms around my neck.

I wanted to pull away, get out of bed and run for the door. Whatever anesthetic was in the soup and the primal scent of Eshe's erotic perfume prevented my doing so. Eshe unbuttoned my shirt and began probing my nipples with supple fingers. It was the last thing I remembered as I floated in and out of consciousness.

Chapter 9

When I opened my eyes, I was naked on the floor at the foot of my bed, the morning sun shining through the window. Eshe was gone, though someone had rifled through my wallet and traveling bag. My skull pounded as I threw up in the toilet.

Though I needed a strong cup of coffee and a handful of aspirins, I knew better than to eat or drink anything from the Bell House. I felt better, though not much, after taking a long shower and changing clothes. Tiana was waiting for me in the open doorway to the office when I came down the stairs.

"Is your room acceptable?" she asked.

"Love it," I said.

"Your complimentary breakfast is waiting for you," she said.

"Never eat breakfast," I said.

"Coffee?"

"I have to watch my caffeine intake," I said. "Rapid heartbeat."

I could tell from Tiana's smile she knew I was lying. It made me wonder why I wasn't already lying naked beside Latitia on the third floor of the Bell House.

"Suit yourself," she said.

71

"I'm going for a bike ride along the Tammany Trace to check out the area and take a few pictures."

"If you're doing a travel article on the region, why go further than the Bell House? You can take some stunning pictures from your balcony," Tiana said.

"I want to capture a few peripheral shots of the North Shore to complement the article."

"Will you return before dark?" she asked.

"That's my plan," I said.

"Did Eshe make you feel at home last night?" she asked.

Tiana smiled again when I said, "Mrs. Brown, you have a lovely daughter."

As I pedaled away from the Bell House, I had little doubt that Tiana had helped Eshe strip me naked and rifle through my possessions.

The temperature was warm, the weather humid, as I left the city streets of Mandeville and entered the Tammany Trace. I'd gone no more than a mile when I passed Toni waiting beside the trail. I slowed until she caught up with me.

"It's after ten," she said. "I was starting to worry about you."

"Except for a short-term memory loss and a splitting headache, I'm good."

"What happened?" she asked.

"Long story. Know where I can get coffee and a handful of aspirins."

"Both," she said, "Though we shouldn't be seen together, even on this trail. Give me five minutes, and then follow."

"You aren't going to leave me in the lurch on that rocket of yours, are you?"

Her grin told me she liked my comment. "I'll make sure you don't get lost."

Before following her, I waited five minutes after Toni had sped away down the Tammany

Trace. When I caught up about two miles down the trace, she pointed to a path leading into the woods. We traversed a bumpy path for about a mile before exiting near a scenic river.

"Frankie's fishing camp isn't far from here," she said.

"Is it secure?"

"You kidding me? Frankie's a stickler for security. Though you wouldn't know by looking at it, the camp is electronically monitored twenty-four hours a day."

Toni led me to a nondescript one-story boathouse moored at a dock on the beautiful river. Stale air gasped when she opened the door.

"No one's been here for a while," she said. "Frankie hasn't visited this houseboat in years."

The outside of Frankie's fishing camp was plain, the inside nothing short of regal. I gazed out one of the picture windows at the pastoral scene. "The river is beautiful. Like a little slice of heaven."

"The Tchefuncte," she said. "Seventy miles of picturesque scenery and the confluence with Lake Pontchartrain not far from here."

"Never heard that name before. Where did it come from."

"I sound like a school teacher, but Tchefuncte is derived from chinquapin, a species of chestnut Indians used to relieve headaches and fevers."

She grinned when I said, "Wish I had some right now."

Toni opened a tin and tapped out two aspirins.

"Take these," she said. "I'll get your coffee."

When the aspirins began kicking in, the air conditioner had overcome the heat and rampant humidity.

"Feeling better?" Toni asked as she handed me a mug of steaming coffee.

"Much better," I said. "Best coffee I ever tasted. What's your secret?"

"If I told you, it wouldn't be a secret. Just enjoy," she said.

"What a place!" I said. "It's not like any fishing camp I've ever visited."

"You know Frankie," Toni said. "No expense spared. The outside doesn't look like much, but he spent a small fortune on the inside. You should see the liquor larder. Too bad neither of us drinks. You hungry?"

"I could eat something," I said

"I'm a better cook than Mom and Grandpa," Toni said. "Please don't tell either of them I told you so.

"My lips are sealed," I said. "Can I help?"

"Relax," Toni said. "Won't take me long to whip something up."

Toni and I were soon feasting on grits, cream gravy, biscuits, and scrambled eggs.

"Wonderful," I said.

"Now, tell me what happened at the Bell House last night."

"The lady who runs the place is Tiana Brown. Her daughter Eshe works for her when she isn't in school. Tiana gave me a complimentary box of chocolates. I took a bite and spat it out because it tasted metallic."

"Oh, shit!" she said.

"I put the truffles in a baggie for testing though forgot to take them with me."

"Should I call Frankie and have the place shut down?"

"There's more to the story," I said.

"Let's go out on the deck," Toni said. "I need a little sun."

Rocking chairs overlooked the Tchefuncte River. Near the shore, snowy egrets fished among the cypress knees. Two otters romped in the shallow water.

"Tell me why you needed aspirins?" Toni asked.

"I had passed out on the bed. Tiana's daughter Eshe shook me until I awoke."

"How did she get into your room?"

"Pass key. She began spooning soup into my mouth. Eshe was young, maybe not even of legal age. Whatever drug was in the soup blunted my senses to the point I didn't care."

"You had sex with a minor?" Toni asked.

I smiled and shook my head. "I was too dysfunctional to move, much less perform. As I said, I woke up this morning naked on the floor."

"You can't go back there," Toni said.

"Maybe I can. Tiana and her daughter were checking my cover story."

"They wouldn't have found anything to make them suspicious," Toni said.

"That's what worries me. My M.O. matches Blanchard's. If they're in on his disappearance, why didn't they take me when they had the opportunity?"

"I need to get out of these shorts," she said. "Wait on me?"

"I'm going nowhere," I said as she reentered Frankie's camp.

Toni returned in a black bikini, revealing an overall tan as far as my popping eyes could see.

"You like?" she asked.

"Baby, you're giving me ideas. Country living has done wonders for you. You're gorgeous," I said.

"I was overly plump growing up and had many body issues. I've fought my doubts for years," she said.

"Life can be a cold nest of insecurities," I said. "We all have them."

"I can't believe you were ever insecure," she

said.

"Some of us just cover it better than others," I said.

"Take off your shirt," she said.

"I'm comfortable," I said.

"To hell with your comfort," she said. "I want to see your body."

I slipped my shirt over my head and dropped it onto the deck. Toni stared at my bare chest. "How old are you?"

"Old enough," I said.

"Pull down your pants. I want to see your ass."

"You're kidding," I said.

"I'm not."

I stood and let my shorts drop to the deck. Toni got out of her rocker, pushed me back down in my chair, sat in my lap, and kissed me.

When she finally pulled away, she said, "What a nice ass. It's the first thing I ever noticed about you."

"You couldn't have been more than eighteen when I met you," I said.

"I was a fat fifteen-year-old who took a while to accept her body image."

"I'm having a hard time thinking of you as anything other than a goddess right now."

"I can see that," she said. "Do you want to have sex with me?"

"The thought's crossing my mind."

"Put your pants back on," she said. "We're working a case. Remember?"

"I'm working a case. You work for Frankie."

"What happened last night?"

"Something unexpected," I said.

Toni returned to her rocker as I pulled up my shorts. "Tell me," she said.

"The Bell House is two and a half stories tall, the upper story permanently shuttered. I decided to have a look."

"How did you get up there?"

"Climbed a tree."

"The roof is so steep."

"I was careful," I said.

"You managed to get inside?"

"One of the shutters wasn't bolted. I had a flashlight and what I found was mostly an empty attic with only a few old chairs and trunks strewn about."

"That's all?"

"Not quite. A naked woman was lying on the floor."

"Get out of here!"

"She had no vital signs, was cold to the touch, and had no pulse."

"A dead person?"

"If she were dead, it was recent because there was no sign of decomposition, bruising, or trauma. She had a tattoo below her left breast I didn't recognize."

"Wait a minute," Toni said. "You knew this woman well enough to know she had a new tattoo below her left breast?"

"Yes," I said.

"What's her name?"

Latitia Boiset," I said.

"The lead singer for Brass & Sass? She's not missing."

"How do you know that?"

"Her show band is headlining at Vodou Nitz. Everyone who has seen the band raves about it. Some friends and I are planning to see them. What about this tattoo?"

"The letter F followed by the number 1232."

"Sounds more like a serial number than a skin ornament," Toni said.

"Like a brand ranchers put on their cattle," I said.

A fishing boat motored past on the river, its occupants waving when they saw us.

"You had an affair with Latitia Boiset?" Toni asked.

"A while back."

"She's the hottest performer in Vegas. How did you meet her?"

"I caught her act years ago at a club in Fat City. It was the same night I met you and your mom."

"Fat City in Metairie?"

I laughed. "How many Fat Citys are there?"

"Only one I know of," Toni said. "Frankie used to own a nightclub there."

"Brass & Sass was playing at Frankie's club the night I met her."

"Are you making this shit up?"

"Everything I've told you is true," I said.

"What next?"

"Visit the voodoo nightclub in Covington."

"I'll tell Frankie. He'll have some men posted in case things get testy. What are you going to do about the Bell House?" Toni asked.

"Haven't decided yet," I said. "If Tiana Brown and her daughter had wanted to control me like they're doing Latitia, they had their chance last night. It's worrisome to me they didn't."

"If you're going to see Brass & Sass, I want to go with you."

"You'll blow my cover," I said.

"You don't trust me, do you?"

"Of course I trust you. I wouldn't be here if I didn't."

"You don't sound very trusting. You think I'm somehow involved in Bobby's disappearance?"

"I didn't say that."

Toni's eyes had turned darker than usual. "Bull shit! It's what you implied."

"I'm sorry if that's what you believe I meant.

It's not."

Our discussion had cooled Toni's ardor, and she covered the bikini with her beach towel.

"You're welcome to stay here as long as you like," she said. "I'm going back to the ranch."

I followed her into the houseboat and watched as she slammed the bathroom door behind her.

"Wait. Can't I even apologize?"

Toni was pissed and didn't bother saying bye. As she pedaled away from the dock, I wondered why she'd become so defensive.

I needed to talk to Tony. Find out what he'd learned and pick his brain a bit. Since I had no cell phone, our conversation wasn't possible. I decided to bike into town and check the post office box he'd rented for me.

Mrs. Brown and her daughter Eshe had probably targeted me thinking no one would miss me if I disappeared like Robert Blanchard, Jr. had. If that were the case, I could see why my insinuation had pissed off Toni. Still, her extreme reaction was unexpected.

I had more questions than answers as I peddled toward Covington. Of one thing, I was sure. I couldn't return to the Bell House and felt uncomfortable in Frankie's Tchefuncte River boathouse. I needed a new base of operation, someplace even the consummate detective Tony Nicosia wouldn't expect.

Chapter 10

Tony had left a pay-as-you-go cell phone in the post office box he'd rented for me. Inside was a fully charged cell phone with a card giving me all the information I might need. When I dialed Tony, he answered on the 2nd ring.

"What's up, Cowboy?" he asked.

"A shit storm," I said.

"What you got?"

"I stayed at the Bell House last night and was drugged. I woke up naked on the floor."

"Sounds like you need to get the hell out of there before you go missing like Bobby Blanchard," Tony said.

"That's what I'm thinking," I said.

"What else?"

"The third floor has no outside entrance. I climbed a tree and got in through an unbolted storm shutter to investigate."

"And?" Tony said.

"I found a naked woman. She had no pulse and was cold as a brick. Doesn't matter because I think she was alive. She was someone I know intimately, Latitia Boiset, the lead singer for a Vegas show band called Brass & Sass."

"Did you check her for tattoos?"

"She had a tattoo that reminded me of a

cattle brand beneath her left breast. F1232."

"What about a voodoo tattoo?" Tony asked.

"No," I said.

"I interviewed the autopsy tech," Tony said. "He told me Bobby Blanchard had a similar tattoo beneath his left nipple. He said the doctor referred to it as Auschwitz-like."

"What about the voodoo symbol?" I asked.

"Mama's helping me," Tony said. "Want to say hi to her?"

"Mama," I said. "How the hell did you let Tony talk you into getting involved in our quagmire?"

"Like you, he's a sweet talker," she said. "We're on our way to check out the live-in girlfriend of Bobby Blanchard."

"What's the deal with the voodoo symbol?"

"Bobby had a Baron Samedi veve tattooed on his wrist," she said.

"So voodoo is part of our problem?" I said.

"There's voodoo involved if that's what you mean. We're checking into it," she said. "I'm handing the phone back to Tony. Be careful, Wyatt."

"I think we're dealing with human trafficking," Tony said. "Maybe an organization using zombie powder to control their captives."

"What the hell is zombie powder?" I asked.

"A drug that takes away your vital signs making you appear dead when you're not."

"Come on!" I said.

"Mama says it's real," Tony said.

"Maybe so," I said. "Latitia might fit that category. What else?"

"There's a voodoo woman from Haiti named Mirlande Casseus who's possibly connected with this caper. She knows about zombie powder."

"You're calling it zombie powder, now?"

"Mama says zombies are real. Mambos and houngans zombie victims to use in various unpaid capacities. Mirlande Casseus may have taken the process to a new level."

"Thanks, Tony," I said. "I'll have to think about it."

"I'm putting this phone back in the post office box. If you have something for me, send me a text message, or leave a voicemail. I'll recheck it tomorrow."

"Watch your ass, Cowboy," Tony said.

"You too," I said.

Tony was correct. After getting drugged and rolled at the Bell House, the risk of returning there outweighed any possible reward. I needed to change my appearance and find another place to stay. I hid Frankie's bike behind a thick patch of shrubbery and hiked to the old part of town. Pancho's little café was empty, and he met me with a smile.

"You must have liked my pizza," he said.

"Best I ever tasted," I said. "I had it a time or two at your restaurant in Metairie."

"I thought I knew you. Help me out here."

"Wyatt Thomas," I said.

"Wyatt's much older than you are," Pancho said.

His comment made me grin. "Toni buzz-cut my hair and then dyed it. These granny glasses are fakes, and I never wear a hat."

I took off the hat and glasses to give him a closer look.

"Why are you in disguise?" he asked.

"I'm working undercover."

"Something is going on in Covington? That's news to me," he said.

"Your son-in-law hired me to find a missing person. Kidnapping is involved, and I suspect there's a connection between the missing person and the new nightclub in town."

"Vodou Nitz?" Pancho said.

"You know about it?"

"I know Frankie owns it," he said.

"You kidding me? Adele, Josie, and Toni don't know he does," I said.

"Toni knows," Pancho said. "She's the one who told me."

"I don't know about Adele. Josie sells real estate all over this area. Why doesn't she know her father owns the biggest nightspot in the parish?"

"He probably doesn't want her to know. There are ways of covering up ownership."

"I understand all too well," I said. "But why?"

Pancho locked the front door and put the closed sign in the window. After motioning me to sit at a booth in the corner of the small café, he grabbed a bottle of ouzo from the bar and joined me.

"I was born in Sicily and came to this country when I was ten with my parents," he said. "My father had a small café, like what I now have. The mafia burned him out because he refused to pay their blood money."

"Let me guess," I said. "The man who burned out your dad was Paco Castellano, Frankie's father."

After pouring himself a glass of ouzo, he took a drink.

"I've never told that story to Adele," he said. "She wouldn't believe me anyway."

Pancho nodded when I said, "Frankie treats his family like royalty."

"He knows why I don't like him," Pancho said. "Though he paid for this café, I have little doubt he'd personally cut my throat if I ever crossed him."

"I don't believe it," I said. "How does Toni know more about Frankie's business than his wife and daughter?"

"Toni works for Frankie. She adores him," Pancho said.

Pancho nodded when I asked, "Have you told her the story about your father's café?"

"She got angry and informed me Frankie would never do anything like that."

"You don't believe her?"

"As I said, I'm from Sicily. Who are you looking for?"

"Bobby Blanchard. The man's dad is a Louisiana senator. Frankie hired another detective and me to find Bobby."

"I read about it in the newspaper," Pancho said. "Bobby's mom is Adele's best friend."

It took a moment for me to remember Adele had shared that little snippet of information with me.

"Let's not worry about Frankie for now. I need to visit Vodou Nitz, and I don't want to be recognized. Will you help me?" I asked.

"Tell me how," Pancho said.

"I need a place to stay for a few days and a new disguise."

Pancho left me alone in the booth, returning with a product called Only for Men. "I can change your hair color," he said. "This will darken your hair."

"Does it work?"

"I use it. Do I look like I'm eighty-three?"

"You aren't that old," I said.

"Oh, yes," he said. "I have a pair of shooting glasses with yellow lenses. Even your mother wouldn't know who you are."

"Except for my clothes," I said.

"Give me your sizes. There's a second-hand store down the street, and my friend Freya will help me fix you up."

Pancho smiled when I said, "Freya?"

I waited in the little café Pancho and an

attractive woman of indeterminate age named Freya arriving with armloads of clothing.

"This is my friend, Wyatt. Can you help me transform his appearance?"

"I'm Freya," the woman said. "I often perform in the local dinner theatre. I've learned a lot about makeup and costuming over the years. It will cost Pancho a bottle of his best Chianti and wonderful pepperoni pizza, though."

Pancho flashed a smile emphasizing his complete set of white teeth.

"You got it, pretty lady," he said.

Freya and Pancho soon had my shirt off, my head under pouring water in the sink as they colored my hair. They dressed me in black pants, a silk shirt, and polished black brogans when they finished.

"No woman will be able to resist you," Freya said.

Pancho brought a large pepperoni pizza from his brick oven. He and Freya toasted with a bottle of Chianti.

"Freya," he said. "Until tonight, no other woman has enamored me like you since my lovely wife passed away thirty years ago."

He grinned when she said, "I'll bet you say that to all the girls."

Freya held a mirror for me to see their creation. "I don't even recognize myself," I said. "How far is Vodou Nitz from here?"

"Too far to walk," Pancho said.

"Pancho and I will take you in my car," Freya said.

"Pancho, I've never tasted better pizza," I said.

Pancho was squeezing Freya's hand. "And you never will," he said.

Freya's car was a baby blue Mazda Miata, a two-seater too small for three. It didn't matter. Freya let Pancho drive, and she sat in my lap as we drove to the giant nightclub on the edge of town. She kissed me before letting me out of the tiny car, and I hugged her.

"How long do you think you'll be?" Pancho said.

"No idea," I said. "Maybe a couple of hours."

I shook my head when he said, "We'll be back in two hours. We'll be waiting in the parking lot."

"You don't have to do that," I said.

"The weather's mild," Freya said. "It'll be fun."

"Then wish me luck," I said as I slipped on the yellow shooting glasses.

"Like we said, your mother wouldn't recognize you."

As I left the Miata, I hoped Pancho was correct. The people at the front door must have thought so because they allowed me to enter without a cover charge.

The club looked familiar, almost like a clone of Frankie's club in Fat City. The primary differences were the voodoo accouterments. A smiling waitress appeared from the darkness to escort me to my table.

"I'm Sindee," she said. "I'll trade you a Skeleton Key for a line of coke."

My drug dealer outfit worked, the yellow shooter's glasses doing the trick.

"No trades until I get to know you, though I'll take that Skeleton Key."

Sindee was a beauty dressed in a wisp of a red velvet outfit, highlighting a pair of legs that went on forever.

"You got it," she said. "I'll be back with your drink."

A blare of trumpets and saxophones from the band almost muted her response.

Like the club in Fat City, tiers of tables surrounded the stage, Brass & Sass in the middle of a number. Eight horn players danced as they played, a wild guitarist and insane drummer keeping the audience captivated. A young woman appeared through the darkness and laid out two lines on the table in front of me.

"Are you buying or selling?" I asked

"Just being friendly," she said.

"I'm busy," I said. "I'll check on you later."

The smiling woman sucked up her line and then disappeared into darkness.

Sindee smiled when she brought me the specialty drink and saw the line on the table. Using a straw, she snorted it without asking.

"Enjoy your Skeleton Key," she said. "I'll check on you in a bit."

Scantily clad Vegas showgirls backed up the band, the dark room reeking of pot and sexual pheromones generated by the rapt crowd.

The club lighting had dimmed to focus on the show onstage. It took a while for my eyes to adjust. When they did, I realized organized crime made up part of the audience.

Everyone at the nearby table was drinking hard liquor and growing louder, and no one in the enthusiastic audience was protesting. One of the saxophone players was the person I'd hoped would be there—Janeen Presley, a girlfriend of mine when I was in high school. She was Latitia's best friend. If anyone knew what had happened to Latitia, it would be Janeen. When the band took a break, I motioned Sindee to return to my table.

"I need to do some business with the young woman playing saxophone. When you have a chance to speak to her, can you have her join me?"

Buzzing from the line she'd snorted, Sindee was more than happy to oblige."

"You got it, handsome," she said.

Chapter 11

The woman who'd laid out the lines on my table returned and scooted into the booth. Though she squeezed my upper thigh, I sensed her motive wasn't sexual. I needed to stay in character. What I didn't need was an unnecessary diversion.

"I'm working and can't play right now," I said.

"No problem," she said. "Another line of coke before I go?"

The young woman's dark hair was a mess, her makeup spoiled, and her grin looked far more than silly. I recognized her as a fellow addict as I pushed my Skeleton Key in front of her.

"You look as if you need a drink. I'll trade you."

After sipping the Skeleton Key, she laid out two more lines of cocaine on the table.

"Will you be around after the show?" she said.

"What's your name?" I asked.

"Sara."

"Get the hell out of here, Sara. I have clients and don't have time for your bullshit."

Tears dripping down Sara's face further spoiled her makeup as she handed me a plastic baggie filled with cocaine.

"I need money. Will you sell this for me?" she

asked.

Pulling out my money clip, I counted out four hundred dollar bills into her hand.

She disappeared into the darkness when I said, "Don't come back."

Sara was a working drug addict and had yet to hit rock bottom. Staying in character grated my nerves, even if I was only acting. One thing I'd learned. When you're working undercover, a conscience will only get you killed.

Forgetting the sad young woman, I glanced around the dark room, hoping no undercover narc had observed the transaction. From the odor of illegal drugs wafting in the refrigerated air, I doubted I had a problem.

Sindee appeared with another drink, grinning when she spotted the two lines. She snorted one without asking and then kissed me before melding into the crowd. Janeen Presley soon approached my booth.

"Sindee said you have something for me."

When I cocked my chin toward the remaining line of cocaine, she scooted beside me and put her arms around my waist.

"I love the way you blow the horn."

"I bet you do," she said.

She grinned when I asked, "What else can you do with those pouty lips of yours."

"Lots of things," she said.

Grabbing the straw Sindee had left on the table, Janeen used it to suck up the cocaine. Her appearance had changed since the last time I'd seen her, blond hair both longer and more brassy. She'd also lost weight, her skin pasty and unhealthy looking.

Though not entirely wasted, she was nervous and babbling as if she were under the influence of several drugs.

It seemed Janeen had no idea who I was as I

checked her hand for a voodoo veve. The lighting again grew dark as I lifted her blouse and used my small flashlight to see if she had a tattoo beneath her left tit. She didn't.

"What the hell are you doing?"

"Sorry," I said. "I have a flashlight tit fetish."

"You're creepy!" she said.

Unperturbed by my creepiness, Janeen moved closer to me and lifted her blouse.

"Don't creep around," she said. "You can see my tits anytime you like as long as you keep serving lines of cocaine."

"Help yourself," I said, tossing the baggie on the table. "Is Latitia performing tonight?" I asked.

Janeen laid out two lines. "Don't know. Haven't seen her in three days. Latitia's a coke whore like me. God only knows where she's at or what she's doing."

"You're not worried about her?"

"She'll be back around."

"Hope so," I said. "I love hearing Latitia sing."

"You and everyone else," Janeen said. "If I had half her talent, I'd be living on a yacht cruising toward St. Marten and not worrying about where my next line was coming from."

"Keep blowing that horn," I said. "You'll be there someday."

"I can blow lots of things if the price is right," she said.

Janeen frowned when I said, "And what is that price."

"I may be a coke whore though I don't fuck for money."

As I pondered the difference between being paid in drugs or money, a change in the lighting signaled Janeen needed to return to the stage.

"I'll be back after the next set," she said.

I grabbed her wrist and pulled her back toward the booth.

"Wait. Any tattoos?"

"Looking at my tattoos will cost you extra," she said with a silly grin.

"I have another line for you if you bring Latitia back with you," I said.

"If she's here," Janeen said before hurrying away.

The lights went down, and the band began playing. An emcee with greasy hair and a sweaty brow appeared from behind the curtains.

"Ladies and gentlemen, it's time for Brass & Sass straight from Vegas. Let's give a big round of applause for New Orleans Creole angel Latitia Boiset."

The crowd went wild as the emcee rushed offstage, and the band fired up a hot number in preparation for the appearance of the show's star. When she danced out onto the stage, no one was disappointed.

White smoke blew up through a grating in the floor, a young woman emerging from it dressed in feathers and a g-string, more revealing than the outfits the backup dancers wore. The dancers joined her in an energetic number leaving the audience in awe. When they finished the song, the lights dimmed again, brightening to reveal Latitia Boiset, clad in a different though still revealing outfit, standing behind a microphone.

I wondered if this was the same woman I'd seen the previous night lying naked and unable to speak on the bare third floor of the Bell House. If it was, it meant my meager understanding of zombification lacked chapters of needed information.

After a short pause, the band began playing a slow melody. Latitia was anything but dead as she belted out a show-stopper. The song ended amid thunderous applause.

Brass & Sass was a classic show band fronted

by a consummate performer. After seeing her in a death-like state the previous night, I could only imagine some drug employing the ultimate in mind control.

Even with the air conditioning on maximum cool, it didn't matter. Everyone was sweating when Latitia finished her final number. The applause continued for five long minutes after she'd departed the stage. The emcee was smiling and admonishing the audience to continue applauding.

He wrung his hands when he said, "Miss Boiset will be back. Don't dare leave."

Though I wasn't a drug dealer, I had to act like one or risk having my cover blown. I laid out three lines of cocaine as Sindee returned with a fresh Skeleton Key.

Seeing the lines on the table, she said, "For me?"

"Go for it."

Sindee sucked up a line and would have taken another. She stopped when Janeen appeared with Latitia in tow.

"Save some for us," Janeen said.

"You got it," Sindee said. "What are you girls drinking?"

"Midnight Gang Bang for me," Janeen said.

"Molotov Cocktail," Latitia said.

Though I'd been a working drunk for many years before becoming a teetotaler, I'd never heard of either drink. I wondered if Bertram Picou ever had.

"There are two lines on the table," Sindee said. "If you girls don't want them, I'll have another."

"Not mine," Janeen said, sucking up her line.

"Take mine," Latitia said. "I have to perform."

"You got it, babe," Sindee said, taking the straw.

When Sindee went for fresh drinks, Latitia slid closer to me.

"I never caught your name," Janeen said.

"No names," I said.

"I'm Latitia," she said, offering me her hand. "Do I know you?"

"I wish you did," I said. "Where were you last night."

"Someplace dark," Latitia said.

"Probably with Philip, our new owner," Janeen said. "A dreamboat."

"He's a dirty little prick," Latitia said.

Someone from the shadows was motioning for Janeen to join them.

"I'll be back," she said as she hurried out of the booth.

When she was gone, Latitia said. "I know it's you, Wyatt. I'm scared shitless, and you have to get me out of here."

"Tell me what's going on," I said.

"A month ago, I was offered the lead in a movie. Management informed me I could never leave the band."

"There's no such thing as a permanent contract," I said.

"Unless you're working for the mob," Latitia said. "Can you help me?"

"Not without busting my cover," I said.

"It's already busted," Latitia said. "The man who summoned Janeen is Philip. I wasn't supposed to leave my dressing room."

"How is he controlling you?"

"Zombie powder. Though I couldn't move a muscle last night, I was aware when you saw me. I wanted to speak, squeeze your hand, and kiss you. I couldn't. It's the most frightening place I've ever been."

"They gave you an antidote so you could sing?

"Yes," she said.

"Why didn't you run?"

"Wyatt, my mom still lives in the 9th Ward. She's raising my daughter. I don't know how Philip found out about her. He's threatened to kill Mom and Aimee if I try to escape."

"You have a daughter named Aimee?" I said. "How old is she?"

"Fifteen, going on twenty-one."

Latitia nodded when I said, "Is she. . . ?"

"She's your daughter, Wyatt. I wasn't ever going to tell you."

"I have a daughter?"

"I'm so sorry," Latitia said. "I thought I was protecting her."

"God damn!" I said.

Latitia squeezed my hand. "I said I was sorry. "I'm going backstage before someone comes looking for me. It would be best if you got the hell out of here. I know I'm going to die. Wyatt, please save Mom and Aimee."

I grabbed her wrist and pulled her back into the booth.

"Don't go so soon. You have at least thirty minutes before your next set and haven't touched your drink."

"I know you hate me now," she said.

"I could never hate you," I said. "What happens to you after the next set?"

"They dose me with zombie powder and put me back in the attic."

"You have to be kidding," I said.

"These people are serious. If they can't control you, they kill you."

"Who is this Philip person?" I asked.

"All I know about him is he's originally from Haiti."

She shook her head when I asked, "Know his last name?"

Latitia blew out the flame burning atop the

Molotov Cocktail and downed the contents of the shot glass in a single swallow.

"Casseus," she said.

"During your set, you changed outfits twice. It couldn't have taken more than thirty seconds. How did you do it?"

"Toward the end of a song, I move to the edge of the stage. When the crew kills the lights, two ladies in wardrobe pull my costume off and put another on."

"Right on stage and with no cover?"

"With the lights out, no one can see anything," Latitia said.

"And you change clothes in thirty seconds?"

"That's how long the lights stay out. I'd be naked for the entire audience to see if something went wrong."

Janeen was smiling when she returned and scooted in beside us.

"Problems?" I asked.

"Philip is jealous," she said. "He thinks you're trying to move in on Latitia."

I grabbed her, groping her tits and nibbling on her neck.

"It's you I'm hot after, not Latitia."

"Something about you is strangely familiar," Janeen said.

She grinned when I said, "We were probably lovers in another life."

Janeen finished her Midnight Gang Bang and said, "I don't believe we ever made love, though there aren't many men with bodies like yours. If we'd had sex, I think I would remember it."

When the lights darkened, Janeen grabbed Latitia's hand.

"Gotta go, sweetie," she said.

I knew I needed to get out of the place before someone realized I wasn't a dope dealer. I also had visions of Latitia lying comatose in the Bell

House attic and knew I wouldn't leave without her. When Sindee returned to the table, I ordered another Midnight Gang Bang and Molotov Cocktail. Doubles.

Not wanting to raise suspicion more than I already had, I said, "Better tab me out."

"Don't leave," she said. "We're open until two."

I handed her the baggie of cocaine.

"For me?" she said.

"I made a couple of big sales tonight. Now, I have work to do."

The band was firing up the crowd onstage when Sindee arrived with the Midnight Gang Bang and Molotov Cocktail.

"Want me to light it for you?" she asked.

When I said, "Do you have an extra lighter?" she handed me a disposable from her apron.

I had a plan. As Latitia belted out a song and before she changed costumes, I made my way toward the stage. When the lights went out, I counted to ten, lit the Molotov cocktail, poured the contents into the 150-proof rum, and tossed it onto the stage.

People began screaming and rushing for the exits when the flaming concoction exploded. I'd gotten a glimpse of Latitia and the two wardrobe women during the flash of light. Grabbing an arm I hoped was hers, I pulled someone off the stage into my arms.

Along with the explosion and resultant darkness, all hell broke loose. A good thing, as Latitia's tiny red g-string, was all she had on. Two men barreled past us in the hallway, trying to stop people from exiting the club. Their presence mattered little as frightened customers, some crying and screaming, pushed through the door. The darkness and ensuing chaos kept the two goons from detaining us.

Chapter 12

My ruse worked as we made it outside Vodou Nitz without detection. Pancho and Freya were waiting in the parking lot in Freya's Miata.

"Get us the hell out of here," I said after piling into the little car.

Freya and Latitia sat in my lap, weighing me down as Pancho squealed out of the parking lot.

"Is anyone chasing us?" he asked.

"Don't know. "Is there a motel near here?"

"My house isn't far. I have a garage," Freya said.

"We're already in danger," I said.

"Not to worry," she said. "I live alone in a huge house and can't remember the last time I had so much fun."

"This fun is serious and could get us killed," I said.

"I accept the danger," Freya said. "Pancho, take us to my house."

The fourth and final super moon of the year filled the horizon, the beautiful orb radiating golden light as Pancho sped through the backstreets of Covington.

We found Freya's house, an old two-story with lots of character on the edge of town. Pancho drove in and parked as sweetly as if Mario Andretti had guided him. Latitia's distressed expression worried me as we piled out of the car.

"It's okay," I said. "No one is going to find you."

"They're going to kill Mom and Aimee."

"No, they aren't," I said. "Freya, do you have a phone I can borrow?"

Freya opened her handbag again and handed me her cell phone. Tony answered on the second ring.

"Who is this?" he said.

"It's Wyatt. Where are you?"

"In bed," he said.

"So sorry. Didn't realize how late it is."

"Lil says to say hi."

"Tell her hi for me. There's something I need you to do."

"Can it wait until tomorrow?"

"It's a matter of life or death."

"Tell me," he said.

"I just rescued Latitia Boiset from Vodou Nitz."

"Who is she?"

"The woman I found on the third floor of the Bell House last night."

"How did you manage that?"

"Long story," I said.

"What do you need me to do?" Tony asked.

"This is complicated," I said. "Latitia and I were lovers. Her mom and daughter live in the 9th Ward. The little girl is my daughter.

"You're shitting me!" he said.

Someone controlled Latitia with zombie powder and threatens to kill her mom and our daughter. You have to get them to a safe place before Latitia is discovered missing."

"You have an address?"

I handed the phone to Latitia. "This is my

partner, Tony. Tell him your mom's address."

When Latitia returned the phone to me, Tony said, "I'll call Tommy Blackburn. He'll send some men to pick them up."

"No," I said.

"What do you mean no?" he said.

"I don't want to involve the police until I see who's complicit," I said.

"Tommy isn't on the take," Tony said.

"I know that," I said. "Can't you get them?"

"Lil and me have been married a long time. I'm trying to keep it that way."

"Do your best," I said.

Tony must have called Mama and given her Freya's number because when her phone rang, it was Mama. Freya handed me the phone.

"What the hell's going on?" she said.

"Did Tony just call you?"

"Woke me and my cats up," she said.

"Your cats, maybe. You never go to sleep before midnight."

"Sometimes I do," she said.

"Mama, I need your help."

"This better be good," she said.

"My daughter and her grandmother live in the Lower 9th Ward. They're in grave danger, and someone needs to get them out of the house before the mob arrives."

"You have no daughter," Mama said.

"Her name is Aimee. I've never met her. Please don't let her die," I said.

"Wyatt," Mama said. "Next time I see you, I'll kick your skinny ass."

"Thanks, Mama."

"One more thing. I did an Internet search and came across something interesting."

"Like what?" I said.

"Someone who arose from the dead. Emile LeCompte. He lives near Covington."

"What does this person have to do with the investigation?"

"He was thought to have died. There was even a funeral. He freaked his family when two years later, he showed up. He gave an interview to the local newspaper claiming he was zombied."

"Sounds like someone I need to talk to," I said. "Do you have an address?"

"I texted the coordinates of his last known address to the cell phone Tony gave you."

"Mama, you're a sweetheart. I'm splitting half my fee with you."

"No need for that," she said. "Tony talked with Frankie Castellano, and I'm now on the payroll."

"Wonderful," I said. "This is turning into a dangerous assignment. Don't get yourself killed."

"You either."

When Mama hung up the phone, I handed it to Freya. I had no doubt she and Tony would find Aimee and Latitia's mom and move them to safety.

"Someone's going for your mom and daughter now," I said. "They'll hide them until we resolve this mess."

Latitia was still crying as she put her arms around me and rested her head on my shoulder. When she pulled away, I realized Pancho was staring, apparently shocked at the sight of Latitia, naked except for her g-string.

"I have some clothes for you, baby," Freya said.

Freya took Latitia into a bedroom. When they returned, a terrycloth robe draped her shoulders.

"So sorry to involve you in all this intrigue," I said.

"I'm good with it," Freya said. "I'm the head witch of the Covington Coven, and nothing much shocks me anymore. I can help you."

Pancho's eyes again grew large. "You're a

witch?" he said.

"Afraid of witches?" Freya said.

Freya laughed when Pancho said. "Only if you're going to turn me into a mouse or a spider."

Freya grinned when she said, "I have other plans for you without resorting to therianthropy."

"That's a big word I don't understand," Pancho said.

"Sorry," Freya said. "I taught high school for thirty years, and sometimes I forget I'm retired. It means a human who takes the form of an animal."

"You mean like a werewolf?" Pancho said.

"Exactly," Freya said. "Let's go to the kitchen. Maybe Wyatt can explain to us what's going on."

Not everything in the house was normal. Freya's old house reeked of must and furniture polish, colorful rugs covering parts of the bare wood floors. She had at least seven cats, and otherworldly-themed oil paintings decorated the walls.

She smiled when I said, "Let me guess. Spirits haunt your house."

"Good guess," she said. "Except for Uncle Ted, most ghosts never bother me."

I didn't ask Freya about Uncle Ted as her curious cats followed us down the hall to her kitchen. Unlike other antique-laden rooms, the kitchen beamed with new light fixtures, countertops, and appliances and looked like the set from a cooking show.

"I'm starved," she said. "I love to cook. Since you're a professional, Pancho, maybe you can help me."

Pancho opened her refrigerator and then checked her pantry.

"You're better stocked than most fancy restaurants," Pancho said.

"Wait till you see the wine cellar. When the

girls come over, one of them always does the cooking while the rest of us get drunk on fine wine," Freya said.

She nodded when I said, "Your coven? How many people is that?"

"Twenty, counting me," Freya said.

"Are you Wiccans?" I asked.

"Pagans," Freya said.

"Love it," I said.

"We witches live by our own rules. Secrecy is imperative because our actions defy the norms of society."

"I'm hip," I said.

"Sounds like omerta to me," Pancho said.

Pancho nodded when Freya said, "The mafia code of silence. Are you good with it?"

"I'll never whisper your secret to anyone."

"I thought so," Freya said.

"If you'll allow us, Pancho and I will whip up something to eat."

"Can't wait," I said."

Pancho began selecting items from Freya's pantry, freezer, and refrigerator. The spicy aroma of linguini and clams soon began filling the kitchen. When it was ready, Pancho dished up the regal meal, serving it on the kitchen table. Even Latitia's sulking somewhat ended as she put the first bite of succulent pasta in her mouth. Her enhanced mood didn't last long.

I shook her shoulders as tears began streaming down her pretty face.

"Snap out of it," Mama's on her way to your mom's. Aimee and your mother will soon be in a safe place."

"I'm praying what you say is true," she said.

"Mama and Tony will reach them before the bad guys even know you're gone. I promise."

Freya pushed her plate aside. "I said I'm a witch. My powers are strong. Please tell me what you're trying to accomplish. I may be able to help."

"A client hired me to find a missing man. My investigation has uncovered much more than a missing individual."

"Like what?" Freya asked.

"Human trafficking on a large scale," I said. "So far, I've only seen the tip of the iceberg.

"Here in Covington?"

"Yes. Latitia performed earlier tonight at Vodou Nitz. Last night, she was lying naked on the third floor of the Bell House in Mandeville."

"I can't even imagine what Wyatt is talking about," Freya said. "Can you help me out on this?"

"I'm paid well but have no contract with the band I front for," Latitia said. "I was offered a movie role. My troubles started when I informed the new owner I was leaving to pursue other opportunities."

"Tell me," Freya said.

"Men were summoned. They held my arms as someone injected me with something that rendered me helpless."

"Zombie powder?" Freya said.

Freya nodded when I said, "You know about it?"

"It paralyzed me," Latitia said. "I couldn't move a muscle. I couldn't cry out or even blink an eye. The men took me to a dark attic, stripped me naked, and raped me. I was consciously aware of their every perversion. I was alone in the dark when they finally finished with me."

"Wyatt found you?"

"He promised to free me," Latitia said.

"Then what happened?" Freya asked.

"This morning, the same men returned me to Vodou Nitz. Philip Casseus, the new owner of Brass & Sass, confronted me after administering an antidote. He somehow knew about my mom and daughter and threatened to kill them if I didn't perform."

"Why aren't the police doing something?" Freya asked.

"They aren't involved," I said.

Freya expressed bewilderment. "Can we trust anyone?"

"Most people are honest. Dishonest people take advantage of those who are."

"One bad apple," Pancho said.

"In this case, lots of bad apples," I said.

"Go on," Freya said.

"I'm working undercover. It's starting to seem as if the person who hired me is at least partially complicit. Pancho's granddaughter is likely involved."

Freya glanced at Pancho and said, "You know something about this?"

"My daughter Adele is married to Frankie Castellano, the Don of the Bayou. She has led a storybook existence since they were married. Adele wouldn't listen to me when I told her Frankie has done many evil things."

"What about your granddaughter?" Freya asked.

"Toni adores Frankie," Pancho said. "To her, he can do no wrong."

"And you?" Freya said.

"I was born in Sicily. I don't believe a word I hear and only half of what I see," he said.

He smiled when Freya asked, "Are you suspicious of me?"

"Yes, though I'm a man with all the weaknesses every man has."

"At least you're honest," Freya said, touching his hand. "I'm going to take you to bed with me. First, I'll see that Latitia is comfortable in her room."

Pancho and I watched Freya lead Latitia away down the hall.

"Damn, Pancho," I said. "Sounds like you're about to get lucky. How old did you say you are?"

"Old enough," he said.

He smiled when I said, "Good luck."

"If she's a witch, it'll be the best night I've ever experienced."

Pancho's sentiments made me smile. "Freya probably has a magic potion, or two, though I feel you'll do fine even without one."

Freya's old house had many bedrooms. She took me to one, tarrying too long as I took off my shirt.

"You have quite the body. Sleep tight," Freya said as she shut the door behind her.

I awakened when the door to my room opened several hours later. It was Freya dressed in a baby blue nightgown, matching the color of her Miata that failed to hide her curves even in the room's muted light. She sat on the edge of my bed. After slipping the sheet down so she could see me, she began softly stroking my bare chest.

"Are you awake?" she said.

"I am now," I said.

Freya may have been close to seventy, though there was nothing old about her body. Her golden hair was no longer in a bun and draped over her bare shoulders. Pheromones filled my nostrils when I took a breath. The strap slipped off Freya's shoulder. She guided my hand to an ample breast and made sure I squeezed it.

"I thought you were taking Pancho to bed," I said.

"Pagans have strong desires. I made love with both Pancho and Latitia," she said. "You're next."

Freya smiled when I said, "You aren't human, are you?"

"I'm a woman with unusual sexual needs," she said. "I want to make love to you."

I'm not sure I could have resisted Freya even if I had wanted to. She let her nightgown drop to the floor, lifted the sheet, and joined me beneath it.

Chapter 13

After talking with Wyatt, Mama called Tony and advised him to return to bed.

"No use both of us going out this time of night," she said. "I'll pick up the woman and her granddaughter."

"You sure?"

"I can handle it," Mama said. "I'll take them home with me."

"If you need me, just call," Tony said.

"Everything will go smoothly."

What could go wrong on a trip to the Lower 9th Ward at two in the morning? Mama didn't want to think about it as she tooled down St. Claude Avenue. The weather was warm enough to drive with the top down. She'd raised it for other reasons.

The Lower 9th Ward was perhaps the poorest district in New Orleans. It had also been the area that had received the most damage during Hurricane Katrina. The levee had broken in several places and had suffered from intense flooding. Following the worst natural disaster in U.S. history, ruined neighborhoods and rat-infested abandoned structures blighted the area for years. Many still exist.

Mama recalled the chaos and devastation as

she turned off St. Claude onto a side street leading to the house where Wyatt's daughter lived with her grandmother.

Though they'd worked together for many years, Wyatt and Mama had always maintained a professional relationship and had never been intimate. Despite their emotional distance, Mama felt jealous because of the daughter Wyatt had had with another woman. The emotion disturbed her as she parked in front of a restored Creole cottage.

Someone had sunk lots of money into the house. Mama suspected Latitia Boiset probably owned it.

Dim lighting, cloaked in early morning fog rolling up from the Industrial Canal, emanated from a lone streetlamp across the street. Careful not to fall on slippery wood, Mama climbed the steps to the porch. When she punched the doorbell, she heard it ring inside the house.

Mama had begun thinking no one would answer when she heard someone in socks padding toward the door. A slightly-built woman opened it without asking who it was. The woman's hair was steel gray, though she looked no older than forty. She grabbed Mama's hand and pulled her into the house.

"I prayed someone would come," she said. "Please hurry."

The woman shook her head when Mama said, "Are you Latitia Boiset's sister?"

"Her mother," the woman said. "I'm Lashonda."

"You don't look old enough to be a grandmother," Mama said.

"I was sixteen when I had Latitia. My skin's darker. Except for that and my gray hair, we could almost pass as sisters. I can't sing and dance like Latitia, though. She must have got those talents from her daddy."

Lashonda led Mama down a darkened hallway to a bedroom illuminated by a single lamp. A girl lay in a four-poster bed, her distressed expression telling Mama something was wrong. She touched her forehead.

"She's burning up. How long has she been like this?"

"An hour or so," Latitia's mother said.

"Do you have an aspirin?" Mama asked.

"I gave her three already."

"Fill the bathroom tub with cold water and put every ice cube you have in it. We must get Aimee's temperature down ASAP, or she'll have brain damage."

"Oh, my God, no!" Lashonda said.

The sound of water pouring into an antique porcelain tub began as Mama lifted the girl out of bed and carried her to the bathroom. Aimee was almost as big as Mama. With difficulty, she put her into the tub, nightgown and all. Mama drenched her head and then began swabbing her face with a washrag.

"Hurry with the ice," Mama said as she patted the girl's face. "Wake up, baby."

Lashonda returned with two buckets of ice which she dumped into the water.

"Thank God Latitia had an icemaker installed last summer. Please don't let her die."

"We have to get her temperature down. Do you have any antibiotics in the medicine cabinet?"

"Some Amoxicillin."

"Get it," Mama said.

The antibiotic was more than a year out of date. At this point, it didn't matter. It would either help save Aimee's life or not.

"What else can I do?" Lashonda said.

"Start praying and keep the ice coming,"

Mama said.

Water from swabbing the girl's head soon soaked Mama's blouse. Lashonda was on her knees.

Morning light peeked through the tiny window when the antibiotic kicked in, and Aimee opened her eyes. She smiled when she saw Mama Mulate. Mama gave her a big hug.

Though Lashonda was a shade darker than Mama, Aimee was as white as a Scandinavian, her eyes pale blue.

"I know who you are," Aimee said.

"How do you know that?" Mama said.

"I've seen you in my dreams," Aimee said.

"You answered my dreams, baby," Mama said.

Lashonda grabbed Aimee when she heard the little girl talking.

"You saved my baby," she said.

"We saved her," Mama said. "I couldn't have done it without you. Dry her off and get her dressed. We have to get her to an emergency room for more antibiotics."

When Mama returned to the front of the house, she found the door half open. A good-looking black man had parked outside and got out of his car. Mama's heart began to race when she saw the pistol in his hand.

Lashonda kept a baseball bat near the entrance to her house. Mama grabbed it and positioned herself behind the door. When the man entered without knocking, Mama nailed him with the bat and watched him crumple to the floor. Lashonda's hand went to her mouth when she and Aimee came out of the bathroom.

"Pack a bag. It's not safe here for you and Aimee. I'll explain when we're in the car."

"I'm not going without Bootsie," Aimee said.

"Who's Bootsie?" Mama asked.

"My kitty."

"Where is she?" Mama said.

"Bootsie is a boy, not a girl," Aimee said.

"Pardon me," Mama said. "Where is he?"

"Tomcatting," Lashonda said.

"Call him and see if he comes," Mama said. "If he doesn't, I'll return later and get him."

Aimee ran to the front porch and began calling her cat, Bootsie. She was in tears when her calls failed to summon the cat. Mama put her hands on Aimee's shoulders.

"Leave him some food and water on the porch. He'll be waiting for me when I return."

"You sure?"

"I promise," Mama said.

Lashonda and Aimee were already in the little car, Mama stowing their bags in the trunk. Instead of getting behind the wheel, she returned to the house to have one last look for Aimee's cat. The man she'd knocked unconscious was lying face down on the floor. Grabbing his shoulder, Mama rolled him over to get a better look at his face.

The man was handsome enough to be a movie star, with a thin mustache marking his upper lip. Something else caught Mama's eye: a tattoo on the wrist of his hand holding the pistol. A Baron Samedi veve. When the man's hand twitched, Mama backed out of the house and hurried toward the car.

They were soon speeding away from the Lower 9th Ward. She stopped at a medical clinic near her house. Mama and Lashonda waited for the results of the blood work. The nurse finally emerged with Aimee.

"Aimee has a sinus infection. We gave her antibiotics." She handed Lashonda a script. "She'll be fine when she completes this round of antibiotics."

"Did the fever harm her?" Lashonda asked.

The nurse smiled. "You kidding? She's as smart as a whip."

Mama stopped at an all-night pharmacy and filled the prescription before driving to her house.

"Oh, wow!" Aimee said when she saw Mama's cats. "How many kitties do you have?"

"Three," Mama said. "Bootsie will fit right in."

Aimee didn't have long to wait before Mama's three cats ran into the house from the porch. They took to Aimee, and it was apparent she was enamored with them. She soon had one in her arms, another rubbing against her legs.

"What are your cat's names?" Aimee asked.

"The orange tabby is Cliffy. Bushy is the white Persian. The little black cat with no tail is Ninja."

"I love them all," Aimee said. "Don't forget you promised to bring Bootsie here."

A single tear dripped down Aimee's face. "What's wrong, baby?" Mama said.

Aimee wrapped her arms around Mama's neck. "I'm so afraid," she said.

"It's okay to be frightened," Mama said.

"It's not okay," Aimee said. "My fear is like a lead necklace that weighs down my soul."

Mama wore two identical necklaces. Removing one, she put it around Aimee's neck. The polished black stone glimmered in the light.

"This is a Locator Stone. It'll keep you safe when it's near you. I'll always find you if you get into trouble," Mama said.

"It's beautiful," Aimee said. "What is it?"

"Enchanted onyx."

"How do you enchant onyx?" Aimee asked.

"Magic," Mama said.

Mama nodded when Aimee said, "Do you practice magic? I want to know how."

Mama shook her head. "You can't just

practice magic, baby. Someone has to instruct you. Even then, the use of magic will change your life forever."

"Who taught you?" Aimee asked.

"The onyx around your neck was Grandmother's and was cut from the same stone as the necklace I wear."

"Does it work?" Aimee asked.

Mama rested her hands on Aimee's shoulders. "We are connected as long as it's near you. It not only wards off evil but also comforts your troubled thoughts."

Aimee smiled and said, "I feel better, except for Bootsie."

Mama hugged the little girl. "Baby, Bootsie will soon be here with the other kitties. I promise."

Mama showed them their bedroom and then fell asleep in her bed. Past noon when her cats awoke her, she found Aimee and Lashonda awake and sitting at the kitchen table.

"Sorry I slept so long," Mama said. "You must be starving."

"I found peanut butter and jelly and made Aimee a sandwich," Lashonda said.

"I'll fix us something," Mama said.

When Tony knocked on the door, Mama and Lashonda were dining on red beans and rice.

"Lashonda, this is Tony. I'm helping him with an investigation that involves your daughter."

"You're the police?" Lashonda said.

Mama grinned and shook her head. "I'm a voodoo mambo when I'm not teaching English lit at Tulane. Trust me when I tell you I'm not the police."

"Him?"

"Tony is a former homicide detective with the N.O.P.D. He's a private detective now with no connection to the police."

"Then tell me why we had to leave our house and what's going on," Lashonda said.

"Latitia was zombied," Mama said. "Our partner Wyatt rescued her. The bad guys were extorting her to perform by threatening you and Aimee."

"Wyatt Thomas?" Lashonda said.

"You know him?" Tony asked.

"He's Aimee's father," Lashonda said.

"You don't like him?" Mama asked.

"He's never paid a penny to support his daughter," Lashonda said.

"Maybe because until last night, he didn't know she existed," Tony said.

"It was a shock to all of us," Mama said. "There's no better person on earth than Wyatt. He risked his life last night to save Latitia."

"I don't know," Lashonda said.

"Latitia's in big trouble. Wyatt, Tony, and I are her only stalwarts. You need to choose a side, and to do it now," Mama said.

"You saved Aimee's life," Lashonda said. "What do you want me to do?"

"Make yourselves at home. There's food in the fridge. Let me show you the back porch."

Mama's house was small, nondescript, and wonderfully livable. Mama showed Lashonda and Aimee her porch overlooking the backyard.

Mirlitons climbed a vine growing up the fence. Corn, kale, and tomatoes grew in Mama's raised truck garden. A dozen hummingbirds would soon be swarming the colorful feeder suspended beside the wind chimes wafting in the early morning breeze.

"I love it," Lashonda said. "I've always wanted to grow a garden."

"There's a fresh seafood market about a mile from here," Mama said. "I love oysters, Creole tomatoes, and avocados. There's also plenty of food in the fridge and freezer. Feel free to pick anything you want, and don't be afraid to get the kitchen dirty."

Lashonda sat in one of the rocking chairs. "This is lovely," she said. "I think I trust you."

"I bought a sack of fresh oysters yesterday," Mama said. Lashonda smiled when Mama asked, "Do you drink?

"Sometimes a little too much," Lashonda said.

Mama laughed. "Don't we all? Do you have a favorite alcoholic beverage?"

"I'm partial to bourbon and water," Lashonda said. "No ice."

"Love it," Mama said.

Mama, Lashonda, and Tony sat in rocking chairs on the back porch, enjoying their drinks as they watched Aimee play with the cats and a rubber ball. Mama soon caught Tony glancing at his watch.

"We have time," she said. "Harvey and Bruno never wake up until after lunch."

"Must be nice," Tony said.

"You'd never sleep late even if you could."

"Right about that," Tony said. "Too many years working for the N.O.P.D."

"You loved every minute of it," Mama said.

"Where are you going?" Lashonda asked.

"The man we're looking for was living in an apartment on Conti with his girlfriend. Someone he knew buzzed in early in the morning. His neighbors found him dead when they arrived home after getting off work."

"They must work in a bar," Lashonda said.

"Actors in a French Quarter drag show," Mama said. "They saw the people who the missing person rang into the apartment. We think they can give us a description of the people they saw."

When they finished their drinks, Mama mixed

go-cups for her and Tony.

Tony and I have work to do," she said. "You're safe here. Make yourself at home, and don't wait up for us."

"You must be exhausted," Lashonda said. "None of us got much sleep last night."

"No rest for the wicked," Mama said.

Chapter 14

Tony's knuckles whitened as Mama sped toward the French Quarter. When she scooted into a parking space near Bertram's, he knew he was again in for a walk. He decided not to raise a fuss and to try to enjoy the sunny day.

"You're in luck," Mama said.

Tony cast a skeptical glance and said, "How's that?"

"No walking required. Stevie Jones is waiting for us at Bertram's. Harvey and Bruno will join us when they wake up."

"I was ready for a walk," Tony said.

"Outstanding," Mama said. "We have time to take a lap over to Café du Monde and circle Jackson Square before hitting Bertram's."

"Just kidding," Tony said. "I'm fine with going straight to Bertram's."

"You liar," Mama said as she followed Tony into Bertram's bar.

Regulars and several tipsy tourists were already crowding into Bertram's booze emporium. Bertram's smile grew larger when he saw Mama and Tony walk through the entrance.

Lady's tail thumped the oiled-wood floor when he said, "Well, look what the cat drug in."

"Are we in time for happy hour?" Mama asked.

"At ol' Bertram's, it's always happy hour. Martini and scotch?"

"You got it," Tony said. Stevie Jones was sitting alone at the bar. "And put this pretty lady's drinks on my tab."

Bertram was smiling and rubbing his hands together as he began preparing drinks for Mama, Tony, and Stevie.

Stevie Jones nodded when Mama said, "Doing all right, baby?"

"Thinking about Bobby is getting to me," she said. "I can't believe he's dead."

"He's not dead, sweetie. He was zombied."

"I'm black, and my mother believes in voodoo. I'm sorry, Mama. I think the whole thing is ignorance and superstition."

"You should always listen to your mother," Mama said with a smile.

Stevie glanced at Tony and said, "You're white. You don't believe in zombies, do you?"

"I'm a detective. I follow the clues and try not to have preconceived ideas," he said.

"You think my ideas are preconceived?" Stevie said.

"You know there are no zombies in the world?" Tony asked.

"Other than in the movies and music videos, they don't sound real to me," Stevie said.

"Not what I asked you," Tony said. "if you have no proof, don't matter what you believe."

"It's not logical," Stevie said.

"Logic and reality are two different things," Tony said. "If you want to, you can believe everyone has two assholes. Don't make it so. It is what it is."

"Mama, can you help me with this?" Stevie said.

"Tony's right, baby. No one knows everything. Don't discount something simply because it doesn't seem logical. Zombies are real. Trust me on that."

"My mind is open though I think you're both full of shit."

"Are your neighbors going to join us?" Tony asked.

"They'll be here," Stevie said.

Seeing the bar was beginning to fill, Mama flagged Bertram. "Two men are joining us, and we need to talk to them privately. Can we use Wyatt's booth?"

"Head back there," Bertram said. "I'll bring fresh drinks."

"Thanks," Mama said.

"How will I recognize the two men?" Bertram asked.

"You'll know," Stevie said.

Bertram said, "I'll take their drink orders and send them your way."

Harvey and Bruno soon appeared. Both were tall, built like Olympic weightlifters, and had closely-cropped hair and prominent five-o'clock shadows. They approached the booth carrying souvenir glasses filled with Bertram's colorful version of the hurricane. When they saw Stevie, they scooted into the booth.

"I'm Harvey," the man in zebra-striped pants said.

"Bruno," his partner in leopard-print pants said.

"I'm Mama, and this is Tony," Mama said. "Your accents tell me you aren't from New Orleans."

"Heidelberg," Bruno said.

"What brought you to New Orleans from Germany?" Tony asked.

"Southern Decadence. We came for the

festival about this time last year and never left," Harvey said.

"Gay Mardi Gras," Mama said.

"Three hundred thousand gay, lesbian, transgender and bisexuals," Bruno said. "What's not to love?"

"Not to mention it's a big financial shot in the arm for the city. I never miss it." Mama said

"You, Tony?" Bruno said.

"I used to work Mardi Gras every year in the N.O.P.D.," Tony said. "Now, I hate crowds. If it ain't on T.V., I don't watch it."

"You a cop?" Harvey asked.

"Not anymore," Tony said. "A private dick."

He almost blushed when Harvey and Bruno grinned. Mama gave him an elbow in the gut.

"Stevie says you are a voodoo mambo," Harvey said.

"I also teach English lit at Tulane. Stevie was one of my most promising students."

"We love Stevie," Bruno said. "She and Bobby were our biggest fans and came to our shows whenever they could."

"Your shows? Where do you work?" Tony asked.

"The Purple Emporium. Bruno and I are part of a drag revue. Three times a week and a Sunday brunch matinee every weekend."

"Best Sunday brunch in the Quarter," Stevie said. "Bobby and I loved spending Sundays with Scarlett Johannesburg and Norma Jean Goldenstein."

Everyone laughed when Tony asked, "Who's that?"

"I'm Scarlett," Bruno said. "Harvey is Norma Jean. Scarlett and Norma Jean are our alter egos. Sometimes we stay in character for days."

"I want to see your show," Mama said.

"Scarlett and Norma Jean are so funny,"

Stevie said.

The words were barely out of her mouth when she started to cry. Bruno and Harvey grabbed her hands and began massaging them.

"That's why we asked you to join us," Mama said. "Tony and I don't believe Bobby is dead."

"I wish it were so," Bruno said. "It isn't."

"I touched his face and felt for a pulse," Harvey said. "He had none."

"His eyes were glassy," Bruno said. "I have a nursing degree. Trust me when I tell you he was dead."

"Tell us how you happened to find Bobby," Tony said.

"We'd come home from work at the Purple Emporium," Bruno said. "It was late, and we were still in costume."

"When we opened the door to the apartment and walked upstairs, we heard a disturbance," Harvey said.

"Robert was lying face down on the deck outside the apartments," Bruno said. "He was naked."

"Someone was crouching over him," Harvey said. "Two other men were standing behind him."

"Three men?" Tony said.

"Two of them were twin brothers."

"Did you get a good look at them?" Tony asked.

"They were black and looked like they were enjoying themselves," Harvey said.

"What do you mean?" Mama said.

"They both had satisfied grins," Harvey said.

Harvey nodded when Tony said, "Can you describe the man crouching over Robert?"

"Hell yes!" Bruno said. "We know who he is."

Tony glanced at Mama when Harvey said, "His name is Philip. He's a regular at the gay bars in the Quarter."

"Describe him for me," Mama asked.

"Good looking. Dark eyes and light brown skin. A pencil-thin mustache," Bruno said.

"Tattoos?" Mama said.

"He had a voodoo tattoo on his wrist," Bruno said.

"You're from Germany. How do you know about voodoo?" Mama asked.

"It's impossible to live in New Orleans without experiencing the past," Harvey said. "This place is mystical. Philip has a Baron Samedi veve tattooed on his wrist."

"What about the other two men?" Tony asked.

"They were about the same size as Philip and had a family resemblance."

"Pardon me?" Mama said.

"They looked enough like Philip to be his brothers," Harvey said.

"Only older," Bruno said.

"What do you know about Baron Samedi?" Mama said.

"There's a voodoo cult mostly in the French Quarter. It's called the Keepers."

"Because," Mama said.

"Baron Samedi is the keeper of cemeteries and the dead," Bruno said. "Harvey and I toyed with joining though we ultimately decided against it."

"Why is that?" Tony asked.

"When we inquired, we learned lots of street people, and many runaways, went missing after joining the group," Harvey said.

"I haven't heard of this group or any complaints brought against them," Tony said.

"The police don't give a fuck about runaway teens," Bruno said. "They just assume they've moved on to another town."

"What else do you know about the Keepers?" Tony asked.

"You know everything we know," Harvey said.

"Let's talk about Philip. What's his last name?" Tony asked.

"Casseus," Harvey said. "We talked with him several times."

"Is he from New Orleans?" Tony asked.

"He used lots of French words when he spoke. His accent wasn't French," Bruno said.

Tony gave Mama a look when she said, "Haitian?"

"Could be," Harvey said. "He was definitely into voodoo."

"Really?" Mama said.

Before Bruno or Harvey could respond, Bertram arrived with fresh drinks. Harvey and Bruno had finished their hurricanes, and Bertram took their glasses.

"I'll put these in boxes for you," he said. "They look good on a shelf filled with Mardi Gras beads and doubloons. You boys having another?"

"Not tonight," Bruno said. "We're already late for rehearsal."

"I'll have the glasses waiting at the door," Bertram said.

"We have to go," Harvey said. "I hope we helped."

Tony said. "Can we contact you if we have further questions?"

"Of course," Bruno said. "You know where to find us."

"One last question before you go," Tony said. "You saw the tattoo beneath Bobby's left nipple?"

Harvey glanced at Bruno and shook his head. "I saw no tattoo beneath his nipple. Bruno?"

"No," Bruno said.

"Stevie?"

"I have no clue what you're talking about," she said.

"You've been a big help. You guys get to

work," Tony said.

After Bruno and Harvey had disappeared down Chartres Street, Stevie said, "Well? Did they give you anything you needed?"

"There's probably a connection with Bobby's disappearance and the Keepers," he said. "Mama, think you can find out anything about it?"

"I'll check my sources," she said.

"Did he discuss his story with you?" Tony asked.

"He called it an exposé and said it was dangerous for me to know the details."

Stevie nodded when Mama said, "He told you that? You never said anything about it to the police."

"I was afraid."

"Of what?" Mama said.

"Bobby said if anything happened to him, leave town for a while."

Stevie shook her head when Mama asked, "Did he tell you why?"

"Maybe you should take Bobby's advice," Tony said. "Do you have family or friends living out of town you could visit for a while?"

"No one," Stevie said. "I can't afford to leave my job."

"Stay with me until we get this resolved," Mama said. "I already have people involved with the case staying there. I have another empty bedroom."

"If these people know where I live, they also know where I work. Leaving the apartment will do me no good. At least Harvey and Bruno are there to keep an eye on me." Stevie glanced at the time on her cell phone. "I have to go to work now. Don't worry about me. I'll be okay."

After hugging Mama, she waved at Bertram as she hurried out of the bar.

"Doesn't matter how confident she is. I'm

124

worried about her," Mama said. "There's also something I need to tell you."

"Hit me," Tony said.

"Rescuing Lashonda and Aimee wasn't as easy as I implied. A man with a pistol arrived at the house as we prepared to leave. I knocked him out with a baseball bat Lashonda kept behind the door. He was Philip Casseus, the same man who zombied Bobby."

"And has the same last name as Mirlande Casseus," Tony said. "What about the missing nipple tattoo?"

"He didn't have one when he was zombied. It first appeared during the autopsy," Mama said.

"Which means?"

"Someone at the hospital tattooed him," Mama said.

"Why would they tattoo a dead man?" Tony asked.

"They wouldn't have."

"Then someone at the hospital is complicit," Tony said.

"Doctor Pompeo's sister, Pearl," Mama said. "Our list of suspects keeps growing."

"Probably what Bobby found when he started digging into the story."

"And maybe what got him zombied," Mama said.

Mama and Tony moved back to the bar and continued drinking. When it came to alcohol, Mama and Tony were pros. They didn't miss a beat until Tony glanced at his watch.

"Lil's pissed at me for missing dinner with her and Tommy. I need to leave before she divorces me," Tony said.

"No problem," Mama said. "Lashonda and Aimee are waiting for me. I'll talk to you tomorrow. Need a ride?"

"I'll catch a cab," Tony said.

After clearing the tab with Bertram, he gave Mama a backward wave as he walked out the door. The sun was gone, neon lighting the sidewalks when Mama strolled to her car.

The night was beginning on Bourbon Street. Mama could hear the roar at Bertram's. Though she loved the nightlife, she had other things on her mind. Aimee's cat, Bootsie, was probably waiting for her in the Lower 9th Ward and Mama decided to find out. Ground fog wafted across St. Bernard Highway blacktop as she pointed her Bug-eye Sprite south, intent on retrieving him.

Chapter 15

New Orleans is a dangerous city, some parts more dangerous than others. The Lower 9th Ward can be risky in broad daylight. Mama realized as much as she pulled her Bugeye Sprite to a stop in front of Lashonda's house.

Mama hurried out of the car, not taking the time to remove her favorite pair of leather driving gloves. She was there to retrieve Aimee's cat Bootsie. When she saw the big black and white cat on the porch, she knew her quest wasn't for naught.

"Bootsie," she said. "Come to Mama."

The cat didn't recognize Mama and was having none of her pleas. He'd already jumped off the porch. Mama stared at the bushes, calling to him.

"Here, kitty, kitty," she said.

Bootsie paid no attention. Intent on recovering the cat, Mama failed to hear the two men exiting the front door until a hand covered her mouth. She struggled, stiffening when she felt the sharp tip of a knife at her neck. Someone yanked up her shirt sleeve.

"Just a little sting," they said. Mama felt the needle go into her arm and became almost instantly woozy. "Something to relax you."

127

Someone handcuffed her, applying pressure to her back until she moved forward. They opened the backdoor of a black Range Rover and pushed her into it.

Both men had dark eyes and coffee-colored skin and were short with receding hairlines. They looked like brothers because they were.

"This woman is hot," one of the men said. "Maybe we should stop by the side of the road and take advantage of the situation."

"You need to keep your hands off of her, Cyril. You know what Mirlande said."

"She's drugged," Cyril said. "She'll never know the difference."

"I don't want to be involved."

"You're a pussy, Cyrus."

"There'll be other opportunities. Now is not the time or place," Cyrus said.

"Chill out," Cyril said. "I haven't touched the bitch."

Mama heard every word the two men spoke. She wanted to say something. She couldn't. The plush seats and rich odor of expensive leather gave her the subliminal message the vehicle must have cost lots of money. Whatever influence she was under caused her to lose track of time. When the car finally stopped, she opened her eyes and gazed out the darkly tinted windows.

The atmosphere was heavy with impending rain, dark clouds cloaking the sky when the Range Rover came to a halt. They followed a blacktop road between rows of sugar cane. Cyril stopped at the entrance to a giant ranch, the lighted sign on the gate reading Faumort Plantation.

Despite the darkness, giant combines with headlights continued cutting sugar cane, and rows of big trucks lined up to receive their load. Mama couldn't imagine how big the farm was but lost track of time when they entered an area dominated by giant live oaks whose branches draped to the rich loam beneath it.

They emerged from the tunnel of trees into a beautiful lighted garden of manicured paths, flowering shrubs, fruit trees, and multicolored flowers of every ilk amid flowing fountains and expensive statuary. They soon reached a southern mansion that could have put Tara to shame.

Servants tuxedoed in white observed from the sweeping veranda as Mama's abductors yanked her out of the car and pulled her up the steps into the mansion. Cyril and Cyrus led her through the house to a large meeting room. When she saw the trappings of wealth and luxury inside the plantation home, she felt like someone had transported her to another place and time.

A regal black woman sat on a carved oak throne cloaked with ermine and velvet. Though she was probably on the backside of sixty, she had the body of an athletic twenty-something. Mama could see because her only clothing was a red net dress with no undergarments. The little-piece-of-nothing dress made her seem even more naked than if she were wearing nothing.

"Greetings, Mama Mulate," the woman said. "Your reputation precedes you."

Though Mama's lips were numb, she said, "Who are you, and how do you know my name?"

"I'm Mirlande. Welcome to Faumort Plantation."

"If I'm so welcome, why have you drugged me?" Mama asked.

"Everyone in New Orleans knows you are a powerful mambo capable of summoning the dead and casting potent spells. I want you to work for me. First, I need to trust you."

"Offers of employment aren't usually

accompanied by force," Mama said.

"I respect your powers. I require absolute loyalty and tolerate nothing less."

In addition to Cyril and Cyrus, many onlookers were in the room with Mirlande.

"Can you say the same for all these people?" Mama said.

"This is a family operation," Mirlande said. "The handsome man beside me is Philip, my son. I come from a large family; all these people are my brothers, sisters, nieces, and nephews. Well, you get the picture. Cyril, remove Mama Mulate's cuffs and bring her to me."

Cyril sat Mama at the foot of Mirlande's throne. When Cyril unlocked Mama's cuffs, he gratuitously felt her rear end. Too drugged to notice, she tried to blink away her stupor.

When Mirlande said, "Bring her out of her drugged state, Cyril gave Mama another injection. I want her fully aware of my proposal."

Someone brought Mama a glass of water. Her stupor began to diminish after a drink.

"Why do you require my services?" Mama managed to say.

"My husband Felix was a powerful houngan in Haiti. He was much older than I when we married, and I was still young when he died. I miss Felix's power and need a powerful mambo to assist me in the dark arts."

"I don't practice dark magic," she said.

"But you could if you wanted to," Mirlande said.

Mama glanced at the man beside Mirlande and realized it was the person she'd knocked out with Lashonda's baseball bat. Philip didn't seem to care that his mother was flaunting her body through the loose weave of the skimpy red dress. Neither did any of the others watching the discourse between Mirlande and Mama.

Mirlande smiled when Mama said, "You are Haitian. I recognize your accent."

"I came to New Orleans years ago. I've since relocated all my family here."

"This plantation is huge," Mama said. Is all your wealth attributable to sugar cane?"

"You ask too many questions. You'll have to wait for the answers. Would you like to see Faumort?" Mirlande said.

"I got a hint during the ride from the front gate."

Mirlande pointed to a man who responded when she said, "Bring the plantation vehicle to the front door. I'll give you more than a hint of how big it is."

Once Mama and Mirlande were situated in the back of an open electric vehicle, the driver headed toward the gardens.

"Beautiful," Mama said.

"A replica of the gardens at the Palace of Versailles?" Mirlande said.

Mirlande smiled when Mama said, "You must have spent a small fortune duplicating it."

"You have no idea," Mirlande said.

"Your gardeners are world-class. Where did you find them?"

Mirlande smiled again. "From the Gardens of Versailles."

"You hired the actual gardeners from Versailles? You must pay them a fortune," Mama said.

"Zombies require no pay."

Mirlande's words chilled Mama because they indicated the scope of this crime family's influence reached much further than simply a few parishes in south Louisiana.

The electric vehicle left the garden, powering into the darkness lighted by working trucks and combines.

"During harvest, work never stops. The combines cut twenty-four hours a day," Mirlande said.

"How large is the plantation?" Mama asked.

"More than twenty-thousand acres," Mirlande said. "The south, Louisiana in particular, has a giant sweet tooth. Faumort is one of the largest sugar plantations in the state."

"The machinery is impressive," Mama said.

"It takes hundreds of men, women, and machines to plant, care for, and harvest the cane. It isn't the only business in which Faumort is involved.

"I can imagine," Mama said.

"It's sometimes overwhelming," Mirlande said. "If you join me, I'll make you wealthy beyond your imagination. If it's power you desire, your authority will be second only to me."

"I'm happy with my life and have no desire for power and wealth and all the baggage that comes with it."

"You don't understand," Mirlande said. "You have no choice."

"Why is that?" Mama asked.

Mirlande didn't answer Mama's question. Instead, she said. "Have you ever experienced death?"

"Not yet," Mama said.

"Felix taught me how to zombie a person. To show me the power, he once zombied me. I was terrified. I now wield the power of life and death over many people. The feeling is intoxicating. Join me, and you will see."

"I'm happy doing what I do," Mama said.

Mirlande's conciliatory tone disappeared, along with the understanding smile on her face.

"You are part of Faumort now. Once you accept the inevitable, your happiness will begin."

"I don't wish to be here," Mama said.

"You are a mambo. You know what a zombie is?" Mirlande said.

Mirlande smiled when Mama said, "There were zombies among your relatives in the plantation house."

"Because I allow the dead to walk as if they were human. There is no fate worse than that of a zombie," Mirlande said. "I think you should spend some time thinking about my offer."

Mama didn't miss Mirlande's thinly-veiled threat.

"I'll consider what you've told me," Mama said.

Rain had begun falling on the open vehicle, a possible violent storm approaching. Mirlande didn't respond to Mama's words as she glanced at the darkening sky.

"Driver, return us to the plantation," she said.

The rain was falling in waves when the electric vehicle driver let Mama and Mirlande off at the porch of the plantation. Mama followed her, accompanied on either side by Cyrus and Cyril. Mirlande's entourage parted as she returned to her throne.

Mama waited while Mirlande drank a glass of iced water. The regal woman's smile had disappeared, and Mama was offered nothing to drink. She failed to see the hand signal to Mirlande's two brothers, who had rejoined the audience. Cyril administered another injection into Mama's arm.

"Take her," Mirlande said. "We'll speak again in a few days. Do not molest her. There will be plenty of opportunities for that if she refuses my offer."

Cyril and Cyrus took Mama to a warehouse and laid her on the cement floor. Cyril began stripping off her clothes.

"What the hell are you doing?" Cyrus

133

demanded.

"I don't care what Mirlande said. I intend to have my way with this woman," Cyril said."

"I won't allow it. You'll get us either killed or worse," Cyrus said."

Cyril pushed his brother away. "Mirlande will never know."

"When Mirlande revives this woman, she will surely tell her," Cyrus said.

"Mirlande is our sister. She'll make an exception for us," Cyril said.

Mama lay almost naked on the cement floor. Cyrus stared at her for a long moment.

"She is gorgeous, and I'm hot," he said. "Let's use her, but make it quick."

Mama had no pain or cold sensation as she lay on the cement floor, unable to speak or move as the two men ripped away what remained of her undergarments. Though mentally braced for the attack, she rued her inability to fight. Cyril's pants and underwear had dropped to his knees, and Mama's legs spread when a hollow voice echoed through the empty warehouse. It was Mirlande's voice.

"I told you not to molest her," she said.

"We're so sorry," Cyrus said. "Cyril took her clothes off."

"So, you're blaming this on your brother?"

"He goaded me into it," Cyrus said.

"You both sicken me," Mirlande said. "Now, you must pay the price."

"We're your brothers," Cyril said. "Pity us."

"You attempted to deceive me. I don't tolerate deceit, especially from family members."

Mirlande wasn't alone. Philip and two zombies were with her. Cyril and Cyrus tried to run. The cat-quick zombies caught them before they reached the door. Philip was smiling as he approached them with two syringes.

"Just a little sting," he said as he administered the injections.

"Leave them on the floor," Mirlande said.

"For how long?" Philip asked.

"Until tomorrow, or maybe eternity," Mirlande said. "Long enough that they never again disobey me."

Chapter 16

Thousands of homicide investigations had left Tony with a pessimistic attitude. Since leaving Mama at Bertram's, he couldn't shake the feeling something was wrong. Getting out of bed, he went to the bathroom, shut the door, and called Mama's house. Lashonda answered on the first ring.

"Is that you, Mama?" he asked.

"It's Lashonda. Mama isn't here. Aimee and I are worried sick."

"We interviewed someone at Bertram's Bar in the Quarter," Tony said. "I left her hours ago. I had a bad feeling about it and couldn't sleep.

"Mama promised to return to our house in the Lower 9th Ward and get Aimee's cat Bootsie. If she did, she should have returned by now."

"I called her cell phone," Tony said. "She's not answering."

"Me, too," Lashonda said. "Should I call the police?"

"Mama's between semesters and may be having late drinks. Let's not panic until I find out and call you back."

Bertram answered the phone when Tony called.

"Mama left hours ago," Bertram said. "Is she

in trouble?"

"Hope not," Tony said. "I'll let you know."

Because of their long marriage, Tony and his wife Lil could almost read each other's minds. Despite the mental connection and many children, the two were as different as night and day.

Lil liked to go to bed with the chickens. Tony was a night owl. Following a midlife crisis where Tony had an affair with a younger woman, he and Lil attempted to compromise to mend their marriage. As heavy rain pounded the roof, Lil opened her eyes, sensing something was wrong. Tony was standing near the window, staring at the closed curtain.

"What are you doing?" Lil asked,

"I can't sleep."

"What's the matter?"

"Nothing."

Then come back to bed."

"I can't," Tony said.

Lil went into the kitchen and began brewing a pot of coffee. Tony soon joined her. He drank his coffee strong and black. When Lil put a cup on the kitchen table in front of him, he took a sip.

"Now," she said. "What's the matter."

"I'm working a case with Wyatt and Mama. Wyatt's undercover in Mandeville. The case involves voodoo, and that's where Mama comes in."

"Voodoo? Is this case dangerous?"

"Not so much for me," he said. "Mama has gone missing."

Lil poured a cup of coffee and sat at the table across from Tony. Unlike Tony, she added a teaspoon of sugar and a splash of milk to the cup, stirring it before taking a sip.

"Maybe you'd better tell me exactly what you're dealing with here," she said.

"Frankie Castellano hired me to locate a missing person." Lil sat her cup on the table and began shaking her head. "What's the matter?" Tony said.

"That man is your problem. He's nothing but trouble every time you work for him," Lil said.

"That's not true at all," Tony said. "You're being unfair."

"He's a mobster. Everyone in Louisiana knows it. How is voodoo connected to this missing person?"

"He was supposed to be dead. Wyatt, Mama, and I believe he was zombied and may still be alive."

"Zombied? What does that mean?"

"Turned into a zombie by using voodoo powder," Tony said.

Lil's hand went to her face. "You don't believe that malarkey, do you?"

"I know it sounds nuts. It's not," Tony said. "I've spoken with medical people who've had experience with it. It's real."

"You haven't been to church in a while," Lil said. "When was the last time you let Father O'Reilly hear your confession."

"Can't remember," he said.

"Maybe you should work on your own religious beliefs and not listen to tall tales like the locals use to make money from gullible tourists."

Tony didn't look up from the table. After years of marriage, he knew her veins and eyes were bulging, and she was frowning.

"There's a little bit of truth in every fiction, and there's more reality to voodoo than you think," he said.

Lil went to the sink and washed her hands for no good reason.

"You need to see Father O'Reilly," she said.

"We'll go Sunday," he said. "I'll wear my best

suit. I'll confess my sins, and then I'll take you to brunch at Brennan's."

"You mean it?" she said.

Tony nodded. "It's been too long since we've had a real date. I look forward to it."

Lil poured Tony more coffee. "What has happened to Mama?"

"Not sure. Wyatt rescued an old girlfriend and needed our help."

"Rescued?" Lil said.

"Long story," Tony said.

Realizing Tony wasn't going to share everything he knew, Lil said, "What help did Wyatt need?"

"The woman Wyatt rescued is Latitia Boiset, the lead singer for Brass & Sass."

"You're right," Lil said. "I've never heard of her or her group. What did Wyatt want you to do?"

"Latitia's mother, Lashonda, lives in the Lower 9th Ward. Lashonda is raising Latitia's daughter Aimee. The men who had kidnapped Latitia had threatened to harm Lashonda and Aimee unless she complied with their demands."

"And?"

"Aimee is Wyatt's daughter."

Lil's hand went to her mouth. "I never knew Wyatt had a child."

"Neither did Wyatt," Tony said. "Latitia kept it from him all these years."

"Oh, my God!" Lil said. "Are they in a safe place?"

"At Mama's. Problem is Aimee's cat wasn't around when they left Lashonda's house. Mama went back earlier tonight to find the cat. Now, she's not answering her phone."

Lil topped up Tony's coffee cup and then poured more for herself. This time, she didn't bother adding milk and sugar.

Tony shook his head when Lil said, "You need

to call Tommy and get the N.O.P.D. involved."

"Can't do that," he said.

"Why not?"

"It's complicated."

"Then what are you going to do?"

"Check Lashonda's house in the Lower 9th Ward. Maybe I'll find something to tell me where to go from here."

"You're going to get killed," Lil said, "You're supposed to be retired from police work."

"When I finish this case, I'll think about doing something else to occupy my time," he said.

"We could travel," she said. "We haven't been anywhere since our second honeymoon to Italy."

"Where do you want to go?" Tony asked.

"Ireland," Lil said. "I've always wanted to visit, and we both have distant relatives who live there."

"You've never said anything about Ireland," Tony said.

"I'm saying it now."

"Okay. When I finish this case, we'll vacation to Ireland."

"You aren't making this up as you go, are you?"

"No way," Tony said.

"And we're still on for church and brunch this Sunday?"

Tony got up from the table, smiled, and kissed Lil.

"I promise," he said.

"You better get dressed and see if you can find Mama," Lil said.

Tony hadn't left his house minutes before midnight in years. He'd had to promise a trip to Ireland, a Catholic confession, and Sunday brunch at Brennan's. Satisfied he wouldn't get chastised when he returned home, it seemed worth it. He called Lashonda.

"I'm on my way to your condo," Tony said. "I need the address."

"Aimee and I want to go with you," Lashonda said.

"Too dangerous. It's half past midnight. I'll call you when I know something."

"Aimee and I can't sleep," Lashonda said. "I'm putting her on the line."

Aimee was speaking before Tony could protest. "Please take us with you," she said. "We feel so helpless here alone."

"Okay," he said. "I'll be there soon."

Tony found Aimee and Lashonda waiting at the front door. The storm had continued, with his top up, and rain battering the canvas as he, Aimee, and Lashonda headed for the Lower 9th Ward.

"I don't expect much," he said.

"We'll find her," Aimee said.

"It's raining so hard the wipers can barely keep up," Tony said.

"Then please slow down," Lashonda said.

The stress in Lashonda's voice instantly affected Tony's speed as he took his foot off the gas.

"Sorry," he said. "My mind was racing, and my foot got heavy. Did Mama mention any other place she was going?" Tony asked.

"Just to get Bootsie," Aimee said.

"You're being very quiet," Lashonda said. "Please tell us what you are thinking."

"I'm worried," Tony said. "Someone was probably watching the house. They could have abducted her."

When they reached Lashonda's house, they found Mama's Bugeye Sprite parked in front, the driver's door open wide. The front seat was drenched with rain when Tony shut the door.

The rain had subsided enough for them to

rush to the front porch. The first thing they found was Aimee's cat Bootsie. When he saw Aimee, he jumped into her arms. Lashonda soon found something else.

"What is it?" Tony said.

"One of Mama's driving gloves," Lashonda said."

"That ain't good," Tony said. "Mama loved those gloves and, given a choice, would never have forgotten one."

"I'll look inside and see if anything is amiss," Lashonda said.

Aimee and Tony followed her into the house. Lashonda took her time and went through every room.

"Anything unusual?" Tony asked.

"Someone's been here," Lashonda said. "There's trash in the cans I didn't leave.

"Someone must have waited here for Mama or whoever else might have shown up," Tony said. "Mama's key was still in her car. Can you drive it back to her house?" Tony asked.

"Yes," Lashonda said.

"I'm riding with Tony," Aimee said.

"You don't trust my driving?" Lashonda asked.

"I have questions for Tony. I can talk to you anytime."

"Suit yourself, little girl," Lashonda said.

"I'm as tall as you are," Aimee said.

Seeing she wouldn't win the argument, Lashonda climbed into Mama's car and started the engine.

Tony pulled out of the driveway and headed to Mama's house. Aimee's cat, happy to be out of the rain, was purring in her lap.

"What questions do you have for me?" Tony asked.

"You know my dad?"

"Very well. What about him?"

"Why isn't he and my mother married?"

"Wyatt didn't know you existed until yesterday," Tony said. "You'll have to ask your mom that question."

Much of New Orleans is below sea level, and even a little rain can cause flooding on the roads. Tony was keeping an eye on Lashonda in his rearview mirror. The ensuing splash washed over the hood of Mama's car when he hit a puddle. He slowed his Mustang and increased the speed of the windshield wipers.

"What's my dad like?" Aimee said.

"An honest, hardworking man. I have nothing but good things to say about him," Tony said.

"What does he do for a living?"

"He's a private investigator. Just like me."

"Is he intelligent?" Aimee asked.

"One of the smartest persons I've ever met," Tony said. "He has a law degree from L.S.U."

"Then why is he a private investigator and not a lawyer?"

The falling rain and clack of the wipers were almost hypnotic. Water from a leak in the canvas roof dripped on Tony's arm, keeping him alert.

"That's a question you'll have to ask your dad," he said.

"If I ever meet him," Aimee said.

"You will."

"Are you married?" Aimee asked.

"Going on thirty years," Tony said.

"Do you have kids?"

"Five and a whole bunch of grand-babies."

"Why is it some people stay married and others don't?"

Aimee smiled when Tony said, "Marriage is like a used car. Something always needs fixing. Some people buy new cars when that happens."

"Lashonda is the only grandparent I have,"

Aimee said.

Aimee smiled again when Tony said, "Well, you got a keeper there. She's one of a kind and good as gold."

"I wouldn't want to lose her," Aimee said.

Aimee's hand went to her mouth when Tony said, "I'm keeping an eye on her. Mama's car is so tiny it could wash away into the canal any minute."

"Maybe we should stop and let her ride with us," Aimee said.

"Your grandmother is a good driver and doing fine."

"If you say so," Aimee said. "We don't even own a car."

Aimee's admission increased Tony's already through the roof anxiety. Despite his concern, they managed to make it to Mama's without mishap. Tony was sitting in Mama's recliner when his cell phone rang. It was Wyatt calling from a phone number he didn't recognize. With the short conversation near its conclusion, Tony conveyed his most important news.

"Wyatt," he said. "Mama has gone missing. Someone involved in our case snatched her."

Chapter 17

Tony had left Mama's when someone began knocking on the door. Lashonda had to stand on her tiptoes to see who it was.

"Who is it?" she said.

"Mama, is that you?" a voice said.

"Mama's not here," Lashonda said.

"Where the hell is she?"

Lashonda opened the door and stared at the pretty black girl in cornrows and cutoff jeans.

"Who are you?" she asked.

"Stevie Jones. Who are you?"

"Lashonda."

"Where is Mama Mulate?" Stevie asked.

"We don't know," Lashonda said. "We found her car at my house in the Lower 9th Ward.

"What was she doing there?" Stevie said.

"Looking for Aimee's cat," Lashonda said.

A white girl with big blue eyes appeared with a cat in her arms.

"I'm Aimee," she said. "Who are you?"

"Stevie," she said. "Mama knows who I am."

Seeing a tear in Stevie's eye, Aimee dropped the cat and put her arms around Stevie's waist.

"We think someone abducted Mama," she said. "We found her car, the door open, in the rain."

"We have to get out of here," Stevie said.

"For what reason?" Lashonda said.

"When I returned home from work, I found my apartment ransacked," Stevie said. "They'll be here before long."

"Who will be here?" Lashonda asked.

"Voodoo People," Stevie said. "We have to leave."

"I'm going nowhere without Bootsie and Mama's three cats," Aimee said.

"They'll be okay," Stevie said.

Aimee shook her head. "Not going to happen. Where I go, the cats go."

"Okay," Stevie said. "Let's gather them up and then get the hell out of here."

"Mama's cats don't trust me yet," Aimee said.

"We're minutes away from capture," Stevie said. "If we can't get the cats, we'll have to leave them."

"I'm not leaving without Mama's cats," Aimee said.

"Then let's try to round them up."

Aimee found a packet of cat treats in a cabinet. When she shook the package, Mama's cats came running. Stevie had stumbled across two cat carriers on the porch, and they soon had the four cats inside them.

"Where are we going?" Lashonda asked.

"I have no idea," Stevie said.

"You know Tony?" Lashonda asked.

"Yes."

"Call him," Aimee said. "He's a good person and knows my dad."

"It's almost four in the morning," Stevie said.

"It was after two when he left Mama's," Lashonda said. "Even if he's in bed, he can't have been there long. I'll give you his number."

"I have it," Stevie said.

Stevie punched in Tony's number, and he

answered on the second ring.

"This is Tony."

"It's Stevie. Lashonda, Aimee, and I just left Mama Mulate's house."

"What's wrong?"

"Someone rifled through my apartment while I was at work. Bruno and Harvey are working late. I was afraid, so I drove to Mama's. Someone followed me, and I wasn't able to shake them."

"I just left Mama's," Tony said.

"We're in my car and have no place to go."

"Who is it?" Lil asked.

"Stevie Jones, Bobby Blanchard's girlfriend. She's just left Mama's house. You were asleep when I got home."

"Who are you talking to?" Stevie asked.

"My wife, Lil. Bring Lashonda and Aimee to my house."

"What about the cats?" Stevie said.

"You brought the cats?"

"Aimee refused to leave without them."

"Bring them," Tony said.

Tony gave Stevie his address and hung up the phone. Lil was sitting up in bed, staring at him.

"Are we about to have a houseful of guests?" Lil asked.

Tony was already out of bed, pulling on his pants. He left the bedroom without answering and was sitting at the breakfast table in his pants and undershirt when Lil appeared in her old cotton robe. She went to the stove and put on a pot of coffee.

"You know, Tony, you're going to go to hell for lying one of these days."

"What?"

"Mass on Sunday and then Sunday brunch in the Quarter."

"How am I lying? Sunday isn't here yet."

"How will we go anywhere with a houseful of

people?"

"They're bringing four cats."

"Are you kidding me? You know I'm allergic to cats."

"What was I supposed to do?" Tony said.

"There are hotels and motels all over town. You told me you're on an expense account. Why can't Frankie Castellano pay for it?"

"It's almost five in the morning. I can't call Frankie now."

Lil just shook her head. "Mother told me I should have married Norris Harris."

"Who the hell is Norris Harris?" Tony asked.

"A millionaire oil man I met when I was in business college. He lives in a mansion outside of Biloxi."

"You keep tabs on your old boyfriends?"

"You never cease to amaze me, Tony Nicosia. You invite people I've never met and their cats to my house at four-thirty in the morning, and you're jealous about one of my old boyfriends."

"You've never said anything about Norris Harris. How did you meet him?"

"What difference does it make? It's all water under the bridge. At least I wasn't married."

Lil's reference to Tony's short-lived affair with a much younger woman shook him.

"I thought we had resolved all of that," he said. "I've told you I'm sorry a thousand times. When we vacationed in Italy, you said it was like a second honeymoon. I thought my little mistake was behind us. Guess it's not."

"Your mistake wasn't so little."

"At least you know about it," Tony said. "You've never told me about this Norris Harris person."

Lil poured coffee and took it to him. "You're hopeless. I love you anyway."

"I love you too," Tony said. "We'll talk about

Norris Harris later."

"I made up that story. It isn't true."

"Yes, it is. I know when you're lying. You were telling the truth."

"I don't lie. What are you insinuating?" Lil said.

"I was a homicide detective for twenty-five years. If there's one thing I learned, everyone has something to cover up and almost always lies about it."

Lil reached for the steaming cup in front of Tony. Tony was smiling when he grabbed it.

"I meant to say I've never heard a lie come from your gorgeous lips."

Lil kissed him on the forehead as the doorbell rang.

"I'll get it," she said.

"What about the cats?"

"I have Benadryl in the medicine cabinet. I'll survive."

Two black women with cat carriers and a white girl with blue eyes greeted Lil when she opened the door.

"I'm Tony's wife, Lil. Come in this house."

The younger of the two black women was almost in tears. Lil took the cat carrier from her, placed it on the floor, and then wrapped her arms around the young woman.

"What's the matter, baby?"

"There was a car tailing us on the way over here. They know where we are. I'm Stevie. Thanks for taking us misfits in."

"Who are you?" Lil asked.

"Lashonda and this is my granddaughter Aimee."

Lil put her hands on Aimee's shoulders. "You are Wyatt's daughter," she said. "You are so pretty. I hope you're as smart as your dad is."

"You know my dad?" Aimee said.

"For almost forever," Lil said. "Let the cats out of the carriers and come in the kitchen. It's not too early for breakfast."

Tony was standing at the kitchen door and quickly noticed the tears trickling down Stevie's face. Grabbing her hand, he gave it a reassuring squeeze.

"You're safe here," Tony said.

"A car followed us. They know where we are."

Tony grabbed his cell phone from the kitchen table and dialed Tommy Blackburn's number. Tommy, sounding groggy, answered on the second ring.

"What's up, boss man?"

"You're the boss now," Tony said. "I need a favor."

"Shoot, Luke," Tommy said.

"Someone's watching my house," Tony said. "I need the cops to start patrolling the neighborhood."

"You got it," Tommy said. "Tell me what's going down?"

"I can't tell you right now. We haven't had a beer at Carlucci's in forever. I'd like to see the old gang again when I get this case behind me. I'll tell you about it when we do."

"Don't get yourself killed, partner," Tommy said.

"Thanks, Tommy. Last thing on my list," Tony said.

Lil and Lashonda were at the stove and smiling when Tony returned the phone to the kitchen table. Stevie was still crying, and Tony wiped her face with a paper towel.

"Cops will be swarming this place in about ten minutes. Whoever's watching us will think twice before attempting a home invasion. Trust me when I tell you we're safe."

Lil's eyes were watering as she downed a

Benadryl tablet at the sink. The curious cats were investigating the kitchen, wondering where they were. They were mostly ignoring Tony's dog, Patch, whose tail was wagging.

Lil and Lashonda had prepared bacon and jalapeño scrambled eggs. Aimee was drinking freshly-squeezed orange juice, everyone else strong chicory, and coffee.

Tony nodded when Stevie said, "What are we going to do about finding Mama?"

"I don't know yet."

"She's in danger," Stevie said. "We have to do something."

"We're working on it."

"We?"

"My partner, Wyatt Thomas, and me. He's undercover in Mandeville."

"Aimee's father?"

Tony nodded. "It shocked his system when he learned he has a daughter he didn't know about."

"Females don't have that particular problem," Stevie said.

"It takes two to tango," Tony said.

"Sorry, I'm so crabby. Stress is beginning to get to me."

"You're doing better than most."

"I'm trying," Stevie said.

"I feel safe here," Lashonda said. "So sorry for the unexpected inconvenience."

"Tony and I have five kids," Lil said. "Our lives are constantly filled with unexpected inconveniences."

"Don't go to any extra trouble for us," Lashonda said. "We can hang out in your living room and try to stay out of your way."

"Nonsense!" Lil said. "Our kids are all grown and gone, and we have many empty bedrooms. Enough for all of you. You're welcome to make yourself at home and stay as long as you like."

"Thank you," Lashonda said.

"Don't know what I'm going to do about my job," Stevie said. "They'll fire me if I don't show up for work."

"Let me call Frankie," Tony said.

"Who is Frankie?" Aimee asked.

"The person who hired me," Tony said."

Frankie was a morning person and already up and drinking coffee when Tony called.

"Tony, thanks for calling," Frankie said when he answered the phone. "Anything new?"

"We're closing in on an answer. I have a request to make."

"Tell me," Frankie said."

"Bobbie was living with a young woman named Stevie Jones. I'll put this to you bluntly. Stevie's black, something Bobby's parents didn't exactly cater to."

"So what's the problem?" Frankie asked.

"The people who zombied Bobby are trying to capture or kill Stevie. I think she can help us in finding Bobby. She can't return to work. She can do us a world of good, and I'd like to hire her until we solve this case."

"How much does she make?" Frankie asked.

"Minimum wage," Tony said.

"Tell Stevie I'm putting five grand in your account for her. There's more if she needs it."

"Thanks, Frankie," Tony said.

"What did he say?" Stevie asked.

Tony smiled. "Will five grand get you through for a while?"

"You kidding me? Really?"

"You're on the payroll starting right now," Tony said. "Call your work and tell them you won't be in for a week or so."

"They'll fire me," Stevie said.

"It's okay," Tony said. "We need you, at least for the foreseeable future. You're on the payroll, and I'll cut you a check tomorrow."

Stevie's tears disappeared, replaced with a beaming smile.

"Thank you, Tony, and thank you, Lil. I'm going to call my boss right now."

"Your eyes are swelling," Aimee said. "I'm so sorry."

"I'll be fine," Lil said. "I have plenty of Benadryl."

"There's a pet motel not far from here," Tony said. "Tomorrow, Aimee and I will check the cats in for a while. They'll love it."

Chapter 18

Mama's abduction had upset me more than I cared to admit, and I awoke worrying about it. Freya had left the door ajar, the aroma of strong coffee and spicy cooking drifting down the hallway. When I glanced in the mirror, I realized Pancho was right. My mother probably wouldn't have recognized me.

Freya and Pancho were flipping pancakes, Pancho in his pants and undershirt, Freya in a purple nightgown. Latitia was only half smiling when I joined her at the kitchen table.

"Smells wonderful," she said.

"You look so sad. What's the matter?"

Latitia clutched my hand. "I'm frightened."

"You're safe here. My partner Tony left a message on Freya's phone and said Lashonda and Aimee are safe and being well taken care of."

"I had a life-changing experience," she said. "I'll never be the same again."

"Tell me," I said.

"I've never thought much about death. That's all changed now."

"How so?"

"Zombie powder renders you motionless. You can't move a muscle. You can't even blink. Your lungs don't work; your heart doesn't beat. Every

154

part of your body shuts down except for your brain. Someone could cut off your finger. You wouldn't move or call out, but you'd still feel the excruciating pain of the blade as it severed your flesh."

"Sounds like a nightmare," I said.

"A nightmare from which you can't awaken," Latitia said. "I don't want to return to that place."

"I'm looking for a missing young man, someone zombied. The person who hired me is possibly involved. We're safe here until I come up with the answers."

Latitia squeezed my hand and said, "I wish I were as confident as you are."

"What do you mean?"

"There's something about Freya," she said.

Latitia smiled when I said, "Her overt sexuality?"

"Freya is different."

"How so?" I asked.

"She's supernatural."

"You can't be serious."

"I sense it. It's something I can't explain, though I can't get it out of my head," she said.

Freya put down her spatula and approached us. "What an intense conversation you two are having. My ears were burning. Are you talking about me?"

"We were discussing your nurturing embraces," I said.

Freya gave me a wink. "Breakfast is almost ready. Eggs Benedict."

"My favorite," Latitia said.

"Mine too," I said.

"See?" Latitia said after Freya had returned to the stove.

"She probably noticed we were talking low and wondered what we were hiding."

"Maybe," Latitia said. "Were you looking for

155

me when you visited Vodou Nitz?"

"I had no idea you were in trouble until I saw you in the attic of the Bell House," I said. "I went there looking for someone else. When I went to the club, I had only an inkling I'd find you there."

"The company that owns Brass & Sass hires dozens of roadies who move the sets, equipment, and musical instruments from show to show. I noticed a new roadie I was wondering about."

"Because?"

"I always make friends with the roadie's because they'll go out of their way to help you. When I introduced myself, he stared at the floor with lifeless eyes."

"You're kidding me," I said. "What did he look like?"

"Young, white, good-looking," she said.

"You know his name?"

"The other roadies called him Zombie Boy. I'm betting he had a dose of the powder."

When Latitia fell into a reflective mood, I turned my attention to the aroma of Freya and Pancho's cooking. This gig was dangerous though I couldn't remember having eaten so well in months. When the meal finally arrived at the kitchen table, it tasted better than it smelled.

Between bites of her eggs Benedict, Freya said, "What's your plan for the day?"

"I left my bicycle on a side street. Now I need it. Once I retrieve it, I have other things on my agenda."

"Will you be staying here tonight?" Freya asked.

"I don't think so. What I'm doing is dangerous. I've involved you enough already."

"I'm aware of the danger, and I accept it," Freya said. "My coven has certain powers. I'll be safe, and so will you and Latitia."

"You sure?" I asked.

Freya put her hand on my knee. "Like I said last night, I haven't had this much fun in years. Please plan on staying here."

"Thank you," I said.

Chapter 19

Questions needed answers as I left Freya's Gothic house in the old Covington neighborhood. Maybe Bobby Blanchard was at Vodou Nitz. I had to retrieve him from the nightclub, take him to Frankie's, and collect the rest of my money. Mama's abduction spoiled that scenario.

Mama's newspaper article about the person arising from the dead might hold some of the answers I sought. I had to find Emile LeCompte and interview him. The bike waited where I'd left it, and I was soon on my way to the post office to retrieve the cell phone.

Mama had texted me the location where I might find Emile LeCompte. The problem was that I had no topographic map and was scratching my head, wondering how to use the coordinates. Looking up from the cell phone, I stared into Toni's dark eyes. She wasn't smiling.

"I thought it was you," she said. "Why are you hiding from me?"

"You said you didn't want to see me again."

"No, I didn't."

"You kidding me? You were so angry I could have lit a match on your forehead."

"I'm over it," she said. "What have you

learned so far?"

"I think I know where I can find Bobby."

"That's wonderful," she said.

"There are problems."

"Such as?"

"He's been zombied."

"We'll take him to a doctor," Toni said.

"They won't have a clue how to revive him. Senator Blanchard would have a non-responsive body on his hands."

"Then what are we going to do?" she asked.

"One of my partners found a newspaper article about a man from Covington named Emile LeCompte, who she thinks was zombied. It's my only lead, and I need to talk to him."

"Not Tony?"

"Mama Mulate. Frankie hired her to help in the investigation. She's gone missing, her disappearance directly related to this case."

Toni snatched the phone away from me. "You're clueless, aren't you?"

She shook her head when I said, "I'll figure it out."

"I doubt it. You think LeCompte has the antidote?"

"Who knows what he can tell me until I talk to him?"

"I'll take you there," she said.

"I don't need your help."

"We're both working for Frankie on this case," Toni said.

"You didn't tell me you knew Frankie owns Vodou Nitz," I said.

Toni stared at me, her mouth open. "Who told you that?"

"Pancho," I said.

I nodded when she said, "My Pancho?"

"I can't see how Frankie's not up to his neck in this situation," I said.

"Bullshit!" Toni said. "Now, I am pissed."

"I'm not trying to alienate you and Frankie. I'm still working for him."

Toni forwarded the coordinates to her cell phone, handing mine back to me.

"Directions by way of the Tammany Trace, Covington, Louisiana."

When the assistant responded, she read the coordinates.

"Take the Tammany Trace two point four miles south," the voice said.

Toni mounted her bike. "Now what?" I asked.

"Try to keep up."

The day was gorgeous, with not a cloud in the sky. A snowy egret drifted in a thermal updraft as Toni poured on the coal, giving me no quarter. I was winded when she pulled to a stop on the Tammany Trace.

"We'll have to go part of the way on a rural road," she said. "At least it's paved. The final few miles are by an unimproved dirt road. Can you make it?"

"Right behind you," I said.

Toni grinned. "You're pretty fit for an old dude."

"Who's old?" I said. "If I were riding your bike, we'd already be there."

"You're not," she said as she powered away.

Toni's tee shirt was damp, sweat covering her neck and bare shoulders. The sand was so deep we were soon pushing our bikes, my legs feeling like rubber when she barreled off the trace.

"It isn't far to the paved road," she said.

I had a canteen in the basket on the back of my old bike.

"Want some water?" I said.

"I'm good," she said.

"Suit yourself," I said as I took a drink from the canteen.

"Give me the damn thing," she said when she saw me smiling.

"You're welcome," I said.

Toni's frown never disappeared as she pushed her bike through the deep sand. When we finally arrived on a rural blacktop road, I wondered if she knew where she was going.

"Don't look at me like that," she said. "I know what I'm doing."

"I didn't say anything."

"You were thinking it," she said.

I handed her the canteen, and she drank a hearty swig before returning it to me. We followed the blacktop for another mile. The dirt road we found when the blacktop disappeared was little more than a trail. The canteen was empty when we reached a clearing in the trees.

"This is it," Toni said.

"I don't see a damn thing."

Before Toni could speak, a big yellow dog came out of the trees, wagging its tail. Toni hugged its neck.

"Did you come to get us, big boy?" she said.

Horseflies dive-bombed our heads as we followed the dog down the dusty country road. A ramshackle, wood-framed house peeked through the overgrown vegetation when we rounded the last dusty corner. If someone lived there, it had been a while since they'd taken care of the yard.

"Looks like we may be too late," Toni said.

The big dog bounded up the steps to the wraparound porch. Toni and I followed him into the house.

The windows were open, a breeze whipping tattered curtains. They'd been open awhile because patches of rainwater spotted the floor. The dog led us into a bedroom, put his front paws on the bed, and licked a man's face. The man opened his eyes.

"Who are you?" he asked.

"Toni and Wyatt. Are you Emile?"

"My friends used to call me Squirrel."

"Used to?" Toni said.

"I'm dead. Ain't got no more friends."

"You look alive to me," Toni said.

A sheet covered Squirrel, and he wasn't wearing a shirt. I pulled back the cover, looking for a tattoo beneath his left nipple. It was there, similar to the one beneath Latitia's breast and Bobby Blanchard's. Squirrel's ribs were prominent on his skinny frame.

"When was the last time you ate?" I asked.

"I ain't eating no more," he said.

Toni cast me a worried glance. "Wyatt, bring me some water."

I'd seen the well on the side of the house, nodded, and backed out of the room. The dog wasn't the only animal living with Squirrel. Chickens were scratching for insects. Two mules occupied a pen behind the house, and several cats were on the porch.

The damp grass around the house was up to my knees, and my pant legs wet from wading through it to the cobblestone well. After cranking a bucket of water, I sat it on the side of the well and filled a ladle hanging from the roof.

The dog had followed me out the door, and I could see he was also thirsty. A trough near the well was dry. When I filled it with water, he drank, the chickens soon joining him. The mules' trough was also dry, and I refilled it before returning to the house. Toni held the ladle beneath Squirrel's mouth until he'd drank all of it.

"I ain't getting out of this bed," he said. "I told you I'm dead."

"You aren't dead," I said. "You were zombied."

"Some voodoo person stole my soul."

"No, they didn't. They controlled you with zombie powder."

"My family thinks I'm dead. They thought I was a ghost or an imposter when I tried to go home."

"You're just as alive as that big yellow dog of yours," I said. "What's his name?"

"Yeller," Squirrel said.

"He was worried about you. He brought us here," Toni said.

Yeller's tail wagged when Squirrel reached down from the bed and rubbed his head.

"He and the other animals are the only family I got left," he said.

"Looks as if they've missed a few meals. Tell me where you keep their food, and I'll feed them," I said.

Mention of his animal's hunger visibly distressed Squirrel, and he got out of bed. Like many inhabitants of south Louisiana, he was of mixed heritage with brown skin and dark eyes. He pulled a worn-out pair of overalls over his boxer shorts.

"You're skinny as a rail," Toni said. "When was the last time you ate?"

"Don't remember," he said.

Squirrel collapsed when he started for the door. "Let's help him into the kitchen and feed him something," I said.

Soon as we had Squirrel in a chair, Toni began searching through the refrigerator and shelves.

"Where do you get the electricity to run the refrigerator?" I asked.

"Propane generator out back," he said. "There's lights and even central heat and air."

"Where's the thermostat?" Toni said. "It's hotter than Holy Hell in here?"

"In the hall," Squirrel said. "There's a shed in

back with barrels of food for the animals. Can you feed and water them?"

"Already watered them," I said. "I'll get them some food."

I soon had the food bowls for Yeller, and the cats filled. The chickens were happy to see me and gathered around as I sprinkled chicken feed on the feeder. When the two mules finished their oats, I led them into the yard to munch on the tall grass. Using tools and lumber from the shed, I began repairing the porch, the house, and the barn. It was getting late when I finished and led the two mules back to their pen. The grass in the yard looked almost professionally mowed, and my carpentry repairs weren't too bad, either.

Squirrel hadn't moved from the chair Toni and I had put him in. All the windows were shut, the air cool, and the dust and mildew removed.

"Looks like you've been busy," I said.

"I made you soup, salad, and a sandwich," Toni said. "The veggies are fresh from the garden."

"Wonderful," I said.

"Thank you for helping an old man," Squirrel said. "Now, tell me why you're here."

"The tattoo on your chest has already answered one of my questions," I said. "You were zombied, the victim of some cruel voodoo practitioner. I want to hear your story."

"This old house can be like a coffin. I don't want to be in it when I talk about the past. Help me out to the front porch," he said

Chapter 20

S quirrel was lightheaded and moved slowly to his rocking chair on the front porch. Before long, two of his cats were in his lap, with Yeller asleep nearby.

"Thanks for giving me the courage to get out of bed," he said. "Before you sit, could you do one more thing for me?"

"Name it," I said.

"There's a jug of shine in the kitchen cabinet."

"I'll get it," I said.

Toni sat on a twisted cane couch as I handed the jug to Squirrel. He hoisted the moonshine to his shoulder and took a drink.

"Either of you want a pull?"

"Not me," I said.

"It's all yours," Toni said. "Enjoy yourself."

"You did a wonderful job on the yard," Squirrel said. "Never thought about letting the mules eat the grass."

"They loved it," I said. "I fixed the fence around the chicken coop and repaired a few holes in the barn's roof."

"I thank both of you," he said.

The sun was beginning to set, and the sky alit in red, filtering through a golden haze. A flock of seagulls above us was heading for Lake

Pontchartrain. The singing of nearby tree frogs and the chirping of crickets signaled rain was on its way.

"I feel your pain and know you have suffered greatly because of your ordeal. Toni and I are working to bring an end to the group practicing dark voodoo. You can help by telling us your story."

Squirrel drank more shine before answering. "I died five years ago this month. My wife found me dead on our front porch in Mandeville."

"How did you die?" I asked.

"Don't know for sure. Sophie called 9-1-1. The EMTs took me to the emergency room, where a doctor ruled me dead. Funny thing, though!"

"What?" I said.

"I couldn't move a muscle or even blink my eyes, but I heard every word said. They took me to the funeral home."

Squirrel shook his head when Toni said, "They didn't embalm you? How can that be?"

"Though disbarred, I'm still an attorney and know the vagaries of Louisiana law," I said. "In Louisiana, embalming is rarely required."

"You're kidding," Toni said.

"I'm not."

"There was a viewing of my body," Squirrel said. "My friends and relatives stood around the casket telling stories about me. They were laughing as if I weren't dead."

"Grief manifests itself in strange ways," I said. It's the price we pay for love."

"I was a spectator to my death," Squirrel said. "I've never felt as horrible as when the coffin shut, stranding me in silence and darkness."

"Jesus!" Toni said. "I don't know if I could have handled it."

"I had no choice," Squirrel said. "My eyes were open, and I stared into darkness until a shovel struck the coffin."

Squirrel nodded when Toni said, "Someone dug you up?"

"They opened the coffin and pulled me out. Baron Samedi, the keeper of the dead, was one of them."

"Who is Baron Samedi?" Toni asked.

"A voodoo deity who wears a tuxedo, a top hat, and smokes a cigar," I said. "In the Vodoun religion, he's the keeper of the dead. Let me see your wrist."

Like Latitia and Bobby Blanchard, Squirrel had a Baron Samedi veve tattooed on his wrist.

"They opened my mouth and trickled some foul-tasting liquid into it. It made me vomit and revived me. Like I said, they identified themselves as Baron Samedi and the keepers of the dead. They were taking me to the place where I would spend eternity."

"You believed them?" Toni asked.

"I was confused and didn't know what to believe. I was herded into a pickup truck and taken to a sugar cane plantation."

"How long were you there?" I asked.

"Years. During planting, I drove a truck. I operated a giant harvesting combine when the crop was ready to cut. It went twenty-four hours a day until the crop was harvested and loaded."

"How many acres of cane?" I asked.

"Twenty thousand," Squirrel said.

"That big?" Toni said. "I didn't know Louisiana still raised sugar cane."

"One of our primary cash crops," I said. There are lots of farms and hundreds of small sugar refineries."

"The plantation was beyond huge," Squirrel said. "It was enormous."

"Did they have to teach you how to operate the combine?" I asked.

"I was a heavy equipment operator before I died. Ain't nothing mechanical I can't operate."

"Maybe that's the reason they chose you. Where did they keep you when you weren't cutting cane?" I asked.

"On the cement floor of a warehouse."

"Were you alone?"

"Me and other dead people."

Squirrel shook his head when I asked, "You knew them?"

"I couldn't speak, and neither could they. The only time we could even move a muscle was after the cook fed us."

"So you were immobile until they needed you?"

"That's right," Squirrel said. "The cook would drizzle something down my throat, causing me to toss my cookies." He smiled. "The cook was smarter than Baron Samedi and always got out of the way."

"How did you feel when they revived you?" I asked.

"Strong as an ox. At least my body. My mind was someplace else."

"Even when you were lying on the concrete?" I asked.

"Only then was my mind active. Being aware and unable to move was pure hell."

"I can only imagine," I said. "How did you escape?"

"The cook revived me when they needed me to work the machinery. She would dribble the liquid down my throat and move out of the way while I threw up and shook off the stupor. One of those times, someone called her after she'd revived me. She left me alone with the bottle. Though it tasted horrible, I drank it all."

"It revived you?" Toni asked.

"I felt alive like I do now. When the men came

to get me, I played dumb."

"How did you escape?" I asked.

"I operated the combine until dark. There was usually a continuous line of waiting trucks. I was cutting a row of cane that paralleled a paved road. Between trucks, I left the combine running and jumped out. I hitchhiked back to Mandeville. It was morning when I got there."

Squirrel nodded when I said, "You went home?"

"My wife screamed and fainted when she saw me. Her new husband made it clear I wasn't welcome there."

"And the rest of your family?"

"As I said, they thought I was either a ghost or an imposter. Either way, I wasn't welcome."

"You gave an interview to the local paper," I said.

"They printed my story though they didn't believe me either," Squirrel said.

"How did you get here?" I asked.

"Uncle Charlie left this land to me when he died. I'd tried to sell it, though it's out here in the middle of nowhere, and nobody wanted to buy it. It's here I came when I realized I wasn't welcome in Mandeville. Been here ever since."

Squirrel grinned when I asked, "How do you support yourself?"

"Uncle Charlie was a lifelong bachelor. I was his favorite nephew. He left everything to me and hired a lawyer to handle the succession."

"How do you know all of this?" I said.

"He left a notebook explaining what he owned and what I needed to do. There was a bank account in my name with almost a million dollars in it."

"Seriously?" Toni said.

"Uncle Charlie owned minerals he'd won in a poker game while working offshore. When an oil

169

company struck pay dirt, the minerals became valuable. I still get big checks every month. One good thing."

"What's that?" I asked.

He grinned and said, "Since I'm dead, I don't have to pay taxes."

Toni ignored his humor and asked, "Why do you live like a pauper?"

"Because until today, I thought I was dead."

"You are very much alive," I said. "When we bust the voodoo ring that zombied you, you'll be able to prove it. You can return to your family."

"I'm never going back. Yeller, my chickens, cats, and mules are my family now."

"We need your help," I said. "Give us the name of the sugar plantation and where we can find it."

"I know the name but not the address. I can take you there," Squirrel said. "I have a truck in the barn."

"That would be wonderful," I said.

"It'll have to wait till tomorrow. My night vision's bad. Can't see much of anything after dark."

"We're on our bikes, and it's starting to rain," I said.

"You can spend the night," Squirrel said. I have a recliner and a couch though no extra bedrooms."

"We don't want to impose on you," I said.

"Where you going to go? The road will be impassable on a bike. If you wait until tomorrow, my four-wheel-drive pickup will get us to the blacktop."

"What's the name of the plantation?" I said.

"Faumort," he said.

"Strange name," Toni said. "I'll fix breakfast in the morning before we go. Wyatt and I will help you to bed."

The wind was blowing, rain falling in sheets when I opened the front door and gazed out.

"I better put the bikes in the shed."

"You'll drown," Toni said.

"I'll make it fast," I said as I hurried out the door.

Half-drowned when I returned, Toni waited with a smile, a cup of hot tea, and a towel.

"You may as well strip down and dry off," she said. "I've already seen you naked."

We were soon sitting on the couch, drinking hot tea and listening to the sound of the storm raging outside the door.

"I'm hungry," she said. "Want another sandwich?"

"Love one," I said. "Biking and carpentry have whetted my appetite.

"Even if we know where to find it, what will we do about the plantation?" Toni asked.

"We'll have to do a deep search of the ownership. Once we obtain that info, we'll be on our way to busting the ring."

"What about the antidote? We can't save Bobby without it."

"Haven't thought that far ahead," I said.

"Legal proceedings can take months, maybe years. Bobby will be dead by then. We have to do something."

"Like what?"

"Have Squirrel take us to the warehouse where they kept him and get a bottle of the antidote," Toni said.

"Risky business. They probably know what his truck looks like."

"Then why haven't they returned for him after all these years?"

"I was thinking the same thing," I said. "Maybe after he gave the newspaper interview, they decided to let well enough alone."

"They've probably forgotten all about him by now," Toni said.

"There's a reason, though I doubt it's because they've forgotten about him."

"You think we need to verify Squirrel's story?" Toni asked.

"The tattoos on his chest and wrist are verification enough for me," I said. "The name of the plantation tells the story."

"Faumort?" Toni said. "How does that tell us anything?"

"Faux mort means fake death in French," I said.

"Damn!" Toni said. "How blatant."

"Probably an indication people are exchanging money under the table. Not unusual when you know the history of Louisiana politics."

"Bobby's daddy is a powerful state senator," Toni said.

"Powerful people have enemies," I said.

"What about Mama Mulate?" Toni asked. "You think she's at Faumort?"

"That's what I think," I said.

"The rain on the roof is lulling me to sleep," she said. "We have decisions to make before we go to sleep."

"Like what?" I said.

"Who will take the couch, and who gets the recliner?"

"I'm easy. Take your pick," I said.

Toni was soon asleep on the couch, cuddled in an old Afghan, one of Squirrel's cats sleeping with her.

An hour passed before the day's events released my psyche into the awaiting arms of Morpheus.

Chapter 21

When I awoke in Squirrel's old recliner, I didn't remember where I was. The pain in my back from one of the chair's broken springs quickly informed me it wasn't the bed in my apartment over Bertram's bar. When I smelled the aroma of sausage, eggs, and biscuits, I realized what had aroused me from a deep sleep.

My damp clothes I'd draped across a coffee table before raising the lever on the recliner were now dry, and I put them on before padding to the kitchen. Toni was cooking at the stove, Squirrel watching from the kitchen table. He nodded though didn't speak when I joined him.

"If I wasn't hungry before, I am now," I said.

"Me too," he said. "Last time someone cooked me breakfast was at an all-night diner on the edge of the French Quarter."

"I can relate," I said.

Cooking had put Toni in a good mood, and she smiled when she brought our steaming breakfast to the table.

"Sleep well last night?" she asked.

She grinned when I said, "Like a ton of bricks," I said.

"I can take you to Faumort. We won't get in," Squirrel said. "It's heavily guarded, especially

173

during harvest."

"Is this harvest season?" I asked.

"Yes, it is. The combines work around the clock. Zombies make the best workers because they never get tired and don't need much food or water."

"Sounds like a corporate dream," I said.

"It was hell though beat lying on the floor, unable to move or even close your eyes," he said.

After breakfast, we helped Squirrel feed and water his animals and were soon on our way to the main road in his truck.

"How far is it?" I asked.

"Quite a way," Squirrel said. "It sits on the banks of the Mississippi. Riverboats once transported the cane to sugar mills. Now, it's taken in big trucks that run twenty-four hours a day."

The trip to the plantation took more than an hour. The fencing around it was made of metal and seemed to go on forever.

"It's huge," Toni said. "The fence must stretch for miles."

"The entrance is up ahead," Squirrel said. "There are guards at the gate, and we won't be able to go in."

"Is there another entrance?" I asked.

"Several," he said. "They're all guarded.

"Is there a way to get inside the fence without going through a guard gate?"

"The river," he said.

"Can we get inside using a boat?"

"With a big enough boat, you could. The Mississippi River isn't someplace you want to be in a small boat."

"Why is that?" Toni asked.

"The currents are strong and unpredictable. If you got capsized, they wouldn't find your body until you reached the Gulf of Mexico. By then, there wouldn't be much left of it."

"Comforting thought," I said. "I'm a strong swimmer. Could a swimmer follow the bank and get in?"

He laughed. "You wouldn't make it fifty feet. I don't care how strong a swimmer you are."

"Not something I wanted to hear," I said. "Are the fences monitored?"

"There's a dirt road around the plantation. A security patrol circles the perimeter twenty-four hours a day. Even if you got past security, you wouldn't know where to go. As you said, the place is huge and has dozens of buildings."

"We can check the Internet for satellite photos," Toni said.

"We'll have to get closer than that," I said.

"You don't use the Internet much. The photos will get us close enough to see roads, sidewalks, vehicles, and buildings."

"They won't tell us what building Mama is in or how to facilitate her escape."

"You don't want to look?"

"Why not? Maybe the satellite photos will give us a clue," I said.

"I have a computer at the house," Toni said.

Our bicycles were in the bed of the truck. Yeller barked as Squirrel made a U-turn on the country blacktop and headed back in the opposite direction. My cell phone rang as we drove down the rural byway. It was Freya.

"Are you okay?" she said. "You didn't return last night."

"Had a change of plans," I said.

"Can I help?" she asked.

"The woman working this case with me was kidnapped. We know where she is within a mile or so. We're on our way to look at some satellite photos to help us zero in on the location."

"We?" Freya said.

"Me, a man name Squirrel and Pancho's granddaughter Toni."

"Who are you talking to?" Toni asked.

"A friend who's helping me," I said.

"How do they know Pancho?"

"He's working with me. Freya, I'll get back to you in a few hours."

Toni crossed her arms, her frown hot enough to raise the temperature in the truck several degrees.

"You didn't tell me you'd involved Pancho," she said.

"He's fine," I said. "In no danger."

"Said the moth to the flame," she said. "Who is this Freya person?"

"An attractive older woman," I said.

"How old?"

"Late sixties or early seventies."

"How did Pancho meet her?" she asked.

"No idea."

"Is she a gold digger?"

"She lives alone in a large house in Covington, has plenty of her own money, and isn't looking for someone to take care of her."

"Sure about that?"

"I'm fairly sure marriage is the farthest thing from their minds. What else are you mad at?"

"You're keeping something from me," she said. "What is it?"

"I went to Vodou Nitz in disguise. The lead singer of Brass & Sass is someone I know. She was zombied, and I rescued her with the help of Pancho and Freya. Latitia Boiset is at Freya's house."

"You know Latitia Boiset?" Toni said.

"More than know her. We have a daughter together."

"Latitia Boiset headlines the hottest act in Vegas. You have a daughter with her?"

"I didn't know it until a couple of days ago," I said. "I've never met my daughter. Latitia's mom Lashonda was raising Aimee in the Lower 9th Ward. Mama took them to her house in New Orleans. Someone abducted her when she returned to find Aimee's cat."

Squirrel didn't interrupt our conversation until he reached the intersection with another highway.

"Sorry to butt in. I need directions," he said.

"Stay on this road for another couple of miles," Toni said. "I'll tell you when to turn."

We soon reached Frankie's horse ranch. Toni flashed her badge as we passed the guard booth and continued beyond Frankie's house to the ranch's original structure.

"Pull in the drive, Squirrel," she said. "This is where I live."

Dogs and cats came running when Toni unlocked the front door. She knelt on the old hardwood floor and began giving hugs and caresses and getting kisses from the pets, happy to see her. She immediately began feeding them. Yeller joined the pack, his tail wagging. Kisses saw me and jumped into my arms.

"Miss me, baby?"

It was evident from her head rubs that she had. She finally jumped out of my lap to get her share of the food Toni was distributing.

"I know they all look hungry and thirsty," Toni said. "They aren't. One of Frankie's employees feeds them when I'm away from the house."

When Toni had finished feeding and watering the animals, I said, "I love your house."

"Me too," Toni said. "Frankie was going to bulldoze it. I talked him into giving it to me instead. Though it's old, I'm remodeling it as I go along."

"Yeller likes it," Squirrel said.

Toni's ranch house featured a covered veranda encircling it. There was a tiny living area, kitchen, and a small side bedroom.

"This is where I sleep," she said. "The house has a full basement. I'm pretty sure it's haunted. I have a little office at the top of the stairs. There are multiple doggie doors and a large yard for all my pets to move comfortably."

"I can see they missed you," I said.

"Every time I leave the house, they want to come. Let's go to my office upstairs."

Toni's office was the only room on the second story of the old ranch house. It had windows in all directions and provided a good view of Frankie's house and the exercise track for the thoroughbred horses he raised and trained.

"Nice view," I said.

"Though I don't drink, I maintain a little bar for when Mom or Frankie comes up," Toni said. "I don't have any moonshine. How about vodka?"

Squirrel nodded. "Love one," he said.

"I usually drink green tea," she said. "Join me in a cup?"

"Sure," I said.

"It's good for arthritis," Toni said.

"I don't have arthritis."

"Neither do I, and that's proof enough for me it works," Toni said.

Squirrel was drinking vodka as Toni fired up her desktop computer. We were soon visiting a website showing satellite images of the earth. Squirrel smiled when Toni zeroed in on the Faumort Plantation.

"Well, I'll be damned!" he said. "That's Faumort, all right." He pointed to a road leading from the entrance into the large ranch. "There's the warehouse where they keep the zombies when they aren't working."

"Do they have the antidote close by?" I asked.

"Can't say," Squirrel said.

"There are no other nearby buildings," Toni said.

"I guess they probably ran the entire zombie operation out of the same building," I said. "I think we should proceed with that hypothesis."

"Logical," Toni said. "I'm on board."

"Squirrel, what do you think?" I asked.

"I'd bet you're right," he said. "I could hear the kitchen noise when I was on the floor."

"Now, all we need to do is figure out how to get into the plantation and get out of it in one piece with Mama."

"Maybe we should talk to Frankie," Toni said. "He'd know how to make it happen."

"Not yet," I said.

"Why not?" she asked.

"I want to convince myself he's not involved before we show our hand."

"You're an asshole," Toni said. "Frankie isn't involved."

"He owns Vodou Nitz," I said. "I'm going there tonight to find Bobby."

"How do you plan to get in?" Toni asked.

"I'm a cat burglar. Remember?"

"It would be easier if we had a key," Toni said.

"But we don't."

"Frankie keeps records, keys, and you name it for all his operations in his office at the ranch house."

"He leaves it unlocked?" I said.

"Frankie trusts me. I have a key."

She nodded when I said, "You're just going to walk right in and find the key? What if he catches you?"

"I'll make something up," she said.

"Fine. Get the key, and I'll see if Bobby is there."

"You're going no place without me," she said.

"I don't need you," I said.

"You smug bastard!" she said. "I'm as athletic as you are and every bit as smart. You aren't going without me."

"Okay," I said. "I don't know how they can do the show without Latitia. Whatever, the last act is after two in the morning. Are you up for it?"

"Don't ask unless you want a fat lip."

"Seems I've heard that before," I said.

"It's getting late, and Yeller and I need to get back to the place," Squirrel said.

"Thanks, Emile," I said. "You've been a big help to us."

Squirrel nodded. "If you need me, I'm available."

Once Squirrel and Yeller were out the door, I said, "What now?"

"We have lots of time to kill, and I'm still on Frankie's payroll," Toni said. "Make yourself at home. I'm going to exercise some horses."

Chapter 22

Tony was at the kitchen table with Lil when his cell phone rang. It was a number he thought he recognized. Since it was a local number, he answered it, hoping it wasn't yet another telemarketer.

"Is this Tony Nicosia?" the voice on the line said.

"This is Tony. How can I help you?"

"It's Jack Dugas, the autopsy tech you interviewed.

"Hi, Jack. You calling to invite me fishing?"

"We'll do it someday. It isn't why I'm calling. You asked me to contact you if I found anything else about Bobby Blanchard."

Suddenly interested, Tony said, "What you got, Jack?"

"I'm still at work and don't want to talk about it while I'm here. I'm off at five. Can you meet me somewhere?"

"If you're a drinking man, I can meet you at Bertram's Bar on Chartres. I'm buying."

"Love the place, though I haven't been there in a while," Jack said. "I'll head over after work."

"See you there," Tony said.

Tony and Aimee had taken the cats to a pet motel. Lashonda, Aimee, and Stevie were still asleep.

"Will you be home for dinner?" Lil asked.

Before the door slammed behind him, Tony said, "Probably not. I'll grab something while I'm out,"

Tony was waiting at the bar, working on his second scotch, when Jack Dugas entered the front door dressed in tennis shoes and blue scrubs. He wasn't alone. An older man as short as Jack accompanied him, a bald spot atop his white hair. Jack waved when he saw Tony and joined him on an empty stool.

"Tony, this is Zane Fleming."

Mention of the man's name brought a smile to Tony's face."Weren't you a reporter for the Picayune?"

"Thanks for remembering," Zane said. "A long time ago."

"You won the Pulitzer. I never missed any of your articles. I always felt informed after reading your stories. Bertram, this is Zane Fleming."

"Bertram and I go way back," Zane said.

When Fleming extended his hand, Bertram grabbed it with both of his.

"Where you been? I thought you was dead."

"Still kicking," Zane said. "Broke a hip a few years back and still not fully recovered. Only now getting out and about."

"You haven't become a teetotaler, have you?

"Not yet," Zane said, "though I have to watch myself."

What you drinking?" Tony asked.

"Scotch, straight up," Jack said.

"Zane?"

"Zane drinks scotch," Bertram said. "He's got a double coming. On the house. Your money's no good at 'ol Bertram's."

"Guess you and Zane already know each

other," Tony said. "This other fellow is my friend, Jack Dugas. I'm on an expense account, so put everyone's drinks on my tab."

"I always like hearing that," Bertram said. "Pleased to make your acquaintance, Jack. Seems to me I've seen you in here before."

"Good memory," Jack said. "It has been a while."

"I never forget a good customer's face," Bertram said. "Zane used to be my best customer. Now, Tony is."

Bertram brought their drinks, and the three men touched glasses.

"How do you two know each other?" Tony asked.

"We met at Doc Pompeo's funeral," Jack said. "The doc's wife asked me to be a pallbearer, so I got to sit with the family."

"I heard it was quite the production," Tony said.

"Even the governor and several senators was there," Jack said. "St. Louis Cathedral was packed. Standing room only. I don't know if I mentioned it, but the doc's sister Pearl Pompeo is the hospital's president. She ended up sitting beside me. That's when things got interesting."

"Tell me," Tony said.

"Pearl has a voodoo tattoo on her wrist. Just like the one Bobby Blanchard had on his."

"You're shitting me!" Tony said.

"That's not all," Jack said. "She was sitting beside a black woman in a wig, dripping in gold and diamonds, and dressed to the nines. It was Mirlande Casseus."

"No way!" Tony said.

"I tried to listen to what they were saying though they were talking lower than the noise in the cathedral."

"Pompeo's sister didn't know who you were?"

Tony asked.

"We've never met, and she had no idea," Jack said. "After the funeral, she and Mirlande Casseus left together. They were on foot, and I followed them. They went into a little bar overlooking Jackson Square. I went inside and sat at a nearby table."

"Did you catch what they were talking about?" Tony asked.

"The weather was nice, and the outside doors opened to the street. The chatter gave me no chance to hear anything. Only thing I knew was they were in a heated conversation."

"Did they leave together?" Tony asked.

"They walked out the door together, exchanged a few words, and then left in opposite directions."

"What's Zane have to do with this?"

"He was also at the funeral and saw me there. Like me, he followed Mirlande and Pearl Pompeo to the little café."

Tony turned to Zane. "What's your interest in Pearl Pompeo?" he said.

"I made my bones as an investigative reporter," Zane said. "I was the best in the city. Toward the end of my career, I had some health problems and fell on hard times."

"You kind of disappeared," Tony said.

"My career was my life. I never married or had kids. Things began falling apart when I started drinking and partying more than normal."

"New Orleans has broken lots of careers," Tony said.

Both Zane and Jack grinned. "That's a fact," Zane said. "I fell and broke my hip one night when I was drunk. I got sick and wound up in the hospital. That's when I met Bobby Blanchard."

Zane nodded when Tony said, "You knew Bobby Blanchard?"

"It was a bad time in my life. I was flat on my back and could hardly breathe because of pneumonia when Bobby stopped by to see me."

"For what reason?" Tony asked.

"He was studying journalism at L.S.U. His passion, he said. He was also the star quarterback for the Tigers, and his dad a prominent state senator. He said one of his professors had talked about me and that he wanted to meet me."

Zane smiled again when Tony said, "That must have made your day."

"I hadn't realized until then how far my self-esteem had fallen. Bobby came to the hospital every day until I got back on my feet."

"Is that why you went to Dr. Pompeo's funeral?"

"I went for answers. Before Bobby disappeared, he talked with me about a project he was working on," Zane said.

"A project?"

"Bobby wanted to be an investigative reporter and had stumbled upon a potential story. As he delved into it, it kept growing larger."

Zane smiled when Tony said, "Let me guess. Did it involve zombie powder?"

"Although I'm old, my mind works the same as it always did. I went to the funeral because Dr. Pompeo was perhaps the last person to see Bobby before he disappeared. I followed Pearl Pompeo and Mirlande Casseus for the same reasons as Jack. Realizing we had something in common, I approached him."

"We started putting two and two together," Jack said.

"I have something to confess," Tony said. "I don't work for an insurance company. I'm a private dick working on a case for someone who hired me to check out the Bobby Blanchard

185

disappearance."

"Does this mean we can't go fishing?" Jack asked.

"Why, hell no!" Tony said. "I wasn't lying about that. I'd love to go fishing with you anytime."

"Hell, Tony," Jack said. "I like you and don't care who you work for."

The conversation stopped when Bertram appeared with another round of drinks. After five, the bar was filling fast, and he didn't hang around to chat.

"Why were you suspicious of Mirlande Casseus?" Tony asked.

"Bobby had learned about several disappearances across the lake in Mandeville. They all had in common the Bell House, a boutique bed and breakfast destination. Mrs. Brown, the owner of the Bell House, is Mirlande Casseus's daughter."

"Really?" Tony said.

"I don't believe in coincidences," Zane said. "When Mirlande Casseus left the funeral with Pearl Pompeo, I realized there's probably a connection needing exploring."

"What else do you know about Mirlande Casseus?" Tony asked.

"She was penniless when she arrived in New Orleans from Haiti. Now, she owns the largest sugar cane plantation in Louisiana and didn't get there working as a nanny.

"Tell me more," Tony said.

"Sugar plantations are mechanized and require lots of warm bodies."

When Zane snickered, Tony said, "What?"

"My guess is most of the bodies working on Mirlande's sugar plantation are anything other than warm."

"Zombies?"

"Lots of them, is my guess," Zane said.

"Where'd she get the money to buy the plantation? Twenty-thousand acres of river bottom ain't cheap," Tony said.

"I have no answer for you," Zane said. "I was hoping you'd have one for me."

Tony grinned. "Maybe some more alcohol will help our thought process."

Jack glanced at his watch. "Not for me," he said. "My old lady expects me home before dark. Hope I helped you at least a little."

"You helped me a bunch," Tony said.

When Jack was out the door, Zane said, "Feels good working again. Don't know why I ever stopped."

"How did you get started in journalism?" Tony asked.

"I was a senior at Tulane in the summer of '69—the Summer of Love. Some of us went to Woodstock to report on the festival. We returned full of piss and vinegar, our hair long, and a tattoo or two we couldn't quite remember getting."

"I was newly married, my wife pregnant, and missed all that," Tony said.

"You probably lucked out," Zane said. "I was set to change the world. The Age of Aquarius never quite dawned. The only thing changing is my age."

"I hear that," Tony said. "I still remember all the music festivals I couldn't attend."

"I never missed one," Zane said. "I went skinny dipping in the Mardi Gras Fountain. The cops were cool and told us to get out of the water. They let the party continue."

"I remember all about the Summer of Love,'" Tony said. "I never went to Vietnam, though I'll never forget the returning vets parading down Bourbon Street."

"I was right there with them," Zane said.

"My life revolved around being a homicide detective for the N.O.P.D. for more than twenty years. You know how many murders we have every year in New Orleans?"

"More than this city cares to admit," Zane said. "While you were solving murders, I was publishing articles in the underground press. Someone at the Picayune finally invited me to join the paper. I loved it."

"Don't mean to be nosy," Tony said. "How do you support yourself now that you're no longer a reporter?"

"I wrote a book a few years back about underground New Orleans. My hefty royalty checks haven't slowed down. You should see my place in the Quarter."

"Must be nice," Tony said. "Want to make extra money even if you don't need it?"

"Doing what?"

"Working with me on this case," Tony said. "You won't be disappointed in the pay."

"Hell, Tony, I'll do it for nothing," Zane said. "I love being active again."

"You'll get paid. You may not like who you're working for."

"Then you'd better tell me who it is."

"Frankie Castellano."

"The Don of the Bayou? Hell, Tony! He's probably involved."

"If he is, we'll deal with it when we can prove it," Tony said.

Zane downed his scotch and then shook Tony's hand.

"Sounds like fun. I'm on board," Zane said.

"You got a plan in mind?" Tony said.

"Visit the parish courthouse and see who owns Mirlande's plantation."

"I better call my partner working undercover in Mandeville and tell him what I know."

Chapter 23

Tony was sitting at his kitchen table drinking coffee when his cell phone rang. It was Zane Fleming.

"Didn't get you out of bed, did I?" he said.

"Been up for a while. It's barely ten. Surely, you haven't been to the courthouse and back."

"I learned long ago there aren't enough hours in the day to do everything needing doing."

"Amen to that," Tony said.

"I used to know every court clerk in the state. I always sent roses, thank-you notes, and boxes of chocolates whenever they helped me out. The new St. John's the Baptist Parish court clerk remembered and answered all my questions."

"She isn't retired?"

"Her mother worked for the parish, and the new clerk worked there during summers. Amazingly, she remembered me."

"What did you find out?" Tony asked.

Zane answered with a question of his own. "What are you doing for lunch?"

Lil turned off the oven and gave Tony a dirty look when he said, "Got no plans. Want me to meet you somewhere?"

"As I told you, I have a townhouse overlooking Bourbon Street. We could have a drink or two

189

before we go to lunch."

Zane gave Tony his address, and Lil frowned again when Tony said, "I'm on my way."

"When are you coming home?" Lil said.

"I shouldn't be long," Tony said.

"That's what you said yesterday, and I was asleep before you got here."

Tony petted Patch, his white setter with a black eye patch, and kissed Lil before hurrying out the door.

"Sorry, Babe," he said. "Hot case. Can you feed Patch?

"What about going to Mass with me and Sunday brunch at Brennan's?" Lil asked.

"I'll try to make it back," Tony said.

"How many times have I heard that?" Lil said.

"Sorry," Tony said. "Duty calls."

Patch tried to follow Tony, whimpering when the door shut in his face. He wagged his tail when Lil scratched behind his ears and gave him a doggie treat.

"Just you and me, Patch," she said. "Now you know how I've felt all these years. At least there's Aimee, Lashonda, and Stevie to keep us company."

Zane Fleming lived in a townhouse in the Quarter on Governor Nichols Street. Zane met him at the door. Tony parked his red Mustang beside Zane's baby blue Subaru, both clashing with the pink building and green shutters.

"Quite a place," Tony said. "I'm impressed."

"Never thought I'd like living in the Quarter. Now that I do, I don't want ever to move."

"How old is the place?"

"Built-in 1843 and less than two thousand square feet. The prior owners completely renovated the old lady's interior."

Tony followed him up the stairs to the

second-floor living room overlooking the narrow street. Opening the French doors, he stepped out on the balcony.

"Great view," he said.

"I love it. Have my coffee on the balcony every morning and cocktails in my courtyard every afternoon."

"You got a courtyard?" Tony asked.

"My little slice of heaven, complete with palms, flagstones, and history," Zane said.

"And probably a ghost or two," Tony said.

"Haven't seen one yet, though I'd appreciate the company. Grab a seat. I'll fix us a drink."

Zane soon joined him, ice and glass clinking when they tapped tumblers.

"Can't get over your place," Tony said. "Lil would love it."

"Your wife? Bring her by sometime. "I have no family or close relatives with whom to share."

"No girlfriend?"

Zane grinned and said, "No steady."

"Why did you decide to move to the Quarter?"

"You have to live someplace. I had the money to do it and no one to leave it to."

"What'd you find out from the courthouse?"

"That Mirlande Casseus owns fifty percent of the Faumort Plantation. What surprised me is who owns the other half."

"Who is?"

"Arthur Wayne Pompeo, Doctor Pompeo's father."

Tony slugged his scotch. "I didn't see that one coming. I don't recall ever hearing about the Pompeo family."

"Me either," Zane said. "Jack Dugas described Doctor Pompeo as a person with no social ambition."

"How did a Haitian nanny end up owning a huge sugar cane plantation?" Tony asked.

Zane poured Tony more scotch from the bottle on the coffee table."

"A property that size is worth a fortune, and I could find no record Mirlande ever paid a penny for it."

"Pompeo just assigned her half the property?"

"Exactly what he did," Zane said.

"From what Jack told me, everyone in the doctor's family except Dr. Pompeo himself loved Mirlande. Maybe they had a sexual arrangement."

Zane grinned again. "Twenty-thousand acres of bottomland abutting the Mississippi River could be worth a billion bucks. A lot of money for a roll in the hay."

"Got that right," Tony said. "I don't understand how Doctor Pompeo and sister Pearl let that slide?"

"Beats the hell out of me," Zane said. "Mirlande and Pearl were thick as thieves at the funeral. Surely she knows how much the plantation is worth."

"It has to cost a fortune to run a twenty-thousand-acre sugar plantation. Where does Mirlande get that kind of money?"

"No clue, though I know someone who might help us fill in the blanks," Zane said.

"Who?" Tony said.

"Candy Daigle."

"I recognize that name from somewhere," Tony said. "Help me out here."

"Candy was the gossip columnist for the paper's society page back when there were no privacy issues."

"Now I remember," Tony said. "She must be pushing. . ."

"Ninety," Zane said. "She hasn't slowed down a bit and is still an item in New Orleans high society. It's de rigueur to include her on the guest list of every fancy party in the city."

"Can she fill us in on the Pompeo family?"

"If Candy can't, no one can," Zane said.

"Will she talk with us?"

"I've known Candy for fifty years. We even had a brief affair when I was a cub reporter. She likes younger men."

"She must be in heaven," Tony said. "Practically everyone is younger than her."

"That's a fact," Zane said. Candy and I have lunch or dinner regularly. Last time cost me more than a thousand bucks."

"Damn!" Tony said. "Is she a drinker?"

They both laughed when Zane said, "Does an alligator shit in the swamp?"

"Are you going to talk to her?"

"Not me, buddy, us," Zane said. "Get your questions ready. We're meeting her around one at the Court of Two Sisters."

"She won't clam up if I'm there?"

Zane chuckled. "You kidding? The more she drinks, the more chatty she gets. Don't be surprised if we're still sitting on the patio at midnight."

"I better call and have Frankie put some more money in my bank account," Tony said.

"What about your wife," Zane said. "I'll be surprised if you make it home tonight. No problem because I have a second bedroom. Want me to call her for you?"

"She'll probably cuss you out over the phone. I promised I'd go to Mass with her Sunday and then take her to Brennan's for Sunday brunch. She ain't gonna be a happy camper."

"I'll give it a shot," Zane said.

Lil answered and said, "Hello."

"Lil, it is Zane Fleming. Tony and I are working a case in the French Quarter." Zane gave her his address. "I have a beautiful old house. Pack some things and join us. You'll have the run of the place until Tony, and I return. I'll take us to Sunday brunch at Brennan's when you and Tony return from Mass. My treat. You game?"

"Sounds lovely. I can't leave Patch here alone."

"Who is Patch?" Zane asked.

"Our dog," Lil said.

"Bring him with you," Zane said. "He'll love my courtyard. My dog, Peaches, will keep him company. Take a taxi. You can return home late Sunday with Tony."

"I don't know," Lil said.

"Please?" Zane said. "We'll wait on you."

"Okay," Lil said. "I'll call a cab and be there shortly."

"You're one smooth-talking son-of-a-bitch. Now I know how you won the Pulitzer."

"Lil's going to love the place," Zane said.

About an hour later, Lil stepped out of a cab with Patch. Zane was at the door with his golden retriever, Peaches, and a smile to greet her.

"Tony said you were beautiful," he said. "He wasn't exaggerating. Let me give you a tour of the house."

Lil had arrived dressed in a flowing red and blue skirt and designer blouse. She'd brushed her hair out and looked sexier than Tony had remembered.

"I've been in the Court of Two Sisters, though never eaten there," Lil said.

"Tony and I are interviewing Candy Daigle," Zane said.

"Are you kidding me? I thought she was dead," Lil said.

Zane laughed. "She's very much alive. We think she has information concerning the case Tony and I are working on."

"Tony never tells me anything about his cases," Lil said. "I love Candy Daigle and never missed any of her articles. Your house is wonderful though I'd like to go to Court of Two Sisters with you."

"This is business," Tony said.

"I won't get in the way," Lil said.

"Candy may resent another woman," Zane said. "She likes being the queen bee when she's holding court."

"I love everything about Candy Daigle. She won't resent me. I'll bow down and kiss her feet. I promise."

Zane glanced at Tony. "This might just work," he said.

"I was a homicide detective for twenty years," Tony said. "Lil never once went with me to a murder scene."

"You are so full of shit!" Lil said. "I lived through every one of those murders right along with you. You'd have never gotten a wink of sleep if it wasn't for me."

Peaches and Patch were already friends, their tails wagging as they roughhoused at the feet of Lil, Zane, and Tony. Tony scratched behind Patch's ear and hugged Peaches.

"Your car or mine?" he said.

"Neither," Zane said. "We'll be shitfaced when we leave. I'll call a cab. Beats passing out on the street."

Foot traffic had started returning to the French Quarter following a lengthy pandemic. A smiling bellman from Court of Two Sisters opened the backdoor of the cab and ushered Tony, Lil, and Zane into the courtyard. Candy Daigle was sitting at a table, waiting for them. She smiled when Zane kissed her.

"Candy, this is Lil and Tony Nicosia."

Candy gave Lil an assessing stare. "Are you part of the detective agency?" she asked.

Lil grabbed Candy's hand. "When Zane and

Tony told me who they were meeting, I begged them to bring me with them. I've admired you forever and never missed a single word you wrote. I always wanted to be exactly like you. Marriage to Tony and five kids sidetracked my ambitions."

"You are lucky," Candy said. "I never married nor had children."

Lil grinned. "You can have all of mine. They get older and needier and never grow up."

Candy wrapped her arms around Lil, crushing her to her bony chest.

"Thank you, baby," she said. "An old woman needs an occasional ego boost."

"You kidding me? You're so beautiful you could be the star model in a fashion show."

"You're lying through your teeth. I love it," Candy said.

When Lil broke away, Tony shook Candy's hand.

"N.O.P.D. homicide detective Tony Nicosia. I've heard about you for years. How many murder cases have you handled?"

"New Orleans is the murder capital of the world. I quit counting after five thousand," Tony said. "Most were easy to solve though there's still a couple I still have no answers for."

"You want some answers from me?"

Candy smiled when Tony said, "I recognize another good detective when I see one."

"Our jobs have different names though we do the same thing," Candy said.

She smiled again when Zane said, "Then tell us what you know about the Pompeo family, and we'll be on our way."

"Kiss my ass," Candy said with a grin. "I'll tell you what I know, which is considerable, but you're not getting off that easily. Lil and I will have the most expensive entrée on the menu and drink until I fall off this chair. I know Zane loves

196

it. Is it okay with you, Lieutenant Nicosia?"

"Nobody drinks Tony Nicosia under the table."

Candy reached and pinched Tony's cheek.

"Lil, your husband, is cute," she said.

"After five kids and all these years," Lil said, "he never ceases to amaze me."

Lil nodded when Candy said, "He's a keeper."

Candy was pushing ninety though you couldn't tell it. Her bouffant hair was hennaed, and her nails polished to perfection. The waiter was there with another scotch and soda when she motioned him.

Lil was drinking a mango margarita, Tony worrying about her staying power as he downed a second scotch. She squeezed Candy's hand again.

"Ms. Daigle, this is the best day of my life."

Chapter 24

With two men hanging on her every word and a super fan in Lil, Candy Daigle was in her element. A waiter hustled to their table when Candy raised a finger.

Live trees and hanging lights added to the ambiance of the patio, a fountain the crowning touch to the impression of a beautiful French Quarter courtyard. The atmosphere was both palpable and irresistible.

"We're going to need more drinks and some appetizers," Candy said.

The waiter was more than happy to oblige. "Whatever you wish, Madame," he said.

"Tell us what you have?" Candy said.

The waiter knew Candy had tried everything on the menu at least once. It mattered little as he began reciting.

"Panko crusted boudin balls. Jalapeno bacon-wrapped duck breast. Barbecue shrimp and crab cakes."

"Bring us one of each," Candy said.

"Oh my," Lil said. "I've wanted to dine here for years. Now, I'm having lunch with not one, but two Pulitzer Prize winners."

"And the crab cakes are to die for," Candy said.

The pace was slow. Candy liked it that way. At least two patrons who recognized her stopped by the table to ask for an autograph, Candy happy to comply.

"Now, tell me what I can do for you," she said.

Tony nodded when Zane glanced at him. "We're hoping you can tell us about the Pompeo family," he said.

"Like what?" Candy said.

"Like, how are they connected to voodoo?"

The restaurant had thoughtfully arranged the tables on the patio so the diners could engage in intimate conversation without worrying about who was listening to them. It didn't stop Candy from glancing over her shoulder to see who might be trying to eavesdrop.

"You come to the point, don't you, Lieutenant?"

"I'd have never gotten through half the yearly homicides playing patty cake with the people I questioned."

"I'm not interested in being sued at my age," Candy said.

"Any info you give us will be privileged. If we use it, we won't implicate you."

"What do you intend to do with the information I give you?" Candy asked.

"I'm no longer a cop," Tony said. "Someone has hired us to find a missing person. That's all I have on my agenda. Whatever crimes we uncover will have to go uncovered. That isn't our job."

"No matter how heinous the crime?" Candy said.

"Call the cops or confide in your priest," Tony said. "I work for those who pay me, and it ain't the N.O.P.D. anymore."

"Good, because if you intend to put away members of the Pompeo family, you're in for a rude awakening. There's not a judge or jury in this town that would indict a Pompeo."

"I've lived in New Orleans all my life and wasn't born yesterday. I'm aware of the city's power structure. Our target is Mirlande Casseus."

"You know what a fer-de-lance is, Lieutenant Nicosia?"

"A snake?"

"A deadly snake. If it bites you, your blood coagulates, and you suffer a painful death. Mirlande Casseus is deadlier than a fer-de-lance, much more painful, and she will make you pray for death."

Candy nodded when Tony said, "Are you talking about zombie powder? Is that how she got twenty-thousand acres of prime sugar cane land from Arthur Pompeo?"

"Did she indoctrinate him?" Zane asked.

Candy grew silent as the waiter brought more drinks. She glanced around the patio again when he was gone before answering the question.

"Mirlande didn't indoctrinate Arthur. It was the other way around."

"Excuse me?" Tony said.

"Secret societies in New Orleans are common. Everyone has heard of the Boston Club. Arthur Pompeo is the founder of one such secret society," Candy said.

"What's the name of this secret society?" Tony asked.

Lil, Tony, and Zane were hanging on Candy's every word. She loved it and grinned, sipping her scotch before answering.

"A group called the Keepers, a name derived for Baron Samedi, the keeper of cemeteries and the dead."

"Arthur Pompeo is white," Zane said.

"All voodoo practitioners aren't black," Candy said. Arthur Pompeo is an example."

"I know Pompeo is old," Zane said.

"A hundred-something, though you wouldn't know it by looking at him," Candy said.

She grinned again when Tony said, "You gotta be kidding!"

"He and his wife travel to Switzerland every year for injections of human growth hormones. He plays golf three times a week, works out at the gym, and looks no older than a healthy sixty-year-old."

"Damn!" Tony said. "Lots of people take growth hormones. What else does he take?"

"That's the sixty-four dollar question," Candy said.

The waiter arrived with their entrees before Candy could finish telling them about Arthur Pompeo's secret to longevity or his voodoo society. Lil was ecstatic when she had her first taste of the crab cakes.

"Oh my God!" she said. "This is wonderful."

"Nothing like it anywhere else in the city," Candy said. "I never tire of coming here."

Tony was like a pursuing bloodhound and had barely touched his crab cakes when Lil elbowed him.

"Eat," she said. "It's lovely, so enjoy. Candy isn't going anywhere, and she'll answer all your questions after you eat.

"Good advice," Candy said. "We work to live and not the other way around. If you can't enjoy the patio, you may as well be pushing up daisies."

Tony took a bite and then another.

"Damn, this is good!"

"Told you so," Lil said.

A jazz quartet in the corner of the patio had begun playing and was the perfect complement to the food. Though Candy had barely touched her entrée, she was enjoying herself.

"You have a captive audience. Don't keep us in suspense," Zane said.

201

Candy slugged her scotch and motioned the waiter for another round. Live jazz reverberated through the patio, not a single person frowning.

"Arthur Pompeo formed the Keepers years ago to honor Baron Samedi. Members have Baron Samedi veves tattooed on their wrists. Like every secret society, the Keepers have influential members who assist each other in achieving their goals," Candy said.

"Such as?" Zane said.

"Influence and money. What else is there?" Candy said.

Candy smiled when Zane said, "You tell me."

"Money and influence are nice," she said. "Sex is better. There are lots of all three when you're a member of the Keepers."

"You sound as if you've been to a Keeper's meeting," Zane said.

"I'm not a member, though I've attended several meetings," Candy said.

"Want to tell us about it?" Zane said.

"I'm considering my options," Candy said.

"You said Pompeo indoctrinated Mirlande," Tony said. "Can you tell us more?"

"By all accounts, Arthur Pompeo is a regular visitor to Haiti. Mirlande's husband was a powerful practitioner of voodoo on the island. Arthur brought Mirlande to New Orleans following her husband's death."

"Because?" Zane said.

"She possessed a secret Arthur coveted," Candy said.

"Which was?" Zane said.

"Mirlande knew her husband's secret for creating voodoo powder."

"You know an awful lot about Pompeo and Mirlande," Zane said.

Grabbing Candy's hand, he flipped it over to see if she had a Baron Samedi tattoo.

"As I told you, I'm not a Keeper," Candy said. "Simply a great reporter."

"That you are," he said. "You look much younger than your actual age. Have you partaken in Arthur's youth potion?"

"You're after all of my secrets, aren't you?" Candy said.

"If you want to tell us, we're all ears," Zane said.

The jazz quartet had crescendoed into another number, the bass strains of the tuba echoing off the masonry walls. Candy drank more of her scotch before answering.

"I've rolled in the hay with Arthur Pompeo on more than one occasion if that's what you're getting at. I've also had a nip or two of his elixir."

Candy shook her head when Zane asked, "Did he tell you what's in it?"

"I didn't want to know," she said. "Arthur is the most perverted person I've ever met. His youth elixir worked so well I wanted more. Arthur goaded me into doing something I've regretted ever since to get a second dose."

Lil, Tony, and Zane had stopped eating and drinking as they stared across the table at Candy Daigle, waiting for her to tell them what Arthur had required her to do.

"Please don't hate me when I tell you what I did," she said.

"Dare we even ask?" Zane said.

"I've wanted to get this off my chest for some time. Now's as good as any to tell it. Lil, you may want to take a break and go to the ladies' room."

"I've been married to an N.O.P.D. homicide detective for most of my adult life," Lil said. "There isn't much I haven't already heard."

"Suit yourself," Candy said. "I participated in a ménage à trois with Arthur and his daughter, Pearl. My priest almost fainted when I confessed

203

to him."

Lil's hand went to her mouth. "Adultery and incest? Oh, my God!"

"I'm ashamed to say I'd do it again for another dose of Arthur's elixir," Candy said.

Ignoring Lil and Zane's shock, Tony crooked a finger for their waiter to bring them another round of drinks.

"So Arthur's a sex freak. Did he sexually indoctrinate Mirlande?" he asked.

"Her and half the population of the Garden District," Candy said. "If you're a member of the Keepers, it's a given you are sexually compromised."

"What's the story on Faumort?" Tony asked.

"It was Mirlande's idea to resurrect the sugar cane plantation, though she did it with Arthur's money," Candy said. "It was Mirlande's idea to make it work with zombie power."

"If you knew this, why haven't you said something?" Zane said. "I can't believe you're somehow complicit."

"I'm old," Candy said. "I'm not ready to spend eternity locked in suspended animation. I decided not to make my knowledge public."

Candy nodded when Tony said, "Then you've experienced the powder?"

"Me and everyone who has come in contact with Arthur and Mirlande. The fear has never left me, and it's the reason their secret is intact after all these years."

"But you just told us," Tony said.

"I've been thinking about it for a long time. I'm frightened, though still a reporter," Candy said. "It's who I am. I had to tell someone."

"Have you ever visited Faumort Plantation?" Tony asked.

"Yes," Candy said.

"And?" Tony said.

"Mirlande rules it like a fantasy kingdom. She has her harem and loves debauchery even more than Arthur."

Candy nodded when Zane said, "Debauchery you participated in?"

"I'm not perfect," Candy said.

"None of us are," Tony said. "Who is the boss, Mirlande or Arthur?"

"Mirlande is good at what she does. The plantation is profitable because of her and has only enhanced Arthur's power. With that said, he is still in control until he dies."

"You've answered my most urgent question," Tony said. "Arthur Pompeo is in charge and not Mirlande."

"That's a fact," Candy said. "You can't stop Mirlande without also stopping Arthur."

"We have another problem," Tony said. "One of our associates is missing. We believe she is at Faumort. Can you help us devise a way to get her out of there?"

"I'm not a military person, though I believe escape is impossible," Candy said.

"There's no way for us to rescue her?" Tony asked.

"The plantation is enormous; Mirlande's home is near its center. It's always heavily guarded," Candy said.

"We need to help our associate escape and get some of the zombie powder antidote," Tony said.

"I wish I could help you," Candy said. "I'm a reporter. You need a strategist who knows far more than I about such things."

The band had returned from a short break and fired up their rendition of 'Sweet Hour of Prayer' when someone appeared at the table. It was Stevie, Lashonda, and Aimee.

"May we join you?" Stevie asked.

Chapter 25

Mama Mulate had never felt so helpless. She had no sensation in her body. Her eyes were open, and she could see though couldn't blink. For all practical purposes, she was dead. The thought kept ringing in her brain.

"What if they leave me like this forever?"

Mama knew she was the victim of zombie powder. She also knew Mirlande Casseus wouldn't keep her in a vegetative state forever. It didn't matter because she kept thinking of the man who'd spent solitary confinement in a tiny, darkened cell for thirty years while a prisoner at Angola. At least he could move, Mama thought.

Mama was in a living hell and hoped her inhumane captivity wouldn't last forever. Between brooding and extreme anxiety, she passed into the land of dreams, escaping her reality until someone spooned a noxious-tasting gruel into her mouth.

Mama's body shook in a frenzy of sensation when the gruel touched her gut. In a moment of extreme nausea, she puked on the floor beside her. When her eyes focused, she found a woman kneeling over her in shorts and a stained tee shirt.

"For a minute, I didn't think you would come out of it," the woman said.

Mama's head was clanging like a church bell, her lungs not reacting when she tried to take a breath. The woman in shorts took her by the shoulders and pounded her back until she could catch her breath.

"Who are you?" Mama asked.

"Honey, I'm Jolene, the cook. I'm damn glad you didn't die on me. Mirlande would have had my ass."

"What did you just give me?" Mama asked.

"The potion," Jolene said.

"I think I need more," Mama said.

Jolene laughed and shook her head. "Ain't going to happen. You drank the last drop I got."

"Where do you get it?" Mama asked.

"Girl, you ask way too many questions. I'm not even supposed to be talking to you."

"Then why are you?"

"Whole lot of things I ain't supposed to do," Jolene said.

Mama glanced around to see where she was. She was lying on the concrete floor of a giant, mainly empty warehouse. A door was open not far from where she lay, and she decided it was probably the kitchen from where Jolene had come.

Jolene smiled again when Mama asked, "Are you a zombie?"

"I work here and live down the road."

"You know what Mirlande is doing isn't legal?" Mama said.

"Mirlande would have my ass if I told anyone what goes on here on the plantation. I don't even talk to my husband about it. Besides, there ain't anyone else in the parish paying twenty dollars an hour."

"I'll give you a thousand if you get me out of

here," Mama said.

"I'd love to take your money. We'd never get away with it. You'd get caught, and Mirlande would skin me alive," Jolene said.

"Two thousand," Mama said.

"Mirlande has bad people working for her. When they finished with me, death would be a blessing."

"Then why do you work for such horrible people?"

"Don't sound like you have three hungry kids and a no-account husband like I do," Jolene said.

"Two thousand dollars goes a long way," Mama said.

"Not far enough," Jolene said. "Besides, you're marked. If you got away, Mirlande would find you and bring you back here."

"Have you heard things?" Mama said.

"I'm not comfortable talking about it," Jolene said.

Mama grabbed Jolene's hand, turning it so she could see her wrist.

"Do you practice voodoo?" Mama asked.

"I'm Baptist. Go to church every Sunday," Jolene said.

Mama removed the gold cross necklace from around her neck and clasped it around Jolene's.

"I'm giving you this necklace. I want something in return," Mama said.

"What?" Jolene said.

"Do you have something to write with?"

"You mean a pen or pencil?"

"Yes," Mama said.

"A mascara pencil. Will that work?"

"Perfect," Mama said.

Jolene removed a plastic compact from the pocket of her shorts and handed it to Mama. Mama opened it and found the stub of a mascara pencil.

"Ain't much left except a stub," Jolene said.

"It'll work," Mama said. "I'm a voodoo mambo. I'm going to draw a veve on your forehead."

"For what?" Jolene said.

"Sit still. It'll only take a minute."

"Are you trying to steal my soul?" Jolene asked.

"Sounds as if Mirlande beat me to it," Mama said. "I'm going to help you get it back."

When Mama finished, Jolene used the mirror in the compact to look at the drawing.

"What is it, and what does it mean?" she asked.

"Mambos don't share their secrets," Mama said. "I have no gris gris with me. The necklace will have to do. It will protect you. Don't ever take it off."

"Not even when I take a bath?"

Mama clutched Jolene's hand and squeezed it. "Not until you're done with this evil place," she said. "Promise me."

Mama nodded when Jolene said, "I promise."

"If you never leave here, then die with it on, or you may die sooner than you wish. It'll protect you from harm. Do you believe?"

"I told you, I'm Baptist," Jolene said.

"You may not know it, but Vodouns and Baptists have the same god," Mama said. "Trust me when I tell you he will protect you."

"What do you want me to do?" Jolene said.

"Can you remember a phone number?"

Mama shook her head when Jolene said, "If you write it down for me."

Mama touched the veve she'd drawn on Jolene's forehead and spoke Wyatt's cell phone number aloud.

"You won't forget," she said.

"You hoodooed me, didn't you?" Jolene said.

"Call the number when you get home. A man

named Wyatt will answer. Tell him who you are and where I am."

"I hear someone coming," Jolene said. "I have to get this voodoo thingy off my forehead."

"The mascara will come off. The voodoo veve I drew on your forehead is there forever," Mama said.

"Mirlande is powerful," Jolene said.

"So am I," Mama said.

Jolene rubbed her forehead when Philip and a zombie walked up behind her. Philip made a face when he saw the vomit on the concrete floor beside Mama.

The zombie had no expression and stared at the floor with impassionate eyes. Philip wore black dress pants, polished shoes, and a purple silk shirt open to his gold belt buckle.

"Is she ready?" he asked.

"Yes sir," Jolene said, turning so he wouldn't see her forehead.

Grabbing Mama's arm, Philip pulled her to her feet and gave her a push in the back.

"Let's go," he said.

The taps on Philip's heels echoed through the warehouse. A backdoor led to a winding path ending at the ranch house where Mama had been the previous night. The zombie pushed her through the door when she slowed to get a better look. When she saw the house in the light of day, she realized she'd underestimated its size.

With Philip ahead of her, the zombie behind, she followed a long hallway to a regal double door encased in gold. Philip knocked twice.

A man with gray features wearing a gold smock and pointed slippers opened the door.

"A guest for Mirlande," Philip said.

The gray man grabbed Mama's arm, the door shutting without admitting Philip or the zombie. Mama followed the man to an open room filled with women, prepubescent males, and girls. They all stopped what they were doing to give Mama an assessing look. The man departed without explanation.

A young woman in harem pants, lots of jewelry, and a transparent blouse stood with her arms crossed, glaring at Mama.

"Who was that man?" Mama asked.

"Ashik," the young woman said. "The chief eunuch."

"Yoh kidding? I'm Mama Mulate. Who are you?" Mama said.

"Vixen," the woman said.

Vixen had blue eyes and short blond hair. Though scantily clad, she appeared perfectly comfortable. Mama wondered if it was a show.

The woman smiled when Mama said, "Tell me your real name."

"Nothing's real about this place," Vixen said. "At least we aren't zombie dead."

"Have you had the powder?" Mama asked.

"More than once," Vixen said. "I no longer resist."

"Resist what?" Mama asked.

"I'm a permanent houri. I service the men, and sometimes the women, who come here to purchase slaves."

Mama glanced around the open room. The women lounged in costumes from another era, specifically the Middle East. Some were topless or completely naked as they reclined on couches or luxuriated in tiled tubs. No one seemed to mind.

"Who are all these people?" Mama asked.

"Mirlande's harem," Vixen said.

"Women don't have harems," Mama said.

"Mirlande does. Most of these women are here for a short time or until sold. Mirlande likes to sample the merchandise before they go."

Vixen laughed when Mama said, "These people are slaves?"

"Of course, they're slaves," Vixen said. "You think a place like this exists in normal society?"

"You sound like an educated person," Mama said. "Why are you here?"

"Kidnapped," Vixen said. "I was kept on zombie powder for three days. After reviving me, Mirlande beat me. It was all part of my indoctrination. Because of the drugs in their bodies, most women aren't aware of what's happened to them."

"Then why are you cognizant?" Mama asked.

"Every one of these women has a price on their head. The price depends on skin color, social status, and education. Some slaves sell for as little as ninety dollars."

"That's crazy," Mama said. "How does Mirlande turn a profit selling someone for only ninety dollars?"

"Many of them sell for much more. It depends."

"On what?" Mama asked.

"I have a Master's degree from Tulane. My eyes are blue, and my hair is naturally blond. My parents are prominently known. My asking price is a million bucks."

"Damn! Who pays that much for a slave?" Mama asked.

"Russian oligarchs, Middle Eastern sheiks, Chinese billionaires," Vixen said.

"Why aren't your prominent parents screaming bloody murder?" Mama asked.

"They think I'm dead. There was even a funeral for me at St. Louis Cathedral."

"No way," Mama said.

"It's hell being immobile in a coffin and having your aunts, uncles, parents, and best friends standing by your coffin telling stories about you. Trust me when I tell you it's an eye-opener."

"Oh, my God!" Mama said. "How long have you been here?"

"Two years," Vixen said.

"And you've yet to be sold? Why is that?" Mama said.

"Mirlande finds me too valuable to sell. The powerful men and women who use me have loose tongues. You can't imagine the things they've told me. I've managed to stay here by making myself indispensable to Mirlande."

"Good for you. Do you have a plan to escape?"

"I've tried more than once, failing every time. After surviving more beatings than I can count, I've spent weeks in the hands of the dead."

"I know exactly how horrible it is," Mama said. "I'm a professor at Tulane. No one thinks I'm dead. People will be looking for me."

"I wish you luck," Vixen said. "I have nothing for which to return. My family and former fiancée think I'm dead. For practical purposes, I am."

"I'm not just a professor," Mama said. "I'm also a voodoo mambo. I have powers Mirlande has never dealt with."

"I've been with her for two years," Vixen said. "No one I know of has ever escaped this place."

Mama put her arms around Vixen and hugged her. The younger woman seemed to dissolve in her arms and began crying.

"I'm going to escape," Mama said. "When I do, I'll take you with me."

Chapter 26

Toni was hot and sweaty when she returned from exercising Frankie's horses. She began removing her clothes before reaching the door to her bathroom.

She laughed when I said, "I'll make us a sandwich while you're cleaning up."

"I didn't know you knew how to cook," she said.

"I can make a sandwich with the best of them," I said.

"Relax," she said. "We need more than a sandwich if we're going to break into Vodou Nitz. I'll whip up something when I finish my shower."

"Suit yourself," I said.

I waited on the couch, Kisses in my lap as Toni exited the bathroom wrapped in a white terrycloth towel. Her blond hair was damp, and she didn't bother drying it as she started pulling condiments from her pantry.

Toni was boiling pasta and frying bacon, her back to me when she asked, "Why are you staring at me?"

"I'm hoping your towel drops to the floor," I said.

She smiled. "You're a pervert. You know it?"

"And you love every minute of it," I said.

Toni didn't respond to my rude comment.

"Too bad neither of us are drinkers," she said. "What I'm making would go well with a nice cabernet."

"Smells wonderful," I said. "If you're eating pasta every meal, how do you keep your figure?"

"Exercise," she said. "Cycling and riding Frankie's horses."

She smiled again when I said, "You're prettier than your mother, and she's drop-dead beautiful."

"You're not getting into my pants, no matter how much you compliment me," she said.

"You have gorgeous legs," I said.

"Shut up or I'm going to feed your pasta to my pups," she said.

She smiled again when I said, "Your eyes sparkle even more than normal when you're angry."

"Put the cat on the floor and come to the table," she said.

Toni was as good a cook as Pancho or Adele. She blushed when I winked at her while eating my pasta carbonara. After dinner, Toni stacked our plates into the dishwasher and returned to the bathroom. Knowing I was watching, she let the towel drop to the floor, pirouetted, and curtsied before shutting the bathroom door.

Toni was dressed in a black tee shirt and camouflage shorts when she exited the bathroom.

"I'm going to the ranch house to get the key," she said.

She was gone for a half-hour, returning with a smile.

"Any problems?"

"Piece of cake," she said. "Mom and Frankie are attending a charitable function in New Orleans. We don't need to search Vodou Nitz."

"Why not?" I asked

"Come see," she said.

I followed Toni back to the main ranch house, wondering what she wanted to show me in Frankie's office.

"There are surveillance cameras everywhere at Vodou Nitz. Take a look."

Toni was seated in front of Frankie's computer, the screen enormous. She began using the mouse to move from room to room.

"Damn!" I said. "Do the cameras cover the entire building?"

"I've checked every inch of it," Toni said. "Bobby isn't there. What do you think?"

"If he isn't at Vodou Nitz, my guess is he's at the Bell House," I said.

"Then let's go see. You've already been there once. It should be easy."

"For me, maybe," I said. "No reason for you to come with me."

"If Bobby is in the attic, you'll need help getting him out."

"Too dangerous."

"You said Latitia was unguarded," Toni said.

"That may have changed. No use taking a chance we both get caught."

Toni ignored me. "We'll take my truck," she said. "We can't get Bobby here on our bikes."

"Okay," I said. "Let's do it."

Toni had restored an old Ford truck, its candy apple red paint job immaculate, and the upholstery professionally restored. The oversized motor purred like a kitten.

Toni beamed when I said, "Beautiful truck."

"Took me five years to get Lizzie to where she is now," she said.

"You didn't restore it yourself, did you?"

"Every nut, bolt, and coat of paint," she said.

"I'm impressed," I said. "Who taught you?"

"Pancho has a '61 Desoto and turns a pretty

mean wrench. I've been helping him work on the car since I was ten."

"You never cease to amaze me," I said. "We're getting ready to see how well you climb."

The moon was bright as we traversed the country road from Murky Bayou Farm to Mandeville. We found a secluded place to park not far from the Bell House, locked the truck, and finished our journey on foot.

The draping branches of a live oak rendered us invisible as I whispered instructions to Toni.

"I got into the attic through an unbolted shutter. We'll have to climb a tree to get on the ledge and then work our way around the building. It's steep and dangerous. Still up for it?"

"Right behind you," she said.

A salty breeze was blowing off Lake Pontchartrain as I climbed an adjacent tree and stepped out on the ledge. Toni slipped, and I grabbed her hand. She didn't panic. I made my way to the shutter where I had previously entered. It opened with a creak when I tugged at it.

Except for the muted light coming through the open window, the attic was dark. After helping Toni through the window, I switched on my flashlight and paned the floor.

"It's Bobby," Toni said.

A man dressed in jeans and L.S.U. tee shirt lay unconscious on the bare floor of the attic, his eyes open in a death stare. I touched his neck, feeling for a pulse.

"No pulse. He's cold as a fish," I said.

"Is he dead?" Toni asked.

"Zombied," I said. "He can hear every word we're saying."

"Bobby, it's Toni Bergamo. Hang on. We'll get you out of here and get you the antidote."

When car lights flashed through the open

window, I peered out to see who it was.

"Philip Casseus and two twin brothers that look like older versions of Philip," I said.

"What'll we do?" Toni said.

I didn't bother answering, grabbing Bobby's shoulders and dragging him to the window. We could hear footsteps coming up the stairs.

"Get on the ledge. I'll lift Bobby through the window. Hold him until I join you."

Someone was lifting the cutout on the floor as Toni climbed out the window. I hoisted Bobby into her awaiting arms and quickly joined them on the ledge. As Toni balanced the young man's inert body against the building wall, I closed the shutter behind us.

"Oh, shit!" Toni said. "We should have brought a rope."

"Get into the branches and grab hold of Bobby when I hand him down to you."

Toni was agile and cat-quick. Bracing herself on the branches of the large tree, she grabbed Bobby when I handed him to her over the roof's edge. I joined them on the limb, hoping our combined weight didn't cause it to break. Toni needed no directions, and we worked our way down the tree until we had Bobby on the ground.

The attic was dark when we exited. Philip and the twins knew the location of a light switch. I could see the light through a crack in the shutter I'd left slightly ajar.

"Oh, shit!" Toni said again.

"Get the truck. I'll drag Bobby to the live oak and wait for you."

Toni was out of sight when Philip, the two twins, and Tiana Brown burst from the front door. Philip and Tiana waited at the door as the twins searched for Bobby around the house. I regretted having told Toni to pick us up near the live oak when her headlights appeared from the opposite direction. She stopped in front of the Bell House and lowered the window of her truck.

"You folks want me to call the police?" she asked.

"Did you see someone on foot just now?" Philip asked.

"Two guys were carrying a body," she said, pointing behind her. "They lifted it into the trunk of a black Mercedes. I was about to call 9-1-1 when I saw you."

The twins appeared from the back of the house when Philip whistled. They piled into his Bimmer and hurried away in the direction Toni had pointed. Tiana went back into the house without saying thank you. Toni stopped about a block from the live oak and waited for me.

"There isn't room in the cab for him," Toni said.

After helping me lift him into the truck's bed, we started toward Murky Bayou Farm. My cell phone rang before we'd gotten out of town.

I didn't recognize the number and said, "Wyatt Thomas."

"I'm Jolene Johnson," the woman on the line said. "I have a message for you from Mama Mulate."

"Tell me," I said.

"Mirlande Casseus is holding her captive at the Faumort Plantation."

"Where on the plantation?" I asked. "The place is huge."

"She's in Mirlande's harem, in the main house."

"Is there a way you can let us in?" I said.

Jolene Johnson hung up the phone after saying, "I can't help you no more."

"Who was that?" Toni asked.

"Tell you in a minute," I said. "I'm getting another call."

It was Freya on the phone, and she sounded frantic.

"Where are you?" she said.

"Pancho's niece Toni and I just rescued Bobby Blanchard. We're on our way to Frankie Castellano's farm."

"Turn around," she said. "Now! Bring Bobby to my house."

"Why?" I said.

"No time for explanations," Freya said. "Your life is in peril if you continue in the direction you're going. Stop and turn around, and do it now."

"Do a three-sixty," I said when Freya hung up the phone."

"Why?" Toni asked.

"Freya said there's danger ahead of us."

"How the hell would she know that?" Toni said.

"She's a witch," I said.

"You aren't funny," Toni said.

"I'm not trying to be. Stop the truck," I said, grabbing the wheel."

Toni slammed on the brakes and slapped my hand away from the steering wheel.

"Have you lost your damn mind?" she said.

"Turn the truck around," I said.

Toni crossed her arms and planted her foot on the brake.

"You asshole!" she said.

I dialed Freya. When she answered, I said, "Put Pancho on the line."

Pancho was standing beside Freya because I quickly heard his voice.

"Hello."

"It's Wyatt, Pancho. I'm handing the phone to Toni."

"What do you want me to say to her?" he asked.

"Tell her you'll spank her ass unless she turns this truck around and heads to Covington."

I put my phone in Toni's hand, not giving Pancho a chance to reply. After a moment, she returned it to me, wheeled the truck around in the middle of the dark road, and started away in a screech of burning rubber in the direction of Covington.

"Pancho never punished me, much less paddled my butt."

We were both grinning when I said, "Maybe he should have."

Freya's garage was open when we reached her house, and Toni parked beside her Miata. Pancho and Freya were waiting for us, helping us get Bobby Blanchard out of the truck's bed as the garage door shut behind us. Freya directed us to an empty bedroom. After depositing Bobby on a bed, we returned to Freya's sitting room.

"Freya, this is my niece, Toni," Pancho said.

Neither Freya nor Toni was smiling as they shook hands.

"Why did you have us come here?" Toni asked.

"People in a black BMW were waiting up the road for you," Freya said.

"How could they have known where we were going?" Toni asked.

"They probably called in your license plate, got your home address, and hurried to intercept us," I said. "Thank you, Freya."

"How did you know?" Toni asked.

"I'm a witch and have extrasensory perception," Freya said.

"I don't believe in witches," Toni said.

"Just because you don't believe in something doesn't mean it isn't real," Freya said.

"Then prove it to me," Toni said.

"In due time," Freya said.

"You can trust Freya," Pancho said. "She's on our side and is everything she says she is."

Toni frowned again when Latitia joined us and hugged me.

"Oh, Wyatt," she said. "You need to brace yourself."

"For what?" I asked.

"Your daughter's in the next room."

Chapter 27

When the door opened, I had little time to draw a breath as a gorgeous girl appeared. My legs had turned to Jell-O, and I dropped to my knees.

"Wyatt," Latitia said. "This is your daughter, Aimee."

Tears began dripping down my face as Aimee approached me. I felt as if everyone in the room was staring at me and knew what I was thinking. Seeing my distress, Aimee put her arms around my neck. It was good, as I had begun blubbering like a baby.

I finally managed to regain my composure and get to my feet. When I did, I grabbed Aimee around the waist and twirled her until we were both dizzy and laughing. I dropped to my knees again and held her hand.

"You have just made me the happiest person in the world," I said. I must have loved you since you were born because the feelings I have for you now can't be explained in any other way."

"Do you like cats?" Aimee asked.

"Love cats," I said. "My tailless cat Kisses isn't far from here."

A black and white cat came strolling into the room, and Aimee picked it up.

"This is Bootsie," she said.

I smiled, and Aimee also did when I said, "If you love cats, then there's no doubt you're my daughter."

When everyone in the room stopped applauding, Freya said, "There's room for everyone in the kitchen. Come with me. I'll introduce everyone."

I was soon in a group hug with Aimee, Latitia, and Lashonda. Toni propped against the kitchen wall, a frown on her face, her arms encircling her chest. I hoped the crowd wouldn't put out Freya. I needn't have worried.

Freya and Pancho had a pot of spaghetti sauce simmering on the stove, smiling as they stirred the concoction. Still, in a daze because of meeting Aimee, I'd failed to notice the person talking with Toni. Toni's demeanor had changed from a frown to a smile. Pulling away from the family crowd, I joined them.

"I'm Stevie Jones," the young woman said. "You must be Wyatt."

Stevie and Toni were about the same height. It wasn't the only thing about them that matched. They both had athletic bodies and toned legs. Stevie's cornrows were dark, as were her eyes. She was radiant in her red blouse and cutoffs.

"Glad to meet you, Stevie. How are you a part of this group?"

"Tony and Mama Mulate interviewed me. I was a student of Mama's at Tulane before I dropped out."

"Why did they interview you?" Toni asked.

"I was Bobby Blanchard's live-in girlfriend before he died. Now, I'm doing everything I can to seek justice."

Toni was looking at me when I glanced at her. "Bobby's not dead," I said.

"I wish it were true," she said.

"You didn't tell her?" I asked.

Toni shook her head.

"Tell me what?" Stevie asked.

"Come with us. We'll show you," I said.

Freya's old house was enormous. Stevie followed us up the grand staircase to the top floor, where we opened the door to a darkened room. Stevie gasped when Toni turned on the light. Seeing Bobby lying inert on the bed, she ran to him, draping herself across his lifeless body.

"Oh my God!" she said. "Bobby hasn't begun to decompose."

"He isn't dead," Toni said.

"He's been zombied," I said when Stevie looked at me for confirmation.

"I don't believe in zombies," she said.

"And you shouldn't believe everything you've seen about zombies in the movies and television. They are real and aren't dead," I said.

Stevie's frown disappeared, replaced by a look of hope.

"Then can we revive him?" she said.

"Not without the antidote," I said.

"What the hell are you talking about?" Stevie said.

"Zombie powder," Toni said.

"Voodoo cultists have a concoction that renders victims into a deathlike state," I said. "The only way to revive someone who has been zombied is to give them the antidote."

"Where can we get it?" she said.

"You know Mama Mulate is missing, don't you?" I asked.

Stevie nodded. "Tony said she's a captive."

"At a sugar cane plantation near the Mississippi River. There's an antidote on the premises," I said.

"Mama's a captive?"

I nodded. "A kitchen worker named Jolene

225

Johnson called and told me about Mama's whereabouts.

"Is Jolene agreeable to working with us to free Mama?"

"I don't think so," I said. "Toni and I are working on a plan."

"Why not just call the police?"

"Mirlande Casseus and her people have broad political connections. We don't want to play our hand too soon and have Mama disappear before we have a chance to save her."

Stevie stroked Bobby's face. "I can't bear to see him like this," she said.

"He knows you're here and can hear every word we're saying," Toni said.

Stevie kissed him. "I'm going to get the antidote for you," she said. "Please hang in there until I do. I love you."

Stevie waited for some reaction from Bobby. Toni and I led her to the door when she got none.

"We'll leave him here in the dark," Toni said. "Maybe he can fall asleep and escape his fate for a while."

The aroma of spaghetti sauce wafted up the stairs, and we were all hungry when we reached the kitchen. Pancho and Freya filled our plates. I grabbed a chair beside Lashonda, Latitia, and Aimee.

"Latitia said your wife died," Lashonda said.

"It's been a while now. I still feel responsible," I said." Her family never forgave me."

"Her cancer killed her," Latitia said. "It wasn't your fault."

"Let's talk about something else?" I said.

"Sorry," Lashonda said.

"What's your story?"

"Mama Mulate rescued us from my house in the Lower 9th Ward. She took us to her house in New Orleans," she said.

"We couldn't find my cat Bootsie," Aimee said. "Mama Mulate went back to the house to try and find her. Grandmother and I were so worried."

"When Tony learned Mama was missing, he took us to the house to check on her," Lashonda said.

"We found her little car. It was raining, and she'd left the front door open," Aimee said.

"That car is Mama's favorite possession," I said. "She wouldn't have left the door open in the rain. At least, not on purpose."

"That's what Tony said. Mama also dropped one of her driving gloves on the front porch," Lashonda said. "Tony tried to hide his shock. I drove Mama's car back to her house. Aimee and I locked the door when Tony went home."

"Where did you meet Stevie?" I asked.

"She was frightened and showed up at Mama's not long after Tony left."

"Because?"

"Someone ransacked her apartment, and she was afraid to stay there. I had her call, Tony."

Lashonda nodded when I said, "You went to Tony's?"

"He told us to leave Mama's and get our butts to his house. He called a friend in the police to patrol the house."

"Good for Tony," I said.

"Bootsie came with us," Aimee said.

"I'm happy you found him," I said.

"He was on Grandma's porch, wringing wet though happy we had found him," Aimee said.

"Good deal," I said.

"Tony's wife Lil is a jewel," Lashonda said. "She was relieved to see us even though she's allergic to cats."

Freya and Pancho collected the dirty dishes and put them into the dishwasher.

"I hope you've saved room for my crème

brulée," she said.

Aimee's eyes told me she'd never eaten anything as extraordinary as Freya's crème brulée. I was happy to give her mine. When we finished, Freya led us to the living room, the glowing fireplace soothing our nerves as we found places to sit on the overstuffed antique furniture.

"Welcome to my house," Freya said. "I'm hoping Wyatt can fill us in on what's happening."

"Two problems," I said. "As you know, Toni and I rescued Bobby Blanchard. He's still under the influence of zombie powder, and we need to secure the antidote. Also, our cohort Mama Mulate is missing and likely in the hands of Mirlande Casseus."

Stevie said. "A voodoo cult called the Keepers is active in the French Quarter. I believe the cult is our key to rescuing Mama."

"What makes you think so?" I asked.

"My two neighbors, Bruno and Harvey, work in the Quarter and are familiar with the people who live there. They've attended some of the meetings. According to Bruno and Harvey, the cult recruits street people, many of who disappear. Mirlande Casseus's son Philip is a sometimes participant."

"You think the Keepers are connected with Mama's disappearance?" I said.

"Tony and Lil had brunch with two local newspaper people who are familiar with the city. Lashonda, Aimee, and I joined them."

"Who?" I asked.

"Candy Daigle and Zane Fleming."

"Are they still alive? They were both old twenty years ago," I said.

"Alive, alert, and active," Stevie said. "They are both familiar with Mirlande Casseus. We had a good discussion of the rumors."

"What else?" I asked.

"Bobby must have joined the Keepers in search of leads because he had their voodoo tattoo on his wrist. He was working on a story, and I believe he got targeted there."

"What's your plan?" I said.

"Infiltrate the Keepers, get abducted, and make contact with Mama Mulate."

"You'll be just as helpless as Mama with no means to escape."

"Not if I have help from the inside," she said.

"You know someone who works there?" Freya asked.

"Wyatt does. A cook at the plantation called him."

"How did she know to call Wyatt?" Freya asked.

"Tell her," Stevie said.

"Jolene Johnson, a cook at the plantation, has access to the antidote. I don't know all the details. I do know Mama talked Jolene into calling me."

"She wouldn't have called you unless she was contemplating helping Mama," Toni said.

Toni's words rang true. "Helping Mama would put her in extreme danger. Why would she help us?"

"Don't know, though it's worth a shot," Toni said.

I dialed Tony's number, and he answered on the second ring. I could hear giggling in the background.

"Am I disturbing something?" I asked.

"Lil and I are spending the weekend at Zane Fleming's place in the French Quarter."

"Sounds like you're having a wonderful time." Tony's unexpected laughter told me I'd probably caught them in a moment of passion. "I can call back tomorrow," I said.

"What you got, Cowboy?"

229

"Jolene Johnson, the woman who called me about Mama. Can you get me some information on her?"

"Like what?"

"Who she is and where she lives. Anything you can find out about her," I said.

"I'll call you tomorrow," Tony said.

Freya, Stevie, and the others were staring at me as I hung up the phone.

"Well?" Freya said.

"Tony will call tomorrow and tell me what he's learned about Jolene Johnson. Maybe it'll give us a clue on how to get her to help us."

"Frankie can make it worth her while," Toni said.

"What are you suggesting?" I said.

"Seems logical Frankie could help facilitate things," She said.

"Are we ready to bring him into this?" I asked.

"Now's as good a time as any," Toni said.

"Let me sleep on it," I said. Tomorrow, we'll know more about Jolene Johnson," I said. "Frankie's paying us to solve this mystery. If I can avoid it, I don't want to put it on my boss."

"Are you afraid he won't pay you?" Toni said with a grin.

"The thought crossed my mind," I said.

"Frankie's not like that," Toni said. "He loves intrigue and would relish being involved."

"Maybe," I said.

"It's getting late," Freya said. "I have plenty of rooms, and no one is leaving tonight."

"Aimee, Lashonda, and I only need a single room," Latitia said.

"Can I bunk with you, "Stevie?" Toni asked. "I have more questions that need answering."

Stevie smiled and said, "Love it. This ordeal has caused me so much anxiety I'm almost afraid to be alone."

"I'm driving Pancho to the apartment above his restaurant. I'll activate the alarm when I return."

"Thanks, Freya," I said. "You're making all of our lives easier."

"You know where your room is," she said with a wink. "I'll situate everyone else.

The bedroom was dark, and I was half asleep when Freya slipped under the covers beside me.

Chapter 28

Mama had little time to commiserate with Vixen because Mirlande had shown up to visit her harem. The women began to buzz about the Sultana having arrived.

"What's all the excitement?" Mama asked.

"Mirlande is in the house. The eunuchs and minions refer to her as the Sultana," Vixen said. "Many of the women here revere her."

"How can they revere someone holding them captive?" Mama asked.

"Because life in the harem is easy and posh," Vixen said. "We are waited on hand and foot, eat the finest food, and only have to perform occasionally. Many people came from the streets and had never had three meals a day."

"Who does the performing? Mama asked.

"Mirlande has her favorites. If you please her, you earn even more perks."

"Such as?"

"Special meals, alcohol, and various drugs," Vixen said. "Mirlande is a control freak and loves nothing more than having people who are subservient to her."

"How do you please her?" Mama asked.

"In case you haven't already noticed, Mirlande is bisexual. She likes men and women."

"She was married and has a son," Mama said.

Vixen laughed. "Mirlande is perverted, and so is her son. Philip," Vixen said. "Neither of them is anywhere close to normal."

"What do you mean?" Mama said.

"Use your imagination. There is no perversion Mirlande and Philip haven't practiced."

Vixen nodded when Mama said, "Incest?"

"Prepare yourself for any sexual perversion if chosen to spend the night with the Sultana."

Vixen lowered her head and nodded again when Mama said, "You've spent the night with her?"

"I'm still here, aren't I," Vixen said.

Mama squeezed Vixen's hand. "Oh, baby, I'm so sorry."

"It's okay. I'm a survivor."

"I'm not judging you," Mama said. "You did what you had to do. Where did Mirlande get the money to buy this place? It must be worth mega bucks. The slave trade may be profitable. This land on the river likely cost mega-millions."

"Have you heard of the Pompeo family?" Vixen asked.

"I've seen their names on the Tulane donors list," Mama said.

"They are one of the wealthiest and most powerful New Orleans families. Arthur Wayne Pompeo owns half this plantation, and Mirlande the other half."

"So he's responsible?"

"She has other benefactors," Vixen said.

"Organized crime?" Mama asked.

"Someone has to handle the sale of the slaves and do the money laundering," Vixen said. "The actual characters involved are part of a complex scenario."

"A scenario you're privy to?" Mama said.

"If I were protected and allowed to testify

233

before a grand jury, I could bust this operation wide open."

"Let's hope you get your chance. How do Mirlande and Philip know a woman named Latitia Boiset?"

"You kidding? Latitia Boiset is a Creole bombshell from New Orleans. She's drop-dead gorgeous and super talented. She headlines Brass & Sass, a Vegas show band."

Mama thought of Wyatt and felt a momentary pang of jealousy. "How are Mirlande and Philip involved in her?"

"Philip spends lots of time in the gay bars in New Orleans. Like his mother, men and women attract him. He caught Latitia's act in Vegas and fell in lust with her. When she rebuffed him, he had Mirlande buy the show band."

"So Latitia Boiset works for Mirlande and Philip?"

"Latitia has a mother and daughter in New Orleans. She's afraid not to perform for fear of her daughter and mother."

"How do you know?"

"I make it my business to know everything going on here," Vixen said.

"They control Latitia Boiset even though she's in Las Vegas?" Mama said.

"Have you heard of the nightclub Vodou Nitz in Covington? Latitia is playing there."

"You sound as if you're a fan," Mama said.

"Latitia Boiset's the sexiest woman alive. Philip zombied her when he heard she had an offer to star in a remake of Cleopatra."

"She must be talented as well as beautiful," Mama said.

"I saw her once in Vegas. She's red hot," Vixen said. "I'd give anything to catch a performance."

Feeling yet another pang of jealousy, Mama

changed the subject.

"What does Mirlande do to deserve half of a going concern like this sugar cane plantation?"

"Until Mirlande came along, farming Faumort was barely profitable. Mirlande convinced Arthur Pompeo there was a better way."

"Slave labor?" Mama said.

"Sugar cane farming is labor intensive. Without slave labor, this plantation wouldn't be so super successful."

"What percentage of the workforce are slaves?" Mama asked.

"My guess is zombies comprise most of the labor force," Vixen said.

"I understand being zombied," Mama said. "I don't understand why they work for Mirlande when they aren't under the influence of the drug."

"That's just it," Vixen said. "As I did, the victims undergo ritual death. Their families mourn them; an impersonator of Baron Samedi digs them up and revives them. Trust me when I tell you it affects your mental health."

"But you know you aren't dead," Mama said.

"Because I have no trace of the zombie powder in my body. Though still partially drugged, the slaves function and perform given tasks. They think they are dead in their controlled minds, maybe in hell."

"They are in hell," Mama said. "I read an article in the Covington paper about a man reportedly dying. He escaped the plantation and walked home. No one in his family would have anything to do with him because they had seen him buried."

Vixen laughed aloud and said, "It's a fact, zombie powder fucks up your life."

Her laughter quickly turned to tears prompting Mama to hug her again.

"When we get out of this place, I'll see to it

everyone understands what has happened to these people. Maybe it'll give them a shot at getting their lives back."

"Thank you, Mama. You've given me hope, which I haven't had in almost forever."

Vixen used her gossamer veil to wipe away the last of her tears.

"If Mirlande wants me as a slave, why is she allowing my escape from the drug?"

"Knowledge has kept me alive. I know exactly why you're here and what plans Mirlande has for you."

"Tell me," Mama said.

"Mirlande desires you sexually. So does Philip. While that is the only reason Philip wants you, Mirlande has other motives."

"Such as?"

"Mirlande's husband was the most powerful houngan on the island of Haiti. She's extremely superstitious."

"And?" Mama said.

"She knows you have spiritual capabilities far exceeding her own. She wants you to be her right-hand man, personal assistant, and advisor."

"I'd have to be stoned out of my mind to accept that role," Mama said.

"Don't ever let Mirlande know how you feel. She is ruthless. I saw her rip a eunuch's tongue right out of his mouth for saying something she didn't like."

"How did she get away with doing that?" Mama asked.

"Everyone is terrified of Mirlande and Philip. The other eunuchs held the terrified man down while she did it."

The memory of the heinous act restarted Vixen's sobs.

"Karma has a way of catching up to you, and despicable people often meet horrific deaths,"

Mama said.

"If I could, I'd kill her with my bare hands," Vixen said.

"Release the hate from your heart," Mama said. "It's the only way to survive this ordeal."

"I had my hands around her neck once," Vixen said. "Mirlande was asleep beside me and snoring. In the end, I couldn't do it."

"Not everyone can slay a dragon," Mama said.

"Could you have done it?" Vixen asked.

"That's a question most of us never have to answer," Mama said.

An approaching eunuch interrupted their conversation.

"Mirlande is in the harem," he said. "She's looking for you. Come with me."

When the tall eunuch dressed in red harem pants and matching turban turned, Vixen knocked him unconscious with a heavy brass plant holder. Mama watched him crumble to the Persian rug on the floor.

"Don't let Mirlande find you," Vixen said.

"Where will I go?" Mama said.

"The harem is extensive. Blend in. Most of the houris are drugged or at least partially drugged and will never notice."

"What about the big eunuch?"

"Who cares?" Vixen said. "I don't intend to be anywhere around when he awakens. Mirlande won't even give him a chance to explain before she has him beaten."

"Where will I find you?" Mama asked.

"You won't," Vixen said. "I'll find you. Put on this veil. Don't take it off even if the rest of you is naked."

The big eunuch was still lying on the floor when Mama took off in one direction, Vixen in the other.

Mama had on the same dress she was

wearing when captured. Even with the veil Vixen had given her, she stood out among the exotically-clad women in Mirlande's harem. She approached a woman wearing a pair of yellow harem pants and a purple blouse. The woman's myopic smile suggested she was under the influence of some drug.

"I love your outfit," Mama said. "I'm new here and want to get rid of my street clothes and into something similar to what you're wearing. What's your name?"

"Sandra," the woman said, surprising Mama when she grabbed her shoulders and planted a wet kiss on her lips. "You are so beautiful."

"Thank you," Mama said. "Do you know where I can get a change of clothes?"

"There are thousands of outfits in the wardrobe room," Sandra said. "You can't go in there like that, though."

"Why not?" Mama asked.

"Everyone is looking for someone dressed like you. If you go into the wardrobe room, Xander will think you are that person."

"Who is Xander?" Mama asked.

"The wardrobe eunuch," the woman said.

"What should I do?" Mama asked.

The woman named Sandra in the colorful costume didn't answer. Instead, she began removing Mama's clothes and tossing them on the rug.

"Go naked into the wardrobe room. Xander will dress you and never even wonder who you are."

"I can't just walk into the wardrobe room naked," Mama said. "What will Xander think?"

"Absolutely nothing. He sees naked women all day, every day. Besides, he's a eunuch."

Except for the veil covering her face, Mama stood naked as the houri gave her a long look.

"Sister, you got a body on you. Mirlande will have a field day when she gets you into her boudoir."

Mama was once a world-class track star at the University of South Carolina and did have an athletic body. Feeling Sandra's stare, she tried to cover herself with her arms and hands.

Sandra smiled when Mama said, "You're making me nervous."

"And you're giving me thoughts," Sandra said.

"Then let's hook up later," Mama said. "Right now, I need to find the wardrobe room."

"You mean it?" Sandra said.

Mama patted her cheek. "We'll have some fun later on," she said. "Right now, point me toward the wardrobe room."

"Through that red-lacquered door," Sandra said. "I'll be waiting for you."

Mama picked her clothes off the floor, gave Sandra a peck on the cheek, and started toward the red door. Before she reached it, she stashed her street clothes behind the brass pots of several palm trees positioned against the wall. She was surprised when she opened the red door and entered the wardrobe room.

Though Mama was six feet tall, she had to look upward into the eyes of someone she recognized. The young, bare-chested man with tattooed arms and an afro hairdo stood at least six-foot-ten. Mama could feel his stare as he began ogling her body.

"Oh my God," the man said. "Not even in my wildest dreams did I ever think I'd see you naked. It is you, isn't it, Professor Mulate?"

Mama tried with little success to cover her nudity with her arms and hands. "You aren't Xander," she said.

"It's my fantasy name," he said. "You know who I am. English 101 two years ago. I thought you were going to flunk me."

"Jimmy Ray Douciere! Quit staring at my nipples and get me something to wear."

"Yes, ma'am!" he said.

Jimmy Ray soon had Mama clad in yellow harem pants and a red sports bra. It didn't stop him from staring at her.

"What are you doing here?" he asked.

"I could ask you the same question." Jimmy grinned when Mama said, "Are you a eunuch?"

"You're not going to send me to the principal, are you, Professor Mulate?"

"Quit staring," Mama said. "I have clothes on now."

"I have a big imagination," Jimmy Ray said.

"Well, stow it and tell me how you got here," Mama said.

"You know I flunked out after my freshman year," he said. "Didn't matter because I'd decided to try my luck in the NBA draft."

"Basketball is my favorite sport," Mama said. "I don't remember hearing your name in the draft."

"I went undrafted," he said. "Got a spot with the G-league Lakers. Had an affair with a Laker's Girl. Thought I was staring at a shotgun wedding, so I hopped a plane back to the Big Easy."

"What are you doing here at the plantation?" Mama asked.

"I was still working out every night, trying to get noticed by the Pelicans. Some pals and I went to a voodoo party in the Quarter, hoping for some fast and dirty sex."

"And?" Mama asked.

"I got voodooed, though not the way I'd planned," Jimmie Ray said. "Wound up here, instead."

"You don't sound drugged," Mama said.

"Never took drugs because of basketball."

"You're not a eunuch?"

"No way," he said. "Want to see?"

"I'll take your word for it," Mama said. "If you aren't zombied, why don't you get out of here?"

"You kidding? I've never had so much sex in my entire life. This place has many beautiful women who can't seem to resist me. I keep thinking I should leave. I haven't reached that point yet."

"What about your dream of making it in the NBA?"

"My odds seem pretty bleak," Jimmy Ray said.

"I know a couple of the assistant coaches on the Pelicans," Mama said. "I could get you a try-out."

"You serious?" Jimmy Ray said.

"It takes talent to make it in the NBA. If you don't already have it, I can't give it to you. Help me get out of here, and I'll see to it you have a shot at stardom. The rest is up to you."

Chapter 29

The morning was nippy, and I wished I'd had a warm bathrobe around my shoulders as I descended the stairs from my bedroom. The aroma of bacon and eggs wafting up the stairway shifted my thoughts from the weather to pangs of hunger. Someone I didn't expect was in the kitchen, laughing it up with Pancho and Freya. Frankie Castellano didn't notice me when I grabbed a chair beside my daughter Aimee.

She smiled when I said, "Hey, baby. Sleep well last night?"

"Freya brought us a tray of warm brownies and a pitcher of cold milk."

She smiled again when I said, "Guess you're too full to eat your bacon and eggs."

"Grandma's a good cook. Freya and Pancho put her to shame."

"Pancho's a pro. Have you tried his pizza yet?" I said.

"He's promised to make his famous pepperoni pizza for us before he heads back for the lunch crowd," Aimee said.

"You like Italian food?" I asked.

"Love it," she said.

"After we rescue Mama, I'll take us all to dinner at Pancho's café."

Aimee's smile disappeared at the mention of Mama.

"Wyatt, I'm so worried," she said. "I can't help thinking this is my fault because Mama returned to the house to find Bootsie."

"I'm worried too, baby," I said. "It's not your fault, and she'll soon be back with us."

"You sure about that?"

"Mama's the strongest person I know. She'll survive whatever life tosses at her. Count on it."

Aimee squeezed my hand as Frankie Castellano saw me and sauntered over to join us.

Aimee smiled when he said, "Who is this beautiful young lady?"

"Frankie Castellano, this is my daughter, Aimee."

Aimee blushed when Frankie kissed her hand. "I don't know where you get your looks. If you're smart as your old man, you gotta lot going for you."

"Grandma says you're a gangster."

Aimee's blunt reply shocked me, and I expected it to anger Frankie. He smiled and said, "Even gangsters aren't all bad."

Aimee shook Frankie's hand. "I knew when you walked up you're a good man. Grandma says I have the touch."

"You're grandma's a smart woman," Frankie said. "I look forward to meeting her."

"I'll go get her," Aimee said as she hurried to find Lashonda.

"Toni called last night. Said there are problems."

"Tony Nicosia and I enlisted Mama Mulate to help us," I said. "She's been kidnapped."

"Catch me up to speed," Frankie said.

"We found Bobby. He's safe upstairs."

"Wonderful. Can I see him?"

"Bobby's under the influence of zombie

powder. He's alive, though you wouldn't know it. Part of the reason we called you is to help us acquire the antidote to revive him."

I shook my head when he said, "Is it money you need?"

"I wish it were the answer. It's not."

"Then what is?"

"Bobby isn't the only one involved. An organized group uses zombie powder to control people. Bobby was doing investigative reporting, and his nosiness resulted in his troubles."

"I know of no crime family operating in this region. You're not pointing the finger at me, are you?"

"Only if your company practices voodoo," I said.

Frankie chuckled. "The only thing I know about voodoo is it's the name of my nightclub. The customers love it. What the hell is zombie powder?" Frankie said.

"A secret concoction given to victims that causes them to appear dead. It's what happened to Bobby."

"Why would someone want to do that?" Frankie asked.

People have been buried by their relatives, thinking they were dead. A gang that then sells them to the sex trade or forces them into physical slavery revives them. Bobby's is only a single example."

"Who else?"

Frankie's eyes widened when I said, "Latitia Boiset was zombied."

"What do you know about Latitia Boiset?" Frankie said.

"Aimee is Latitia's daughter."

"You're shitting me!" Frankie said. "How did you get hooked up with Latitia Boiset?"

"Long story," I said. "Doesn't matter now

because we haven't been a number for years."

Frankie stared at me a moment. "I see it now. She has your eyes."

Aimee, Latitia, and Lashonda joined us as we conversed.

"We're you two talking about me?" Latitia said.

"Miss Boiset," Frankie said. "What are you doing here?"

"Wyatt rescued me," she said.

"From what?" Frankie asked.

"Philip Casseus zombied me when I told him I was leaving Brass & Sass," Latitia said.

"There is no Brass & Sass without you," Frankie said.

"I'm a paid performer like everyone else in the revue," Latitia said. "I have an offer to star in a major motion picture. Philip zombied me rather than let me go. He kept me that way for days until I became frightened out of my mind. When he revived me, he threatened to harm my mom and daughter if I refused to continue performing."

"Philip Casseus is part of the voodoo thing?" Frankie asked.

Before I could answer, Aimee grabbed Frankie's elbow to get his attention. "You met my mom. This is Grandmother Lashonda."

Frankie shook Lashonda's hand. "You have a lovely family. So sorry my nightclub is involved in this mess. I promise I'll help rectify the situation."

Lashonda patted Frankie's hand. "Latitia said you were a handsome man. She wasn't lying."

Frankie knew bullshit when he heard it, and Lashonda's compliment made him smile. He dished back some of his own.

"Thank you, Lashonda. I can see where your daughter and granddaughter got their good looks."

Lashonda was blushing when Freya joined us

with a platter of bacon-wrapped shrimp.

"Lashonda is quite correct. Frankie is a handsome man," she said. "Try one of my hors d'oeuvres."

Frankie bit into one of Freya's hors d'oeuvres and licked his lips as he glanced around to see my reaction.

"Tasty," he said. "I need to get your recipe for my wife, Adele."

Frankie posed an impressive figure, but he was about as handsome as a bulldog who'd participated in one-too-many dogfights. I tried not to smile. Lashonda, Aimee, and Latitia stared at Frankie when Freya returned to the stove. It seemed apparent Frankie had invoked Adele's name because he was both attracted and intimidated by the striking older woman.

Sensing everyone was looking at him, he said, "What?"

"I see your wedding ring," Lashonda said. "Do not spend the night here if you want to stay married."

"You trying to tell me something?"

"Freya's a certified carnivore, and she was eyeing you like a piece of raw meat," Latitia said.

"Should I be worried?" he said.

"She'd roll you in the bed before you had a chance to sneeze," Lashonda said.

I wiped the smile off my face when Latitia cast me a dirty look. The appearance of Stevie and Toni halted any further discussion of Freya's sexual appetite.

"Did we miss something?" Toni asked.

"Where have you been?" Frankie asked. "Your mom is worried sick."

"I'm a big girl and can take care of myself," she said.

"It wouldn't hurt to check in every once in a while. Who is this lovely young lady with you?"

"Frankie Castellano, this is my friend Stevie Jones. She and Bobby were living together when he disappeared."

"Were you now? Can I be so crass as to ask if Bobby's parents know about your relationship?"

"We talked to them on the phone," Stevie said. "My relationship with Bobby is no secret."

"Bobby's parents are close friends of me and Adele. They're. . ."

"Racists?" Stevie said.

"You said it, not me," Frankie said.

"Why are people like that?" Toni said. "You don't have a racist bone in your body, Frankie."

"Hell, little girl. Being Italian, I've been on the other end of the stick more times than I can count."

Frankie spoke the truth. Though rich as any person in the Boston Club, he was unable to join because of the group requirements.

"I'm also Italian and have experienced my share of discrimination," Toni said.

"Try being black for a day," Stevie said.

"Wyatt explained what's going on and why I should be involved," Frankie said. "Help us out here."

"Bobby's mom is my mom's best friend," Toni said. "Bobby's dad came to you for help in finding his son. I'd say you're invested."

"I hired Wyatt, and he found Bobby," Frankie said.

"Have you seen him?" Stevie said. "He isn't even alive."

"Tell me what I can do. I'm all ears, little girl," Frankie said."

"Stevie and I have a plan," Toni said. "We're going to get captured, sent to the plantation, and then help Mama to escape."

"And bring some of the antidote back with us," Stevie said.

"Plantation? What are you talking about?"

"Mirlande Casseus, Philip Casseus' mother, operates a sugar cane plantation in St. John's the Baptist Parish.

"Mirlande is the head of the crime cartel I told you about," I said.

"Is she dangerous?" Frankie asked. Before Toni or I could answer, he said, "You're not going anywhere. I'll send in some men."

"Frankie, no," Toni said. "That won't work."

"Why not?" he asked.

"The operation is too big and too widespread," I said. "The other Tony is working with a couple of investigative reporters. They're compiling a timeline to present to the police."

"I won't let you risk your life," Frankie said.

"I'm an adult. I've made my decision," Toni said.

Unable to ignore the conflict in her kitchen, Freya joined the fray.

"Allow me to make a suggestion," she said.

"I'm listening," Frankie said.

"I can help, though only if we're all on the same page," Freya said.

"We all want to rescue Mama," I said. "It would be icing on the cake to get some of the zombie powder antidote."

"I can help you accomplish your goal," Freya said.

"Please explain," Frankie said.

"I'm a dark witch," she said.

"Pardon me?"

Freya showed him a quartz crystal attached to a gold chain. "This is a Locator Stone. It can lead us to Mama Mulate."

"Then what?" I said.

"With the stone in Mama's possession, I'll cast a spell to see she escapes."

"How's that going to happen?" Frankie said.

"Toni and Stevie will take it to her."

"Too dangerous," Frankie said. "Toni's mom will kill me if I let her go."

"Call your wife and daughter," Freya said. "I'll convince them. We can use their energy to make this work."

"That's crazy," Frankie said.

"Wyatt, call your friend Tony and the people with who he works. We can do this."

Pancho came out of the kitchen and took Freya's hand. "You and me have our differences, and we haven't always seen eye to eye, but we were both born in Sicily. If Freya tells you she can make something positive happen, you better heed her advice."

"Toni is blood," Frankie said. "Your blood and mine."

"She's never been to the old country though she's as Sicilian as you and me," Pancho said. "Give her a chance."

When Frankie gave Freya a nod, she slipped the quartz necklace over Stevie's neck.

"This stone is our eyes," Freya said. "We'll track your progress and intervene by casting a spell if you encounter problems."

Stevie grabbed Toni's hand and pulled her to the door.

"How do you intend to monitor the stone?" I asked.

Freya showed us an identical quartz necklace to the one she'd placed around Stevie's neck.

"I have the Locator Stone's sister," she said.

"I don't know," Frankie said. "I'm Catholic. Catholics used to burn witches at the stake."

"Because witches had powers," Pancho said. "Freya has powers and is on our side."

"Don't be afraid of me," Freya said. "Use me now and confess to your priest on Sunday."

"Will your dark magic protect Toni?" Frankie

asked.

"She's in danger," Freya said. "I won't lie to you about that. That said, I'll do everything I can to protect her."

"Okay," Frankie said. "Let's do it. I don't know about calling Adele and Josie."

At that moment, Frankie's cell phone rang. It was Adele.

"Frankie," she said. "Where are you? Are you okay?"

"I'm in Covington with Pancho, and I'm good," Frankie said. "Can you and Josie join us?"

"Is Toni with you?" Adele asked.

"I'll explain when you get here. Wyatt found Bobby. And Adele, bring Robert and Alice. There's a problem; they need to be here for him."

Chapter 30

Stevie's car and Toni's truck sat on the street in front of Freya's house. Toni followed Stevie to a dented Toyota with a large crack in the windshield.

"My truck's older than your car. At least you can see out the windshield. I'll drive."

"Whatever," Stevie said. "I'm still waiting on my dream car. Until then, my old Toyota gets me where I want to go."

Stevie was grinning when Toni opened the door of her candy apple red Ford truck.

"Stevie, meet Lizzie."

"Did Frankie buy you the truck at a collector's car auction?"

"Hell no!" Toni said. "I restored this baby myself."

Stevie slid into the passenger seat. "Get out of here!"

"The only part of Lizzie that isn't stock is the seat belts. Buckle up."

Stevie soon held on to the seat as Toni sped south on the Causeway.

"Girl, you're going to get us arrested," she said.

"The police don't arrest pretty girls who aren't drunk or drugged," Toni said.

"White girls, maybe," Stevie said. "It's a fact you'll never get a DWB."

"What's that?" Toni asked.

They both laughed when Stevie said, "Driving While Black."

Stevie shook her head, not answering when Toni said, "You're joking, aren't you?"

"I live in an apartment on Conti, in the Quarter. We can leave your truck parked in front and walk from there."

"You know where this place is?" Toni asked.

"The Keepers operate out of a little shop on Royal Street. They sell voodoo paraphernalia to tourists in the front. In the back, they conduct ceremonies and initiations. It's where Bobby got his Baron Samedi tattoo."

"How do we get invited into the back?" Toni asked.

"We could both use a couple of shots of vodka to calm our nerves though I doubt we'll have any trouble getting an invite into the back room."

"There's a liquor store at the end of the Causeway," Toni said.

There is no shortage of liquor stores in New Orleans. Toni pulled up to the door of a wood-frame standalone building topped by a neon sign that said liquor.

"Stay here," Toni said. "I hate vodka. I'll get tequila instead."

She soon returned with a fifth of tequila and a six-pack of Abita Beer.

"We don't want to be out of control, just loose enough to convey that appearance," Stevie said.

Toni opened the bottle of tequila and made a face when she took a swig. "We don't have to drink it all," she said.

Foam spewed out of the can when Toni popped the top of one of the cans of Abita and chased the tequila with it.

"We'll be drunk on our asses before we get there," Stevie said.

"You were the one who suggested the tequila, not me," Toni said.

Stevie was shaking her head as she slugged a tequila shot and then finished Toni's tequila.

"We'll park your truck in front of my apartment and walk to the voodoo shop. The beer can go in the fridge."

Toni had another shot of tequila and an Abita chaser before starting the truck. Stevie was glaring at her when she turned around.

"What?" Toni said.

"I didn't mean for us to get shit-faced. We need to keep our wits about us, and you're already drunk. You can't hold your liquor."

"Because I don't drink," Toni said.

"Then what the hell do you think you're doing?"

"I won't blow our cover," Toni said. "I'm Italian and have a large tolerance for alcohol."

"My ass!" Stevie said. "You've already had too much. Don't take another drink. My apartment is just a few blocks from here."

Stevie knew Toni was well lubricated when she slid to a stop at her apartment."

"What?" Toni said when she saw Stevie staring at her.

"You're drunk. Give me the bottle," Stevie said.

Toni took another drink of the tequila, followed by more cold beer before handing the bottle to Stevie. Stevie shook her head.

"You need to sleep it off in my apartment. I'll take care of things from here."

Toni hiccupped. "I'm good to go. I promise."

"Sure about that?

"I'll let you do the talking," she said.

The voodoo shop on Royal wasn't far from

Stevie's apartment. It still took longer than expected. Toni kept giggling and leaning on Stevie's shoulder."

"You sure you're okay?" Stevie said.

"Do you have the crystal?"

"I've got it," Stevie said.

The voodoo shop was similar to the many other voodoo shops in the French Quarter. The smell of burning sage accosted their senses, Linda Ronstadt and Aaron Neville singing a duet from speakers hidden somewhere amid the crowded rows of voodoo paraphernalia. Toni's eyes grew wide when she saw the African death masks and pin-pierced voodoo dolls.

"This place is creepy," she said.

"Have another shot of tequila," Stevie said.

"I'm okay. I won't screw things up."

"Good, because someone's coming over."

The little man with a pencil mustache had a Midwestern accent and didn't look like he knew anything about voodoo.

"We got a special today on voodoo dolls," he said.

"A friend told us we could meet Baron Samedi here," Stevie said.

"Did they?" the little man said. "What's your friend's name?" he asked.

"Bruno," she said. "I don't know his last name. He's a performer."

"Wait here," the man said. "Be right back."

When the little man disappeared around a row of herbs and roots packaged in cellophane, Stevie grabbed Toni's hand.

"You okay?" she asked.

"I think I need to throw up," Toni said.

"I'll find you a bathroom."

The little man returned before Stevie could make good on her promise. He was smiling as he rubbed his hands together.

"Come with me," he said.

Pop music disappeared, morphing into African drumming when Toni and Stevie passed through the door in the back. A group of bare-chested men aligned in a circle played the drums. Observers, swaying to the music, sat on the floor in a semicircle. Their eyes were glazed, and they all seemed high on something. Stevie grabbed Toni's forearm and found a place to sit amid the circle of observers.

"I need to find a bathroom," Toni said.

A young woman in a flowing, flower-print dress didn't stop swaying when she pointed to an exit sign. Stevie helped Toni to her feet and into the nearby bathroom, waiting outside the stall to the sound of Toni throwing up into the toilet. Toni had no color in her cheeks when she exited the stall.

"I'm sick," she said.

Stevie helped her to the exit and into the alleyway behind the voodoo shop.

"You can sleep it off in my bed," she said.

Cyril and Cyrus, the Casseus twins, were at the Keeper's meeting. Cyril glanced up from the ongoing ceremony when Stevie and Toni came out of the bathroom.

"That's Bobby Blanchard's girlfriend," he said.

Cyrus watched the two women as they headed for the exit.

"Shit! Look who she's with," he said.

"Who?"

"The bitch in the old truck that gave us wrong directions the night we tried to take Blanchard from the Bell House."

"Sure about that?"

"You kidding? She's beautiful. I don't forget faces like that. Let's go after them before they get away."

255

Stevie and Toni were halfway up Bourbon Street when Cyril and Cyrus exited the alleyway. The chilly morning had turned sunny, and dozens of tourists lined the sidewalks on both sides of the streets. Drunken revelers were common on Bourbon Street, and no one seemed to notice Stevie helping Toni up the sidewalk. Cyril grabbed his brother's arm.

"They're headed toward the bitch's apartment on Conti. We'll meet them there and have some fun before we take them to Mirlande's. The blond is so drunk we won't even have to inject her."

"I don't know," Cyrus said. "You know what happened last time we did something Mirlande told us not to do."

"She's not here and will never know," Cyril said. "Grow a set of balls."

"Don't know about you. I like my balls and don't want to end up another eunuch in Mirlande's harem."

"Mirlande is our sister. She wouldn't cut off her little brothers' balls."

"You kidding? She'll do it herself and enjoy every minute of it," Cyrus said.

"Let's get the car. The apartment has no eyes, and we can worry about what we do once we get there," Cyril said.

⊰⊱

A young man in an L.S.U. sweatshirt didn't bother saying sorry when he bumped into Stevie and Toni. Stevie got a better grip around Toni's waist and pushed ahead without responding.

"I'm okay," she said. "Let's go back to the meeting."

"You can barely walk, dribble coming out of your mouth, and you're slurring your words. I'll take care of the Keepers after I put you to bed."

Toni was too drunk to argue, and it took them twenty minutes to reach the entrance to

Stevie's apartment. She didn't notice the two men exiting the black B.M.W. The twins reached the heavy door before it rotated back on its hinges and slammed shut. They waited halfway up the stairs as Stevie opened the door to her apartment. She didn't bother locking it as she dragged Toni to her bed. After removing her shoes, she pulled the covers up around her neck. Toni's eyes were closed when Cyrus and Cyril entered the bedroom.

Stevie was unaware someone had followed her into the apartment until Cyril put his hand over her mouth.

"Just a little pinch," Cyrus said as he injected the zombie drug into her veins.

Cyril and Cyrus weren't the only ones on the second floor of the apartments. Harvey and Bruno were walking up from work, still dressed in drag, when they saw Cyrus and Cyril slip through the lower door. The two twins entered Stevie's apartment as Harvey and Bruno reached the top of the stairs.

"What the hell?" Bruno said.

They entered the bedroom in time to see Cyrus injecting Stevie with a hypodermic needle. Bruno and Harvey watched Stevie slump to the floor before reacting.

Bruno dropped to his knees and placed a finger on Stevie's carotid artery. Harvey grabbed Cyrus's wrist holding the needle with one hand, wheeling him around with the other. He dispensed of him with a vicious head butt. Harvey grabbed Cyril's hair, yanking it back until his neck snapped and he dropped to the floor along with Stevie and Cyrus.

"She's dead," he said. "These fuckers killed her. Better call 9-1-1."

"What if she's not dead?" Harvey said.

"I have a nursing degree. Don't you think I know if someone's dead or not?"

"You thought Bobby was dead. According to Stevie's friends at the bar, he was zombied. We saw Philip at the Keeper's meeting. These two could have zombied Stevie."

"Maybe. What do you suggest we do?"

"Call the detective we met at Bertram's," Harvey said. "I'm going to check the bedroom."

Harvey stuck his head through the door and saw Toni passed out beneath the covers.

"What?" Bruno said.

"We have a woman I don't recognize in Stevie's bed."

Bruno dialed Tony's number, and he answered on the second ring.

"Tony Nicosia, here. How can I help you?"

"It's Bruno. You and Mama Mulate met me and Harvey at Bertram's bar. We're Stevie Jones's neighbors."

"What you got, Bruno?"

"We're in Stevie's apartment. We were returning home from rehearsal as two men were attacking Stevie."

"Is she okay?"

"She looks dead to me though Harvey seems to think she's only zombied."

"Do you recognize the two men?"

"They're the twins with Philip the night Bobby had his problem. Want me to call the cops?"

"Are the twins alive?" Tony asked.

"Unconscious but alive," Bruno said.

"Tie them up. Don't call the police. I'm not far away and will be there in a few minutes. Hang tight until I do."

"Tony, there's another woman here we don't recognize."

"Is she zombied, too?"

"Passed out drunk in Stevie's bed," Bruno

258

said.

"Don't call the cops. Be there in a few," Tony said.

"What'd he say?" Harvey asked.

"He'll be here in a few minutes, and you can ask him yourself. Find something we can use to tie up these two goons."

Harvey found a roll of light-duty rope in one of Stevie's cabinets, and Cyril and Cyrus were soon bound and sitting upright in the corner of the apartment, beginning to regain consciousness when Tony burst through the door.

Lil, Candy, and Zane accompanied Tony. Lil knelt beside Stevie and tried to take her pulse.

"Tony, she's dead," she said.

"She ain't dead," Tony said.

Lil glanced at Bruno and said, "I'm Lil, Tony's wife."

She backed up when Bruno replied in his deep voice, "I'm Bruno."

Candy Daigle had an ear-to-ear grin on her face. "Bruno and Harvey headline the best drag show in the universe at the Purple Emporium."

"Sorry," Lil said.

"No problem," Bruno said, "Happy to meet you, Lil. Harvey and I already know Candy and Zane."

"Any idea who the two gents tied up in the corner are?" Tony asked.

"Cyril and Cyrus Casseus," Candy said. "Mirlande Casseus's little brothers."

"What now?" Zane asked.

"Don't know," Tony said. "Let me call Wyatt."

Chapter 31

For the first time in my life, I enjoyed being a father. Aimee's head rested on my shoulder as we occupied one of Freya's overstuffed couches and watched television. Aimee's eyes opened when my cell phone rang. It was Tony Nicosia.

Freya appeared from the kitchen when she heard my phone ringing.

"Who is it?" she asked.

"My partner, Tony. Stevie's been zombied, and Toni's passed out drunk. Stevie's neighbors have captured her assailants."

"That it?" she asked.

"Candy Daigle and Zane Fleming, the two greatest Big Easy investigative reporters of all times, are with them, along with Tony's wife, Lil."

"Give them directions and tell them to join us," Freya said.

"You sure?" you already have a houseful of guests," I said.

"I'm good with it. The Tracking Stone is useless to us since Stevie and Toni didn't make it into the plantation. I have a feeling someone in our group will provide a solution to the conundrum."

"Hope you're right," I said as I punched

260

Tony's number on my cell phone.

Aimee heard us talking and rubbed her eyes. "What's a Locator Stone?" she asked.

"Something we witches and other magicians use to locate people and keep tabs on them."

"Stones have powers?"

"Yes, baby," Freya said. "The quartz crystal I gave Stevie could communicate with my quartz crystal. It would have helped us contact Mama Mulate."

Aimee fingered her black onyx necklace around her neck. "Mama said I would always be safe as long as I keep this stone around my neck."

Aimee nodded when Freya said, "Mama Mulate gave it to you?"

"This one belonged to her grandmother. She wears its twin. Will it help us?"

Freya hugged Aimee and said, "Hell, yes it will! If you'll let me borrow it, I promise I'll take good care of it."

Aimee removed the necklace from around her neck and handed it to Freya. "I trust you."

"Thanks, baby. Tonight, the Covington Coven will free Mama Mulate and get the antidote."

The sky over Pontchartrain had darkened when Tony and his entourage arrived from the city. The crowd was eclectic: a crime boss, his wife, and daughter; two French Quarter private dicks and a long-suffering wife; a pop star, her mother and daughter; and two drag queens in costume.

There was also Candy Daigle and Zane Fleming, both of whom I'd long admired. Tony and his crew had also brought the two prisoners who we locked in the basement. Stevie lay on the bed beside Bobby and caused a disturbance when Senator Robert Blanchard and his wife Alice arrived.

Alice Blanchard stood an inch taller than her distinguished husband, with long, peroxide blond hair draping her shoulders.

"Can we see Bobby?" she said.

"I'll take you," I said.

Aimee went upstairs with me to the bedroom where Bobby and Stevie lay. Alice, Robert, Frankie, and Adele followed us through the door. When Alice saw her son's lifeless body, she crossed her arms tightly across her chest and started to cry.

"Why is that woman on the bed with Bobby?" she asked.

No one answered until Aimee said, "Because they love each other."

"Interracial relationships never work," Alice said.

"Not true," Aimee said. "My Grandmother is black, my mother Creole, and my dad white. I have no clue what I am, though I know we're all people."

"You can't know how I feel," Alice said.

Aimee took her hand. "We're from Louisiana. We know about broken hearts."

Alice began to cry when she hugged Aimee. "My poor son," she said.

"He can hear every word you're saying," Aimee said. "Take him in your arms and tell him how much you love him. It'll make all the difference in the world."

Alice reclined on the bed and put her arms around Bobby. Adele joined her.

"He's going to be fine," Frankie said. "I promise you we'll get him the antidote."

Alice moved to the other side of the bed and put her hand on Stevie's face.

"I don't know if you can hear me. If Bobby loves you, then so do I."

Adele ushered us out of the room. "Let's give

262

them some space. I'm worried about my daughter."

Toni's over-indulgence had worn off, and we found her sitting in the kitchen, Pancho preparing her a hangover cocktail.

"This will make you feel better," he said.

Toni made a face when she tasted Pancho's concoction. "Horrible!" she said. "What's in it?"

"If I told you, it wouldn't be a secret," Pancho said.

"I get the tomato juice," she said.

"One ingredient of many," Pancho said.

"Tell me."

"No way," Pancho said. "I'll put the formula in my will for you."

"You're not dying anytime soon. I might need more before then."

"Then I'll be here to help," Pancho said.

Zane Fleming and Candy Daigle smiled as they enjoyed bloody marys and listened to Toni and her grandfather's banter. Aimee hadn't left my side as we approached the table.

I'm Wyatt Thomas, and this is my daughter, Aimee."

"Join us," Zane said.

Candy shook Aimee's hand. "You know you have a famous relative, don't you."

"You mean my dad?" Aimee asked.

"Your great-granddad was governor of Louisiana many years ago," Candy said. "Sit by me."

I pulled up a chair beside Zane at the plank table. "You are heroes of mine. I miss reading your articles."

"High praise coming from the grandson of Louisiana's most notorious governor," Zane said. "What all did he teach you?"

Zane and Candy smiled when I said, "How to dodge questions I don't want to answer."

"Touché," Candy said.

"What's the story of the two men we have locked in the basement?" I asked.

"Cyril and Cyrus Casseus," Zane said. "Tony didn't want to call the cops."

"They would have bonded out in an hour," Candy said. "Bringing them with us keeps Mirlande in the dark."

"Smart," I said.

"What's your plan?"

"Witchcraft," I said.

"You're joking, right?" Candy said.

"Freya is the head witch of the Covington Coven. She thinks we can use magic to free Mama Mulate. I have no better plan."

"What do you think, Aimee?" Candy asked.

Aimee showed Candy the Locator Stone around her neck. "Mama Mulate gave me this black onyx necklace. Freya said it's magical. I believe her."

Candy introduced everyone when Harvey and Bruno, still dressed in costume, joined us.

"This is Scarlet Johannesburg and Norma Jean Goldenstein," she said. "Stars of the best drag revue in the Quarter."

Tony and the others soon occupied Freya's plank table. Frankie became involved in a heated conversation with Zane. Everyone's conversations ended when Pancho served wine and his famous pepperoni pizza. Soon, members of the Covington Coven began arriving. They went straight to a room in the large house without bothering with introductions.

Freya joined us and said, "Enjoy. At midnight, you'll witness the Locator Ceremony; something non-witches rarely, if ever, have a chance to see. Until then, make yourselves comfortable here in the kitchen or the living room."

"I have a few questions," Candy said.

"No questions. Remain in the kitchen with Pancho if you can't comply. Agree by answering either yes or no."

"Yes," everyone said.

"Aimee, I'll need your help. Are you okay consorting with witches?"

"I'm not okay with it," Lashonda said.

"Aimee clasped her grandmother's hand and said, "Please?"

"Well. . ." Lashonda said.

The older woman's eyes told Aimee it was okay. After a hearty hug, she followed Freya out of the kitchen and down a darkened hallway.

❧

The rest of us spent the next few hours exchanging small talk.

"The priest won't be happy when I confess to attending a witch's ceremony," Lil said.

Lil gave Tony a dirty look when he said, "

"Then don't tell him," he said.

"Is that what you do?" Lil asked.

"You can wait in the kitchen with Pancho," he said.

Tony didn't answer when she said, "Have you ever attended a ceremony like this?"

Latitia touched Lil's wrist. "It's okay. Mom and I also have a problem getting our heads around this ceremony. If it weren't for Aimee, we'd both skip it."

"I don't mind telling you I'm a bit frightened," Josie Castellano said. "Adele?"

"I'm more than apprehensive, though I'll go where Frankie goes."

Frankie had a crazy look in his eyes. "What's the matter, Papa?" Josie asked.

"When I was ten, my family returned to Sicily for a few months to visit relatives. I watched a priest perform an exorcism. It still gives me

265

nightmares."

"I saw my mother's ghost the day after she died," Harvey said. "She kissed my forehead and told me she loved me."

"You've never told me that story," Bruno said.

"Because no one ever believes it when I tell them," Harvey said. "I started doubting it was real myself."

"Was it?" Zane asked.

"Very real," Harvey said.

"Most of the people I knew and loved are dead now," Candy said. "They converse with me in dreams I only half remember in the morning."

"Let's stop talking about it," Adele said. "We're accomplishing nothing except scaring ourselves."

Alice Blanchard was as pale as a ghost, her hands trembling.

"I'll stay with you if you decide to skip the ceremony," Robert Blanchard said.

"We have to go," she said. "Bobby's life may depend on it."

"What about you, Zane?" Candy said. "Do you have a story?"

"I live in an ancient house in the Quarter. One night I was reading when the tortured sound of a young person in pain shook me to the bone. Though whatever or whoever made the sound couldn't have been more than ten feet from me, my dog, asleep at my feet, never awoke."

An old grandfather clock behind us chimed twelve times. A woman none of us recognized appeared from the dark hallway.

"It's time," she said. "Come with me."

We followed her to a circular room with a row of chairs, where we took seats. The floor was bare wood, with nineteen marks encircling a flat surface podium. The room was otherwise empty. When Alice started to speak, the woman who had directed us to our seats shook her head and put a finger to her lips. She returned to the darkness of the hallway. Because of the strange acoustics of the room, the door made no sound when she shut it behind her.

There were no visible lights in the room though an ephemeral radiance allowed us to see. The light danced in slow, green waves, transfixing my thoughts and those around me. There was absolutely no sound.

Someone dressed in a dark robe entered the circular room from a door covered with a black curtain I hadn't noticed. A loose hood covered their face. Though I didn't know for sure, I assumed it was probably Freya. With rapt attention, we watched her walk to the circle's center and approach the podium.

An unlit black candle appeared in her palms. When she lifted her arms to the ceiling, the candle ignited. As she lowered her arms, another dark-robed woman appeared from behind the black curtain. After taking the lighted candle from Freya, she moved slowly in a counter-clockwise direction until she returned to the top of the circle.

The procession of dark-robed women continued, each circumnavigating the circle and then handing the candle to another woman who circled in the opposite direction. Soon, nineteen dark-robed women were rotating in opposite directions from Freya standing at the podium. The women took stationary positions when Freya began a rhyming chant.

Detect, discover.
Unearth, uncover,
Occur, appear.
Attain, draw near.

After repeating the verse three times, someone else exited the black curtain. It was

Aimee dressed in a dark robe without a hood. The hands of both Lashonda and Latitia went to their mouths.

Aimee walked to the center of the circle and faced the woman standing there. Two black candles were in her palms, one lighted and the other unlit. When she extended her arms, the unlit candle ignited in a flame, kissing the ceiling, followed by smoke covering Aimee and Freya. The black onyx pendant around her neck began to glow when the smoke dissipated.

I couldn't believe my eyes as a holographic image looking like a scene from 1,001 Arabian Nights began filling the center of the circle. It took me a moment before I could see Mama Mulate.

Chapter 32

Mama Mulate turned away from Jimmy Ray Douciere when a young woman, barely dressed in a pink nightgown, entered the red door. The young woman exited with a smile on her face. It seemed she was more interested in arranging a sexual encounter with Jimmy Ray than getting fitted with a new seductive costume. She'd kissed him when he agreed to spend the night with her.

It was Jimmy Ray's turn to smile when Mama said, "My, oh my! Aren't you the popular one?"

"Not much competition here in the harem," he said. "You think you can get me a tryout with the Pels?"

"I promised, didn't I?"

"I don't need guarantees, only a chance," he said.

"I'll help you get your foot in the door," Mama said. "The rest is up to you, though if you can score baskets the way you do women, you'll be an all-star your first year,"

"Easier than getting the hell out of this place. It's an armed fortress."

"You've thought about it," Mama said.

"Some of the guards have cars," he said. "I'll have to steal one."

"You know how to do that?" Mama asked.

"Hell, Professor Mulate. I stole my first car when I was ten years old."

"I don't want to hear about it. I don't condone thievery," Mama said.

"Make up your mind," he said. "We can't walk out of this place."

"One last time, then," Mama said. "You'll have to promise me it'll be your last car theft."

"I promise."

"I can tell by the smirk on your face you're lying, Jimmy Ray."

"You don't survive on the street for long without knowing how to lie and steal."

Jimmy Ray smiled when Mama said, "You need to go into politics."

"I'll get us a car and hide it near here," Jimmy Ray said. "What then?"

"Have a gun?" Mama asked.

"Do we need one?"

"What we need is a diversion to cause confusion and cover our escape."

"I'll think of something," Jimmy Ray said.

When more women arrived at the wardrobe room, Mama gave Jimmy Ray a wink.

"Looks as if your business is picking up. I'll be somewhere in the harem," she said.

Mama bumped into Vixen when she exited the wardrobe room. At first, the young woman didn't recognize her.

When she did, she said, "Mama, is that you?"

"It's me, baby," Mama said.

"You look beautiful and so exotic."

"No time for small talk. Do you know Jimmy Ray Douciere?"

"Me and every other female in the harem," Vixen said. "If Mirlande knew he wasn't fixed, she'd kill him and all of us along with him."

"I can't believe she hasn't already found out,"

Mama said.

"Who's going to tell her?" Vixen said.

"Guess you're right about that," Mama said.

Neither Mama nor Vixen heard someone approaching from behind until Mirlande rested her hand on their shoulders. Jimmy Ray peeked from behind the red door, seeing what was happening.

"Well, look what I've found. Two of the most beautiful women in my harem," she said. "Might be fun to choose the two of you for my bed tonight."

Vixen fondled one of Mirlande's breasts. "We don't need her," she said. "Aren't I more than a handful?"

"You are one of my favorites, my lovely," Mirlande said. "I'm the Sultana and can have more than one pretty in my bed at a time."

Mirlande smiled when Vixen said, "You are all-powerful, Sultana, and can do whatever you wish."

"Right about that," Mirlande said. "Mama Mulate hasn't quite yet accepted her situation. Tonight, I will instruct her, and you will help me."

Vixen kissed her lightly and said, "I can hardly wait."

Mirlande's smile disappeared as she turned her attention to Mama.

"How did you enjoy being dead, my lovely?" she said.

"Horrible," Mama said. "I was praying you wouldn't leave me in limbo forever."

"Was it enough to convince you to join forces with me?"

"I'm ready. I fantasized about you while I was zombied," Mama said. "There is nothing I would rather do than help you every way I can and pleasure you and myself."

"You're a bad liar," Mirlande said. "Doesn't matter. You will be mine before the night is over."

"I'm ready now," Mama said.

"I don't think so," Mirlande said. "Tonight, you, I, and Vixen will realize the ultimate sexual nirvana."

The harem's concubines watched as Mirlande led Mama and Vixen to one of Mirlande's zombies. Mama winced as the he yanked her hands around her back and put handcuffs on them. Vixen had a horrified look on her face when Mama gave her a wink.

"Why are you cuffing me?" Mama said.

Mirlande didn't turn around as she started down the hallway.

"I talk. You listen," she said.

Mirlande's sudden display of anger worried Mama as the zombie gave her a push in the back.

The harem was spectacular. Mirlande's bedroom was like something out of an erotic fantasy, the bed large enough for a dozen people, a steaming pool of water occupying the center of the room.

"Do you like my boudoir?" she asked.

"Spectacular," Mama said. "Uncuff me, and I'll show you some love."

"Not quite yet," Mirlande said. "I'm going to take a dip in my hot tub."

Mirlande's clothes dropped to the floor before she stepped into the hot water.

Mirlande's smile disappeared when she said, "Strip her."

With her hands cuffed behind her back, Mama could only close her eyes as a zombie ripped off her clothes.

"Why are you doing this?" Mama asked. "I'm ready to be your slave. What must I do for you to believe me?"

"You'll get your answer before long," Mirlande said.

Through a door, Mirlande's son Philip appeared. As the zombie held the cuffs securing Mama, Philip rubbed his hand down her naked body.

"I still have a goose egg on my head where you hit me with the baseball bat," he said.

"You're lucky I didn't kill you," Mama said.

"I'm in no danger of that happening again," Philip said.

Philip wasn't the only naked person preparing to join Mirlande in the water. An older white man and a younger white woman tiptoed into the hot water.

Mirlande smiled at her son and said, "Join me. We have all night to deal with the deceitful mambo."

Philip faced Mirlande, then wheeled around and slapped Mama so hard she sank to her knees. Mirlande laughed.

"Resign yourself, Mama Mulate. Before the night ends, you'll please Philip and me and be happy to do it."

"I'll do it now," Mama said. "Free my hands."

Mirlande nodded to a zombie who unlocked the cuffs. As Mama massaged her wrists, trying to restore feeling, Vixen knelt beside her.

"You okay?" she asked.

Mama nodded and said, "Who are the two white people?"

"Arthur Wayne Pompeo, the person who owns this plantation with Mirlande, and his daughter, Pearl," Vixen said. "He's more than a hundred years old."

"He doesn't look over sixty," Mama said.

"He has the hands of a dead man," Vixen said. "Skeletal and covered with coarse hair. Brace yourself because he likes to touch."

The two naked couples were already groping each other in the hot pool of water.

"Good God almighty!" Mama said. "I've died and gone to hell."

Vixen gave Mama a perplexed glance when Mirlande said, "Get naked and join us. We'll have you first."

Mama clutched Vixen's hand, keeping her from descending into the hot water.

"Don't go. Make up an excuse," Mama said.

"I have no choice," Vixen said.

Mama's heart was racing, the black onyx pendant around her neck pulsating.

"Something bad is about to happen," Mama said. "Don't get in the water."

"I have to go to the bathroom," Vixen said.

"Then hurry," Mirlande said. "Join us, Mama."

"My wrists hurt," Mama said.

"One thing you will learn before the night is over," Mirlande said. "Pain is better than death. You might even decide you like it."

⊱⊰

The witch's ceremony was like nothing I'd ever imagined. There was no sound, no secret language. Every movement seemed like a choreographed dance. Aimee's black onyx pendant was glowing bright red and pulsating. The nineteen witches drew closer and clasped hands. As one, they moved to the center of the circle. When they reached it, they raised their arms, along with Aimee and the head witch, toward the ceiling. Flames burst from their

274

extended fingers. My heart was pounding, and for a moment, I thought the house would catch fire and burn to the ground.

Mirlande, Philip, Arthur, and Pearl Pompeo were groping each other in the hot tub. Their smiles disappeared, replaced by the looks of horror when the water began bubbling, steam filling the room. Mirlande shrieked, almost passing out from the pain before crawling out of the water and collapsing on the rug. Philip wasn't so lucky, his eyes bulging in disbelief as he sank beneath the boiling water.

"Pull him out!" Mirlande cried.

A eunuch grabbed Philip by his hair, yanked him out of the boiling water, and laid him beside Mirlande. He also pulled Pearl from the hot tub that had become a boiling cauldron. Arthur, his skin lobster red, wasn't so lucky. He floated on his back, his eyes closed, in the bubbling water.

The violent scene had left the eunuchs, zombies, and concubines in disarray. Mirlande managed to raise her head off the rug and point at Mama.

"She did this. Kill her"

Before the guards or zombies could react, Jimmie Ray Douciere burst through the door. Yanking a spear out of a guard's hands, he began swinging it in an ever-expanding pendulum. Mama's pendant continued to glow as she got to her feet and ran to the door. Jimmy Ray followed her.

"There's an exit behind you," he said. "Let's get the hell out of here."

"Not without Vixen," she said. "Where's the bathroom."

"Near the exit," he said.

When they found the bathroom door locked, Mama said, "Vixen. Let me in."

Jimmy motioned Mama to get out of the way and then kicked the door off its hinges. Vixen was in tears, on her knees. Mama grabbed her arm.

"No time for tears," she said. "We're blowing this place."

Mama pulled Vixen to her feet and out the bathroom door. Jimmy was facing the opposite direction, swinging the spear as guards and zombie's tried to subdue him. Mama let go of Vixen's hand and hurried to his side, pointing the black onyx pendant at the attackers. They ran when a burst of flame strafed the hallway.

"What the hell?" Jimmy said.

"Magic," Mama said, directing him toward the exit sign,

A vintage lime-green Dodge Charger, the motor rumbling, waited outside the exit door.

"Get in," Jimmy Ray said.

Mama pulled Vixen into the old muscle car, grabbing the seat when Jimmy Ray cranked the engine and hit the accelerator. Bullets began ricocheting off of the vehicle. Losing control for a moment, Jimmy Ray held on as the Charger did a three-sixty before straightening and heading for the front gate.

"Someone's shooting at us," Mama said.

"No shit!" Jimmy Ray said. "Stay down."

"We have to get the antidote," Mama said.

"No time," Jimmy Ray said.

"Make time," Mama said. "I'm not leaving without it. Take us to the warehouse."

Jimmy quickly outran the armed men pursuing them and spun to a stop in front of the giant warehouse where Mama had lain zombied. Mama found the door open. Lights glowed in the kitchen though it was on the opposite end of the warehouse

Mama's voice echoed when she called, "Jolene! It's Mama. Bring me the antidote."

Jolene heard her and came running, meeting her in the middle of the empty warehouse with a bottle of antidote. Mama grabbed her shoulders.

"Bad shit's going down! Get back in the kitchen and get under something," Mama said.

Jolene nodded, turned, and sprinted back to the kitchen. Jimmy was waiting outside the door.

"The main entrance is blocked," he said. "We'll have to get out of here some other way."

"What other way?" Mama said.

"There's a dirt road on the other side of the river berm. Hang the hell on! I'm going to jump it."

Bullets were flying, and a dozen vehicles converged on them as Jimmy gunned the engine, spun the tires, and sped away. Mama had no idea how fast they were going when the Charger hit the berm at an oblique angle. The car flipped, flew over the ridge, and landed on its wheels. Under power, they fishtailed to the blacktop.

"Didn't know you had a pilot's license," Mama said.

"Which way?" Jimmy Ray said.

"Take a right," Mama said.

Jimmy Ray didn't slow the Charger for ten miles down the road. Mama finally patted his knee, smiled, and gave him a high five.

"Screw the NBA," she said. "I think you have a real shot driving in NASCAR."

Chapter 33

No one in the circular room uttered a sound as we watched the flames shooting from the witches' extended fingers. When the blaze dissipated, they lowered their arms as one, clenched hands, backed out of the center of the circle, and returned to their starting positions. The witch closest to the black curtain had one of the candles in her hands, its flame extinguished.

One-by-one, they began exiting the room, returning to the black curtain after circling the room in a clockwise direction. Soon, only Freya and Aimee remained in the circle's center. When the last witch walked through the curtain, Aimee snuffed the remaining candle and ran to her grandmother's arms.

"What now?" I asked.

"It's over," Aimee said. "Mama is free and has the antidote."

"How do you know that?" Lashonda said.

Aimee grinned and said, "I know."

"All I know is I need a drink," Frankie said.

"You and me both," Tony said.

We followed Aimee out of the circular room to the kitchen, where we found Freya sitting at the plank table, her head in her hands as Pancho massaged her shoulders.

"You okay?" I asked.

Freya smiled and said, "Except for the knots in my neck and a splitting headache."

"Were you the head witch?"

"Ask me no questions," she said. "I can tell you Mama Mulate is on her way here."

"Aimee told us. How does she know where we are?" I asked.

"She has the twin of Aimee's Locator Stone. The black onyx stones served us well. Mirlande, Philip, and Pearl were boiled alive and are on their way to a hospital. Arthur Pompeo is dead, the plantation in chaos."

Reports of gunshots and explosions at the Faumort Plantation were coming into the police. Tony called Tommy Blackburn, remaining silent as Tommy gave him a lengthy report. Like Frankie and Robert Blanchard, Candy Daigle and Zane Fleming were also on their phones. The stories they heard were all similar to what Freya had told them: Mirlande, Philip, and Pearl Pompeo were on their way to a nearby hospital with severe burns.

"I have an aide working with a judge to obtain a search warrant," Robert said. "The Faumort Plantation will soon be swarming with the Louisiana State Police Bureau of Investigation, the FBI, and the US Marshals Service. It'll prevent local shenanigans from attempting to cover up this mess."

"The bar is open," Freya said. "Pancho's making me a bloody mary, though I have anything you may want in my liquor cabinet."

Pancho laid out bottles and mixers on the kitchen cabinet. Frankie and Tony were smiling as they took advantage of Freya's offer.

"Don't mind if I do," Tony said. "I'll play bartender. Can I get you anything, Sweetheart?"

"Vodka," Lil said. "Straight."

The open bar soon took the edge off of everyone, even Lil. Everyone except Freya and Pancho convened in the living room. Pancho made me a pitcher of lemonade, and I sat beside Freya.

"You sure you're okay?" I asked.

"Witching takes it out of you," she said. "I'll survive."

"Where are all the other witches?"

"Gone home. Most of them have to work tomorrow."

"What do they do?" I asked.

"School teachers, librarians, secretaries, you name it. Witches have a bad reputation, although everyone I know is salt of the earth and there when you need them."

"The ceremony was so complex. How did you learn to do all that?"

"Witching is something you don't learn overnight. I apprenticed with one of the best. After all these years, I'm still learning."

When a car with a loud motor pulled up out front, I squeezed Freya's hand and said, "Thank you."

"I'll be fine," she said. "Go join your partner."

Mama, a very tall man, and a beautiful young woman were coming through the front door. They were all dressed in colorful and revealing costumes. The first person Mama saw was Aimee. Pushing through the crowd of welcoming people, she went straight to her and gave her a big hug.

Aimee smiled when Mama said, "Baby, you saved my life."

Following introductions, Jimmy Ray Douciere handed Mama a one-liter bottle filled with something other than soda.

"You might want this," he said.

"Where are Stevie and Bobby?" Mama asked.

"Upstairs," Alice said. "I'll show you."

"This could be disturbing," Mama said. "You might want to wait downstairs."

"I'm coming with you," Alice said.

Robert Blanchard and I followed them to the bedroom where Stevie and Bobby lay comatose. We watched as Mama dribbled antidote into Stevie's and Bobby's mouths. They both awoke with a start, pained expressions on their faces as they threw up on the sides of the bed. Neither of them smiled until they'd washed their faces with the washcloths I brought from the bathroom. The first thing Bobby and Stevie did after that was to embrace each other.

"Baby, you saved my butt," Bobby said.

"This is Mama Mulate," Stevie said. "She was my English Lit professor when I was at Tulane. She saved both our butts."

Bobby glanced at Mama's harem costume and said, "Is it Mardi Gras?"

"Seeing the two of you alive, it feels like it."

Bobby's mom and dad stood in the open doorway. When Bobby saw them, he got out of bed and hugged his mother.

"Mom, what are you and Dad doing here?"

"We were told you were dead. We never believed it," Alice said. "I'm so happy."

"Mom and Dad, this is Stevie Jones. I'm the luckiest man in the world to have you and Dad as parents and Stevie as the woman I love."

Mama was ignorant of the conflict between Alice and Stevie. I wasn't and waited for an angry reaction from her. It didn't happen as Alice hurried to the bed and embraced Stevie. In a moment, they were both crying.

Bobby's mom and dad weren't the only ones standing outside the door. Zane Fleming and

Candy Daigle entered the bedroom, Zane pumping Bobby's hand.

"Mr. Fleming. What are you doing here?"

"Bobby, this is Candy Daigle, one of the best journalists ever to grace a newspaper in Louisiana."

Candy shook Bobby's hand and said, "Way before your time."

"You kidding me? I learned all about you in a journalism class at L.S.U."

"Jesus!" Candy said. "Now, I do feel old."

"You can't imagine how honored I am to have two Pulitzer Prize recipients visit me."

"When you break this story, you'll have your chance at fame," Zane said.

"You can't believe the amount of research I've done on this project," Bobby said.

"If you need help, Zane and I are here for you," Candy said.

"You mean it?" Bobby said.

"It's your story, not ours," she said.

"I don't mind sharing," he said.

I was the last person the leave the bedroom, all the others heading downstairs to enjoy Freya's hospitality. Toni was waiting at the stairs.

"What's the deal with the gloomy expression?" I said.

"I feel like an idiot," she said.

"For what reason?"

"I've made a fool of myself."

"You kidding me? We'd have never resolved this case without you, not to mention you risked life and limb on more than one occasion."

"Thank you," she said. "It's more than that."

"Tell me," I said.

"All this time, I thought you were attracted to me. Seeing you react with Latitia, Mama and Freya, I realize now I was fooling myself."

"You must be blind," I said.

282

"What do you mean?"

"Latitia is an ex, Mama, a business associate."

I grinned when she said, "What about Freya?"

"When it comes to sex, Freya is a supernatural being. She has cravings and needs far more than an average human. She used me, and I let her. She's a remarkable woman but whatever we had between us is gone."

"Sure about that?" she said.

"Did you see the way Pancho was massaging Freya's shoulders? They're a number, now."

"Should I be worried for Pancho?"

"Hell!" I said. "Pancho should be worried and not you."

"I'm so sorry I misjudged our relationship," Toni said.

"I must have the best poker face in the world," I said.

"Why is that?" Toni asked.

"I've had a thing for you since we first met at your mom's restaurant in Metairie."

I was holding Toni's hand, and she didn't pull away.

"What now?" she asked.

"I'd forgotten how much I like bicycling. I want to spend more time on the Tammany Trace with someone who likes cycling as much as I do."

Toni smiled. "What about fishing?"

"I'd love to spend a few days at Frankie's camp on the Tchefuncte River. If a special someone was there to do a little fishing with me."

Toni's frown had disappeared. "I'm returning to the ranch to take care of the animals. Call me next week?"

"Yes," I said.

Toni kissed me and then hurried down the stairs. I saw Tony and Lil heading for the front door when I reached the ground floor.

"What's up?" I asked.

"Come Sunday, Lil and I are going to church, and I'm going to confess to the priest for the first time in ten years."

He smiled when I said, "That'll take a while."

"After church, Lil and I are having breakfast at Brennan's. We're heading back to Zane's house on Bourbon Street right now."

Lil squeezed Tony's hand. "We'll have the house all to ourselves."

"This case has worn me smooth," Tony said. "After this weekend, I'm going to take a few days off and go fishing with Jack Dugas."

"Then, we're going to Ireland for a vacation," Lil said.

"Have fun," I said."

The party was just getting started behind me. Freya's anxiety had disappeared, and she and Pancho mingled with the guests. Frankie motioned me to join him, Adele, and Josie."

"I almost didn't recognize you," he said.

"I've had lots of help on this case," I said.

"Thank you for finding Bobby," Adele said.

"It's what I do, and your husband paid me well to do it."

"Wait'll you see your bonus," Frankie said.

"You don't have to do that," I said.

"Hell, Wyatt, I don't have to do anything. You did a wonderful job, and I'm giving you, Tony, and Mama a bonus."

"I need a glass of lemonade," I said, pulling away from Josie's grasp.

Mama was on the couch, sitting with Aimee, Latitia, and Lashonda. I joined them.

"Wyatt," Mama said. "I'm in love with your daughter."

"You and me both," I said.

"Don't get too attached," Latitia said. "I'm taking the lead role in the remake of Cleopatra.

We'll sell the house in the Lower 9th and move to
LA to make movies. Mom and Aimee are coming
with me."

"I look forward to living in LA, though I'll be
back in New Orleans to spend next summer with
you," Aimee said. "Mama's going to teach me how
to be a voodoo mambo."

"Maybe so, little girl," Latitia said. "Right now,
it's past your bedtime. Go upstairs and go to
bed."

"Are you coming?" Aimee asked.

"In a while," Latitia said.

Lashonda took Aimee's hand. "I'll go with
you., baby," she said. "I can hardly keep my eyes
open."

After watching Lashonda and Aimee ascend
the stairs, I said, "Now what?"

"Latitia's going to tell me all your secrets,"
Mama said.

"She'd better hurry," I said. The night's
almost over."

Leaving Mama and Latitia on the couch, I
grabbed a slice of pepperoni and glass of
lemonade from Pancho, and headed upstairs for
some much needed sleep.

End

Book Notes

Years ago, I read a book about Haitian secret societies. *The Serpent and the Rainbow,* written by Harvard University Anthropology professor Wade Davis, chronicled Davis's visit to Haiti to try and prove the existence of zombies. Later adapted into a schlocky horror movie, the adaptation bore little resemblance to the book.

The book is excellent, and I won't spoil it by telling you what he discovered. Davis's book got me thinking about zombies. What if they do exist? I knew how to find the answer though it took me years to assign the case to Mama Mulate and Wyatt Thomas. As always, they led me on a circuitous pathway through magical and mysterious places I never knew existed.

I hope you enjoyed reading *Half Past Midnight* as much as I enjoyed writing it and that you liked Wyatt Thomas, my moody private investigator. Please consider leaving a review and reading the other nine books in the series if you did.

You may also like the *Paranormal Cowboy Series* featuring Buck McDivit, my modern-day cowboy detective who likes horses, cowgirls, and Australian sheepdogs. Buck's younger and more rowdy than Wyatt, though he always manages to become involved in paranormal mystery and adventure.

Oyster Bay Mystery, my newest series, features lighthouse keeper Jack Wiesinski, Grogan 'Chief' la Tortue, the last Atakapa Indian, and former Bourbon Street stripper Odette Mouton. Set on an almost deserted island off the Louisiana Gulf Coast about fifty miles from New Orleans, the series features rougarous, ghosts, Cajun witches, and many more paranormal entities, and frequent visits from many of the characters in the *French Quarter Mystery Series*.

Thanks for being a fan. Without wonderful readers like you, my stories would be little more than morning fog wafting across a forgotten lawn before disappearing forever into the Great Unknown.

About the Author

Born near a sleepy bayou, Louisiana Mystery Writer Eric Wilder grew up listening to tales of ghosts, magic, and voodoo. He's the author of fifteen novels, several cookbooks, many short stories, and Murder Etouffee, a book that defies classification. His series features characters who often find themselves involved in the paranormal.

Eric lives in Oklahoma near historic Route 66 with his wife, Marilyn, two beautiful dogs, and one remarkable cat. Please check out Eric's books on his Amazon homepage.

CPSIA information can be obtained
at www.ICGtesting.com
Printed in the USA
LVHW110553220323
742254LV00002B/334